Thoroughly Southern Mysteries

WHO INVITED THE DEAD MAN?
WHO LEFT THAT BODY IN THE RAIN?
WHO LET THAT KILLER IN THE HOUSE?
WHEN WILL THE DEAD LADY SING?

WHO KILLED THE QUEEN OF CLUBS?

}⋅ A THOROUGHLY SOUTHERN MYSTERY ⋅{

Patricia Sprinkle

A SIGNET BOOK

SIGNET
Published by New American Library, a division of
Penguin Group (USA) Inc., 375 Hudson Street,
New York, New York 10014, USA
Penguin Group (Canada), 10 Alcorn Avenue, Toronto,
Ontario M4V 3B2, Canada (a division of Pearson Penguin Canada Inc.)
Penguin Books Ltd., 80 Strand, London WC2R 0RL, England
Penguin Ireland, 25 St. Stephen's Green, Dublin 2,
Ireland (a division of Penguin Books Ltd.)
Penguin Group (Australia), 250 Camberwell Road, Camberwell, Victoria 3124,
Australia (a division of Pearson Australia Group Pty. Ltd.)
Penguin Books India Pvt. Ltd., 11 Community Centre, Panchsheel Park,
New Delhi - 110 017, India
Penguin Group (NZ), cnr Airborne and Rosedale Roads, Albany,
Auckland 1310, New Zealand (a division of Pearson New Zealand Ltd.)
Penguin Books (South Africa) (Pty.) Ltd., 24 Sturdee Avenue,
Rosebank, Johannesburg 2196, South Africa

Penguin Books Ltd., Registered Offices:
80 Strand, London WC2R 0RL, England

First published by Signet, an imprint of New American Library,
a division of Penguin Group (USA) Inc.

First Printing, March 2005
10   9   8   7   6   5   4   3   2   1

CAST OF CHARACTERS

MacLaren Yarbrough: Georgia magistrate, co-owner of Yarbrough Feed, Seed & Nursery

Joe Riddley Yarbrough: MacLaren's husband, co-owner of Yarbrough Feed, Seed & Nursery

Ridd and Martha Yarbrough: MacLaren's older son and his wife
Cricket (4) and *Bethany* (17): their children

Walker and Cindy Yarbrough: MacLaren's younger son and his wife
Tad (10) and *Jessica* (12): their children

Clarinda Williams: MacLaren's cook and housekeeper

Hollis Stanton, Tyrone Noland, Smitty Smith: teenagers in town

Bailey "Buster" Gibbons: Hope County sheriff

Isaac James: assistant police chief

Alexandra James: Isaac's cousin, director of the Hope County Library
Natasha (4): her daughter

Edith Whelan Burkett: clubwoman, bridge champion, now library assistant

Genna and Adney Harrison: Edith's stepdaughter and her husband

Olive Harrison: Adney's sister, also a librarian

Donna Linse: children's librarian

Shep Faxon: local attorney

Valerie Allen: young adult who lives with Edith

Frank Sparks: biker, friend of Valerie's

Henry Joyner: Edie's pecan grove foreman

Daisy Joyner: Henry's mother

The second Friday morning in November, I wasn't thinking about murder. Two weeks to Thanksgiving with Christmas pounding along right behind, I was helping our clerks make our store festive with chrysanthemums, straw bales, and pumpkins. When the phone rang, I stumbled over a bale of straw answering the danged thing. "Yarbrough Feed, Seed and Nursery. MacLaren Yarbrough speaking."

"This is Alexandra James. Would you happen to have a spare hour to come by my office? I really need to talk to you." The syllables that rolled over the line were large, round, and perfectly enunciated. You could tell she didn't grow up in Georgia.

I cringed like a kid invited to the principal's office. I knew Alex as the first cousin of my friend Isaac James, Hopemore's assistant police chief, and as the mother of Natasha, my grandson Cricket's favorite preschool chum. But Alex was also the director of the Hope County Library, and she'd never called me before. "I thought I returned all my books."

We'd recently moved into a new house, though, and I kept forgetting where I put things. Were a couple more library books stuck on a bottom shelf somewhere? Was there a limit to how many times you could return books late in a three-month period before they took away your card?

Alex laughed. "I don't do overdue books. That's handled

by the front desk. This is something else, if you can spare me about an hour."

Spare hours were scarce on the ground right then. Joe Riddley and I were spending most of our waking hours trying to sell hundreds of pumpkins, chrysanthemums, and a parking lot full of pine straw before a superstore opened at the edge of town on Thanksgiving Friday. In addition, as a Hope County magistrate, I was busier than a monkey picking fleas. You don't have to be a lawyer to be a magistrate in rural Georgia, so except for the chief magistrate in each county, a lot of us fit magisterial duties around the edges of regular jobs. With the holidays approaching, we'd had more bad checks passed in the last week than in the whole month of July, and a sad number of couples had revved up their holiday spirit by pounding on each other.

Still, I'd never been invited to meet with a library director in her office before, and I was tired of shifting bales of straw and pumpkins. "Would right now suit you?"

"Great. I'll put on a pot of tea."

Hope County is located in that wedge of Middle Georgia between I-20 and I-16, where November is a lovely month. Our fall is subtler than the flaming ones farther north, but equally lovely and a whole lot warmer. The sun blessed my shoulders as I walked the four blocks. Only dogwoods were rusty red as yet. Sweet gums were turning gold from the top down, and Bradford pears were making up their individual minds—some were red, others still green. Birds sang for joy at being back home for the winter, and the sky looked like it had been washed, hung out, and blown dry by sweet breezes. We'd had a long spell of chilly rain, so the air had that fresh, happy smell it always gets rising up from wet ground to meet the sun.

At the library, I admired fat pumpkins lining the library steps and smiled at a scarecrow reading in the new children's wing. Donna Linse, the children's librarian, was on the lookout for me. She came to take my elbow and steer me toward the back. "Miss James is expecting you."

As we passed the checkout desk, I waved to Olive Harrison and Edith Burkett, thinking how odd it seemed to see Edie there. Edie was one of Hopemore's few claims to fame. She had competed in bridge tournaments all over the world and was expected to come in at least third in the U.S. Women's Bridge Championship in May. In addition, for years she had been one of Hopemore's leading clubwomen. There wasn't a club in the state worth belonging to that Edie hadn't held office in. She'd even won a Georgia Woman of the Year award for her work with literacy. The previous April, however, her husband—who owned our local drugstore—had closed his pharmacy one night, gone into the back room, and taken an overdose of his own pills. Within three weeks, Edie had gone to work full-time at the library.

She still served as president of the local literacy council and headed up a bridge club that was hosting a big regional championship tournament in January, but she had resigned as chair of the library board when she started work. As I pattered after Donna, I wondered how it felt to move from board to staff and how well Edie fit in with the other librarians. Of course, Edie and Olive Harrison had been friends and played bridge together before Edie went to work, and they were practically family, since Edie's stepdaughter, Genna, had married Olive's brother, Adney.

Donna tapped on the director's door, peeped in, and announced, "The judge is here."

It wasn't me Donna was in awe of, it was her boss. Alex stood five foot ten in her stocking feet, taller in the spike heels she preferred. She piled satiny black curls in elaborate styles on top of her head, poured her caramel curves into exotic clothes, and sported nails that were more like talons. Some people might be misled by her glamour into underestimating her intelligence, but her coworkers weren't among them. Alex had her master's in library science. I just hoped she didn't spend spare moments reading the classifieds, looking for a better-paying job.

I stepped through Alex's office door and saw Natasha

smiling from at least two dozen frames. How had the child had time in her four and a half years to do anything but pose?

Across the room, Alex towered over a credenza, pouring boiling water from an electric kettle into a china teapot. An enameled tray held a matching china sugar bowl, creamer, four cups with saucers, a plate full of cookies, orange napkins, and silver spoons.

"Welcome, Judge." She turned with a smile, setting pumpkin earrings swinging. Colorful cornucopias were knitted into her black cotton sweater, and it looked real good with a long black skirt and boots. "Thanks for coming."

"You sure do this in style." I could admire the china cups and saucers, but had to repress a shudder at the tea. I hadn't drunk tea from a pot since a memorable incident nine months before, when a pot-brewed cup nearly ended my life.*

"I don't tolerate mugs, tepid water, or tea bags in my office. Tea is a ritual I take seriously." Alex put the lid on the pot and covered it with a yellow cozy to let it steep. "I'm real glad you could come. Won't you sit down?" She gestured toward one of two visitor's chairs, and I saw that even her long nails were painted orange with little gold pumpkins on them.

She had lived in the South long enough to know not to rush into a conversation, so while we waited for the tea, we talked about our dogs. Alex's Poe Boy was the son of my beagle, Lulu. Finally Alex shifted and settled back in a way that made me think we were getting down to business. I figured she had some legal question and didn't want to pay a lawyer when she could get the same information free from a judge. She surprised me.

"I called you because you've known Edie longer than I have, and I need your opinion. Olive claims Edie is worrying about something, and it's beginning to interfere with her work. She forgets to run books over the magnet, which scares the pants off patrons when they start out the door and the alarm sounds. At least twice she has sent somebody to the

Who Left that Body in the Rain?

wrong section, when she knows this library as well as anybody. And yesterday she shelved three books somebody donated to the library book sale. I want to get this straightened out so she can get her mind back where it belongs." Alex tolerated nothing that interfered with the library running smoothly.

"I'm not her priest or her doctor," I protested. "Edie doesn't call to tell me her problems."

Alex reached for her phone. "But you do know her, right?"

"Sure. We've served on a lot of boards and committees together, and when Wick was alive, we saw them pretty often at the country club and various events."

"Then let me call her in and ask her to tell us both what's bothering her. Afterwards, I want you to tell me what you think. Isaac says you have a good head for solving mysteries."

While she turned her attention to the phone, I wondered uneasily what, exactly, Isaac had meant. The last time I'd gotten involved with a mystery, I'd nearly got myself and Clarinda, my housekeeper, killed.* He hadn't been particularly complimentary at the time. Was it likely he'd tell Alex I was good at solving mysteries so she'd involve me in another one?

*When Will the Dead Lady Sing?

Edie Burkett was neither plain nor pretty, but had what my
mama described as "a pleasant face." Her short brown hair,
dusted with gray, fell from a side part to turn under above her
collar except for what she called "that one bullheaded curl"
that always flipped up at the back. We were about the same
height, but she was still slender while I—well, Joe Riddley
kindly calls me voluptuous.

"I hate women skinny enough to look good in long denim
jumpers," I greeted her, "but if that cardigan ever goes missing from your closet, you'll know where to look for it." It
was navy, with a snow-dusted village knit into it all around
the bottom.

She smiled. "I'll stop by Shep Faxon's office after work
and leave it to you in my will."

I tremble to remember how we all laughed at that.

Alex got up and went to pour tea. Edie held up a hand.
"None for me, thanks. I can't stay long." She bent to remove
a stack of files from the other visitor's chair. "What are
these?"

Alex screwed up her mouth in disgust. "That grant proposal. You would not believe how much piddly information
those folks want in it."

"I told you I'd do it over the weekend." Edie put the files
on the floor, settled herself in the chair, and crossed her ankles. "What did you want to see me about?"

"In a minute." Alex bent to strain tea into two cups and brought one to me.

Mama always said, "Eat and drink what you're offered, even if it kills you." She never imagined that one day it nearly would. However, I spooned in sugar, poured milk, and took a nervous sip. It tasted good, whether it killed me or not, and drinking from real china was a nice change on a workday morning.

However, if I didn't get back soon, our employees would begin to think I'd absconded to Brazil with their paychecks. I told Edie, "I understand something's been bothering you."

Edie frowned at Alex. "Did Olive tell you that?"

Alex sipped her tea and avoided Edie's eyes. "She said something to make me think you've joined the hereafter club. You know"—she waved to show it wasn't real important—"the one where you go into a room and ask, 'What did I come in here after?' "

Edie didn't crack a smile. "I hope you didn't drag Mac all the way over here to talk about something that stupid." Her voice was cross.

Alex sipped her tea before replying. "Isaac says Mac's real good at puzzles."

Edie gave me a sour look. "Alex and Olive ought to mind their own business."

My employees didn't talk to me like that, but then, none of them ever chaired my board.

"Since I haven't," her boss replied, "why don't you go ahead and tell us about it?"

Edie heaved a sigh that came from the tips of her clogs. "It's so *silly*. But since we're here—I got in my car last Sunday and couldn't reach the pedals. Since nobody ever drives the car but me, I must have put the seat back to get out and forgotten I did it."

"I put my seat back almost automatically," I reassured her. "Don't you wish somebody would make a car short people could drive without the dashboard bumping our knees and the steering wheel removing our digestive tract as we get out?"

She nodded. "Or one where the seat belt didn't cut off your windpipe?"

Alex stretched long arms above her head and preened like a cat. "You all should have taken your vitamins. But Olive said something about a door."

Edie's returning good humor evaporated in a huff of disgust. "I left it unlocked that same night. I'm usually careful about locking both the door and the dead bolt since Daddy left, but I guess I forgot the night before."

Her daddy, Josiah Whelan, hadn't exactly "left." Edie had put him in Golden Years Nursing Home up in Augusta the past September, after a massive stroke left him paralyzed on the left side and unable to speak.

"What was most puzzling," Edie continued, "was that the cat was inside. He's an outdoor cat. He *never* comes inside."

No wonder she was troubled, if she was forgetting to lock her door. Hope County isn't the crime capital of the South, but isolated women are vulnerable wherever they live. Still, there could be a rational explanation. I suggested one possibility. "Could Genna have used your car while you were asleep?"

Like I said before, Genna was Edie's stepdaughter—Wick's child by a previous marriage. When her husband, Adney, was out of town on business, Genna often slept over with Edie. My daughter-in-law Cindy, who was Genna's friend, said Adney was nervous about Genna sleeping in their house alone.

"Genna wasn't there that night." Edie's fingers twisted like mating worms. "Olive should never have mentioned this. Now you all are worried, and Genna and Adney will have one more reason why I ought to sell the grove and move into a nice little town house in town." Her tone said exactly what she thought about a nice little town house in town and that she was quoting somebody—probably Genna. "Forget it, okay?"

She rose, but before she could leave, Olive stepped into the office after the slightest of knocks. As a judge, I had no business convicting Olive of eavesdropping without evidence, but she convicted herself when she joined our conversation right away with no apology. "What about that girl who lives with you?"

Edie gave her the impatient look she gave persons who attended board meetings uninvited and spoke out of turn. "Valerie is good about locking up. She also has a car."

Edie had been a lot more willing to consider Genna than Valerie, but she was irritated enough with Olive right then to reject anything she suggested. Olive must have understood that, for her pale, plain face flushed, and she said, in the same drab, uninflected voice that never held the children's attention when she took over story hour for Donna, "I was just trying to help."

Poor Olive was less like an olive than anything I could imagine. A woman named Olive ought to be sophisticated and interesting, with sleek dark hair worn in a knot at the nape of her neck, slim little black dresses that cost a fortune, and a face you could put on a magazine cover. This Olive had a square jaw and eyes like unpolished pewter, and she invariably wore a black skirt, a light gray sweater with long sleeves and a V-neck, a single gold chain, and small gold balls in her ears. For winter she added black blazers. For summer she substituted short-sleeved gray cotton sweaters with scoop necks. For dress-up she wore gray silk blouses. For golfing she changed the skirt for black pants and the V-neck for a gray polo shirt or sweatshirt.

She even drove a gray car, a Nissan SUV exactly like her brother's, suitable for rough-track adventures, although I doubted Olive ever took hers anywhere more adventurous than the Bi-Lo. Cindy said Adney bought her the car soon after he bought his own. Apparently they were the only two left of their family, and very close. She had certainly moved to Hopemore not long after Adney and Genna.

Joe Riddley claimed Olive had a secret desire to be a nun.

I suspected she had drawers full of red bikini underwear and a closet full of slinky negligees. However, I was unlikely to ever know. Olive never invited anybody to her apartment except Adney, Genna, and Edie. She didn't seem to have any other friends. It wasn't just that she was a newcomer. She made it clear she preferred books to people. She also apparently preferred solitary rounds on the golf course to foursomes, if the gossip was right down at Phyllis's Beauty Parlor.

"She's real good at golf," I'd heard one woman say, "but when people ask her to play with them, she says she prefers to play alone. Can you imagine?"

"She plays bridge like that, too," said another. "Makes it clear it's cards she likes, not the company."

"Poor honey, can't you do something about her hair?" a third asked Phyllis. "I mean, that short straight look doesn't do a thing for her, thin as she is, and that color of red—Well, all I can say is, if you and she are trying to match Genna's color, one of you is color-blind."

Phyllis frowned over the head of a permanent she was rolling. "They don't use the same color at all. And I give people what they ask for. You know that." Her critic was a woman well past fifty who kept her own hair an improbable shade of yellow, too long for her age, and teased to look like Texas. "Olive favors a French waif look, and she brings her color with her."

As soon as Phyllis stepped into the dryer room to check on another customer, the last woman snorted. "French waif, my foot. That chopped-off crop makes Olive look like she's trying out for the fire scene in *Joan of Arc*."

"With her head already ablaze," said the first. They all laughed. They didn't so much dislike Olive as resent that she wouldn't let them get to know her.

All that went through my head in Alex's office, until I suddenly realized Olive was staring at me. Had I quoted some of that out loud? Probably not. She looked more like we were teammates on *Jeopardy!* and she was willing me to ask the winning question. I gave it a try. "Could Valerie have let anybody else drive your car?"

Edie gave an impatient huff and stomped to the door. "She wouldn't. And I can't see that this is anybody's business but mine. Is that all?" she asked Alex. "I need to get back to the desk."

I was sorry we'd upset her. Edie had been deluged with despair that year, between Wick's death and Josiah's stroke. "None of this sounds like much to worry about," I said. "Stress makes all of us forgetful, and you have every reason to be worn out, with all you've been through. Are you still driving back and forth every evening to see your daddy?"

"Yes." One short, abrupt syllable.

I was ready to end the conversation and head back to the store, but Alex must have wanted me to have the full picture. "You're still president of the literacy council, right?"

"Just until June."

"And tutoring every week?"

"Just one student right now."

"And playing bridge?"

Olive put in her oar. "She doesn't have to run the tournament. I told her I'd be glad to—"

"You don't know all that's involved," Edie said impatiently. "It would take longer to explain it than to do it myself."

How many times have I heard that from women who claim they are doing too much, but never let go of anything because they don't really believe anybody else can do it as well as they can? It's such a small step from knowing you are competent to believing you are indispensable.

Olive's eyes narrowed into dime-sized slits. "But with that new committee you agreed to serve on at your church—"

Edie's color flared high. "That's just for a year, while we raise money for repairs."

"Honey!" I exclaimed in dismay. "Between 'just this' and 'just that,' it's a wonder you aren't plumb nuts. You can't do all you used to do and work. And you don't need to see Josiah every day. That's two hours round-trip, plus time to visit. Your daddy doesn't want you killing yourself coming to see him."

Edie sighed. "I keep hoping one day he'll talk a little, or move his hand. I don't want to miss being there that day." Her voice trembled, and she took deep breaths to steady herself.

Olive made a movement with one hand like she wished she could help but didn't know how. "I'd better get back to the desk. I came in to see if I could take an early lunch." Nobody believed that, but when Alex approved the request, she backed out of the room.

I couldn't offer Edie much hope that her daddy would get better. Instead, I asked, "Speaking of nuts, are you going to be able to get in this year's crop without Pete?"

Josiah Whelan owned a thousand acres of pecan trees that had to be harvested between October and February if he was to have any income for the year. Harvest required at least thirty workers to bring in the crop, run the cleaning and sorting operation, and keep the machinery going, and Pete Joyner, Josiah's harvest foreman, had suffered a fatal heart attack the same morning Josiah had his stroke. Nobody knew exactly what had gone on out at the grove that day, but something terrible had blown up between them after a lifetime of working together.

In addition to my concern for Edie, I had a personal interest in her answer. Yarbrough's might weather the superstore, but if Whelan Grove went under, we'd have a hole in our bottom line. A thousand acres of pecans need a lot of herbicides, pesticides, and fertilizer in a year, and Josiah purchased them all from us.

"This year's crop will be okay if the rain lets up. Henry came home for his daddy's funeral, and he said he'll stay to get the harvest in."

Henry was Pete's son, and he must be about thirty now. Pete used to bring him to the store when he was a toddler, and

I don't think I ever saw a prettier child, with his daddy's big gray eyes and long, curling lashes in a face the color of coffee laced with pure cream. As soon as he could push a wheelbarrow, Henry started helping in the grove. Our older son, Ridd, who taught at the high school, had expected him to go to college, study horticulture, and maybe one day buy a grove of his own. Instead, right after graduation, Henry got married and moved over to South Carolina. By Christmas, Pete was flashing pictures of a new granddaughter.

I hadn't heard anything about Henry since then, but I did remember that he used to be a real tease. When Pete brought him down to the store, we'd find smiley faces drawn in the zeros on sale signs, or signs that belonged to big potted plants stuck in front of seed packets, jacking up their price considerably. "Henry sneaked a plastic ice cube in my cup once, with a fly in it, to be funny. Could he have altered your car seat and let the cat in for a joke?"

Edie shook her head. "Henry doesn't joke since he came back. Maybe it's losing his daddy, but it's all I can do to get him to say good morning."

Alex set her cup down in the saucer with a click. "Weren't you saying you all had a fight this morning before you came in?"

"Do you mind keeping my business private?" Edie blazed. "Henry and I had a little disagreement, that's all." She gave another irritated huff and a flap of a wave. "Forget this. It's not worth making a fuss over, and I need to get back to the desk. Donna's got story hour."

"If you want an office in the hereafter club, let me know," I offered. "I'm running for president, but you can be secretary."

The way she slammed the door behind her, I got the notion she didn't find that funny.

﹩3﹪

Alex drummed her nails on a stack of papers on her desk. "So. What do you think?"

What I really thought was that Alex and Olive were antsy because of all the wet, soggy weather we'd been having. When folks can't get out to exercise their bodies, their imaginations work overtime. What I said, though, was, "I don't think there's anything to be worried about, but Edie's under a lot of pressure with Josiah right now. Maybe she shouldn't be working."

Alex stopped drumming and started rubbing a bare spot on her desk with one finger. Afraid I'd offended her, I added quickly, "You were brilliant, though, to get her working so soon after Wick died. Fifty is young to be a widow. She needed a new interest."

Alex hesitated, then said bluntly, "She needed the *money*." She held up a hand to forestall my protest. "Everybody thinks Edie sold her nice house and moved out with her daddy so neither would be lonesome. They think she got a fat stock portfolio from the sale of the house and the pharmacy, and works to take her mind off things. I wouldn't tell you if I weren't so worried, but Edie's broke. Wick Burkett was a drug addict who spent every penny they had—and borrowed a good many dollars they didn't—to feed his habit."

That sure took the starch out of my britches. "Why would

you think that? Wick Burkett was a *fine* man." There's no higher accolade in Georgia.

Alex chewed her lower lip. "How much has Isaac told you about me?"

"That you're his first cousin and were in the army before you came here."

"That's true, but it's not the whole truth. I grew up in a Chicago housing project. Mama, who was Isaac's daddy's sister, was a drop-dead drunk, and I was the oldest of five kids she got from five different men who supplied her with liquor. I joined the army as soon as they'd take me and was lucky enough to get a sergeant who kicked some sense into the only part of me that knew how to listen back then. He convinced me I could handle college, and that got me so hooked on learning, I finished my master's before I got out. But I know drugs. One of my brothers is in jail for dealing. Another died of an overdose when he was twenty. I recognized Wick's symptoms several months before he died, I just didn't realize how far he had gone down that road until I went over to Edie's a week after his funeral, with some library business. Since we worked pretty closely on the library board, I took a risk and mentioned I'd lost a brother to drugs. She started pouring her heart out. Said a doctor prescribed pills several years ago for a ski injury, and Wick got hooked. First he took them to get relief. Eventually he took them because he liked how they made him feel. Then he started mixing his own prescription cocktails. Even getting drugs wholesale, it eventually took every penny he made and then some to support his habit. The last year of his life, Edie was frantic—both because of the money and because she was terrified he'd make a mistake on somebody else's prescription. After he died, she discovered his debts would take every penny she got for selling the business, her house, and most of her furniture. All she took away from that marriage was some collection or other his mother had. According to his will, she can't sell them—they're to go to Genna upon her death."

"Eighteenth-century American snuffboxes," I contributed. "But I'm surprised Wick didn't sell them, too."

"He would have if Edie hadn't hidden them, along with some jewelry her mother left her. She said he was furious, but she told him they ought to go to Genna one day, and she was determined to see that they did." Alex's face was grave. "Another month or so, and he'd have been bankrupt. I guess he tried to do the honorable thing by killing himself before things went that far." She bit her lower lip again. "She's never told another soul, and I wouldn't have told you, except it may be related to all this. She could be still worried about money."

I hardly heard her. I was thinking of all the times I'd been with Wick and Edie during his last two years and never guessed a thing was wrong. Do we ever really know what lies behind another human face? "Does Genna know all this?"

"I'm pretty sure she doesn't know about the drugs. I don't know if Edie told her there wasn't any money or not."

I doubted it. Edie was a private person. I'd also recalled how angry my daughter-in-law had been on Genna's behalf after Wick died. "He made a new will just a week before he died," Cindy had said, "and he didn't leave her a blessed thing. Can you believe that? His entire estate went to Edie. He even left her Genna's grandmother's snuffboxes, after promising them to Genna all her life."

Drugs change people. Had Wick, in his last desperate week, taken petty revenge on Edie for hiding the boxes, saying, in effect, "Since you hung on to the danged things in my lifetime, you can jolly well keep them until you die—and put up with Genna grousing about it"?

Alex was still talking. "I think Genna's still under the misapprehension that Edie's rich, because I overheard Edie on the phone a few weeks back refusing to give her a loan. It wouldn't occur to Genna to get a job. Can you imagine two women more dissimilar than those two?"

"Not right off." Genna was a social butterfly who worshiped at the temple of the elegant lifestyle according to the gospel of *Southern Living*. Except for painting birdhouses to sell in benefit craft shows, she seemed to do little that didn't involve the tennis court, golf course, chic restaurants, women's clubs, a new women's gym, or the beauty parlor.

Alex took a sip of tea, found it cold, and leaned over to pour the rest into a potted ficus. "Were Genna and Edie close when Genna was growing up?" she asked over her shoulder.

"No. Genna was eight when her parents divorced and her daddy bought the pharmacy and moved here. He had custody, for some reason, and Genna arrived furious that he'd moved her away from Memphis, where her mother still lived. Possibly she hoped her parents would get back together, I don't know, but when Wick married Edie the next year, you wouldn't believe the devious tricks that child tried—first to block the marriage, then to sabotage it. I felt sorry for Edie, and just as sorry for Genna. The only woman she related to was Sally Whelan, Josiah's mother, who had moved back in with him when his wife died. Old as Sally was, she and Genna got along like two little girls. They both loved ruffled dresses and big hair bows, elaborate tea parties with baby dolls, painting their fingernails and trying out new shades of lipsticks. I sometimes thought Genna was the granddaughter Sally wished Edie had been."

"Did that bother Edie?" Alex held up her teacup with a silent question and I nodded. While she refilled both cups, I kept talking—as much to myself as to her.

"No, I think both Genna and Edie would have been glad for Genna to stay out at the pecan grove until she went to college, but Josiah had to put Sally in a nursing home when Genna was sixteen. Genna got so upset she asked to live with her mother. Wick took her back to Memphis, and he and Edie breathed a sigh of relief—until she came back six months later."

"Why?" Alex asked the question without turning around.

"Nobody ever said, and I never heard her mother mentioned again. Genna was nicer to Edie after that, for what it's worth, but she didn't come back to Hopemore after college. She worked in Birmingham for years, in a hospital records department."

Alex handed me my tea. "Makes me nervous to think of somebody that fluffy working on people's medical records. Was that where she met Adney? He sells hospital supplies, right?"

"Back then it was pharmaceuticals, and Wick's store was in his territory, too. Wick was delighted when Adney and Genna met and got married five years ago. He was higher than a stockbroker's promises when they moved to Hopemore three years later and bought one of those big houses by the golf course out on—" I stopped, embarrassed. Joe Riddley had called the street "High Mortgage Lane" for so long, I'd forgotten its real name.

Fortunately, Alex was too busy savoring her own tea to wonder why I'd cut off in midsentence. "Well, I don't think Genna is Edie's problem." She settled back in her chair. "They seem to get along okay now." She offered me the cookies, took a piece of shortbread, and bit off a sizeable chunk. "I do love this stuff," she said through a mouthful of crumbs. "And I am a devious person. The real reason I invited you over here was so I could justify eating it."

"Joe Riddley already warned me you were devious. He said you pulled strings to get Edie elected chair of the library board so you could get what you wanted in the new children's wing."

She threw back her head and laughed so hard I saw her back teeth. "Whoo-ee, girl, I sure am glad that man is married to you, not me. He sees too much. But Edie and I got an outstanding children's section, didn't we?"

"Outstanding," I agreed.

"This town is entitled to a good library, and I am devoted to seeing that people get what they are entitled to. Take Edie, now. She has thirty years' experience in administration as a volunteer, but I can't pay her her fair worth because she's only had three years of college and never worked except one summer, for Wick."

"And married him the next Christmas," I added.

"Is that right? Well, I am dedicated to making sure that woman finishes her degree and gets the salary she's entitled to. She had already gone back to college before Wick died, thinking she might need to work and support them both if his addiction got worse. When she came to work here, she changed her major to library science, and she's been working real hard."

"School on top of the rest she's doing? Even Edie can't do *everything*."

"She makes a good stab at it. She dropped out this semester when her daddy got sick, but she only lacks six credits to graduate. Once her daddy gets better, she ought to be able to whip out that degree in one more semester. Then I want her to go for her master's. She ought to be running a library—here or somewhere else."

I brushed crumbs from my lap. "I'd rate Josiah's chances of getting better about the same as my winning the lottery—which I never enter."

Alex drained her cup and set it on the tray. "Well, I wish Edie would stop feeling guilty about putting him in that place. I keep telling her she did what she had to do."

"She has bad associations with the place. Her grandmother died there."

Alex swivelled around to give me a long level look. "What was the matter with her?"

"Alzheimer's, probably, although back then they weren't sure enough to call it that."

"I heard something about that. What were her symptoms?"

"First she got forgetful. Then she got real belligerent over any little thing. Finally she got so she'd wander off, show up places and have no idea where she was. Josiah tried to keep her at home. He hired Daisy, Pete Joyner's wife, to stay with her, and Genna watched her some after school, but Sally would slip away. When Josiah came back from the grocery store one day and found her out by the road naked as the mockingbird singing above her, pitching nuts at cars passing on the road, he knew he couldn't keep her at home any longer."

Alex shoved back her chair, got up, and started pacing. Back and forth, like a caged lion, darting looks my way now and then. I waited, figuring she'd get around to whatever she wanted to say in her own time. I hoped it wouldn't take up much more of mine.

Finally she stopped, gripped the back of her chair for support, and demanded, "You don't reckon Edie could be getting what her grandmother had, do you?"

Alzheimer's is like cancer. A lot of people think if they don't say it, they won't get it. But I could tell by Alex's intense tone that this was, finally, the question she'd brought me across town to ask.

I thought it over and gave her my best shot at a reply. "I doubt it. Sally was past eighty before she showed any symptoms, and nobody else in the family has had it." I set my cup on the desk. "I appreciate the tea, so here's my valued opinion: You are making a forest out of a couple of pinecones. Either Edie's under too much stress or she's getting forgetful like the rest of us."

I picked up my pocketbook and headed out. As I opened the door, Olive was standing so close she had to have been eavesdropping again. She didn't apologize, but pushed past me and stormed, "You two don't get it, do you? Edie isn't forgetful. This is all Valerie's doing—and that jerk she's going around with."

I'm not used to accepting opinions as evidence. "Why should you think that?"

"What does anybody know about that girl?" Olive flung back.

Alex and I exchanged a look. Alex shrugged. "I know what Edie's told me. Valerie rents an upstairs bedroom with a bath, and they share the kitchen. Edie likes her. I know that.

She says Valerie cooks dinner for her some nights, and Edie's teaching her to sew."

"She works for Meriwether DuBose's new company," was all I had to contribute.

Meriwether's Pots of Luck sold pots of all sorts, shapes, and sizes by catalogue and Internet. Most of her employees were young adults, and Meriwether had arranged the work schedule so they could attend community college classes in the morning, then work from noon until eight. She'd confided to me, "That will be better for me, anyway, once the baby comes. I'll be home in the morning, we'll have a sitter for the afternoon, and Jed will take over at suppertime." Her first child was due in a month, and curiosity was running high. Meriwether and Jed, who hadn't married until they were past thirty,* refused to say if the baby was a girl or a boy.

"I don't care who she works for, I don't think she's safe to have around." Olive looked like she was willing to stand with her back against the door and discuss this forever.

Alex nodded toward her telephone. "Could you call Ms. DuBose, Judge, and ask what she thinks of Valerie?" She didn't add "to satisfy Olive," but it hovered in the air.

I was one of Meriwether's grandmother's oldest friends and had known her all her life, so after I'd checked to be sure she wasn't in labor, I didn't mind saying, "I wanted to ask about one of your employees—Valerie something or other, who lives out with Edie Burkett."

"Valerie Allen. Is she in trouble with the law?"

"Not that I know of. But Edie's been having a few things happening out there that make her think she's getting forgetful, and I wondered if Valerie could be playing practical jokes or something."

Meriwether was highly amused. "Not likely. Valerie is real sweet and conscientious, and I think she and Edie get

*Who Invited the Dead Man?

along real well. Besides, Valerie's the flakiest person I ever knew. She wouldn't know a practical joke if she met one."

After I hung up, I repeated what Meriwether had said. Olive asked, "She didn't mention Valerie's new boyfriend? She's started hanging out with a biker who has tattoos all over him and plays in a hard-rock band. Heaven only knows what kind of trouble he's been in."

That was a kind of trouble Alex understood. Her forehead furrowed. "Edie didn't tell me that. She just said Valerie has a friend from school who comes over and fixes things."

Olive sighed. "Edie sees what Edie wants to see. Frank is helpful, so Frank is fine. To hear Edie talk, you'd think he was Saint Peter himself. What I see is a man who looks like a Hell's Angel hanging around my best friend's house. And now Valerie has started playing keyboard and singing with the band, which means they go out almost every night to practice or play."

Alex leaned against her desk and gave Olive a thoughtful look. "Do you think Valerie may be getting in with somebody who could endanger Edie?"

Olive hesitated, then nodded. "What's to keep Valerie from letting him in at night? Edie goes to bed early. Maybe Valerie forgot to lock the door after he left last week. She could be letting him use Edie's car, too. Edie sleeps soundly. She might not hear it driving out. The two of them could use it to deliver drugs, or they could rob Edie blind before she knew a thing was happening."

Alex turned to me. "What do you think, Mac?"

I thought it was time for some common sense. "Ask Isaac to check the man out. If he has a criminal record, Edie ought to be informed. If he doesn't, I'd wait and see if there are any more developments." I nodded toward Alex's window. "And speaking of developments, while I've been in here, clouds have been rolling back in. By now, it looks like the sky angel has had a serious accident involving bleach. I need to run if I don't want to get soaked walking back."

Alex looked, then sighed. "Lordy, I hope it won't rain

again. Edie will have kittens. She said they need sunshine and wind to dry things up fast, so they can get back to harvesting." She took my elbow to see me out, and murmured so Olive couldn't hear, "Thanks for coming. I was scared Edie might be getting—you know. You've put things in perspective. Isaac was right. You are good at solving mysteries."

"I think it's just stress," I assured her. "If she cuts back, she ought to be fine."

Oh, Edie, how could I have been so wrong?

That afternoon I held traffic court in the west end of the county then returned to town via Whelan Grove Road. The new superstore had been built where Whelan Grove Road dead-ends into Oglethorpe Street, and I wanted to see if our business owners' association prayers had been answered and that dratted superstore lay in a smoking ruin.

I know those weren't charitable thoughts, but I still couldn't believe how eagerly our county commissioners had bought the corporation's claim that the new store would stimulate our economy by creating jobs. Most of the jobs it created would pay minimum wage, and all the profits would slide out of town into the pockets of distant corporate officers and stockholders. Meanwhile, folks like us, who owned or managed businesses and had invested our lives, our money, and sizeable civic and charitable contributions in Hopemore, would watch our livelihoods dry up and die. I felt like a Roman watching Goths and Vandals climb over the wall.

The weather deteriorated along with my mood. Mist had settled low on the shoulders of the sky, blurring the line where treetops met the clouds. I kept needing my wipers, but they just made a streaky mess of the windshield.

About the time I reached Whelan Grove, the mist turned to drizzle. For those who know pecans only as sweet halves in tins or bags, a rainy grove in November is lovely. Pecans keep their leaves until the first frost, and soft evergreen grass is planted between the rows. The road split Josiah's thousand acres, so on both sides, mammoth trees planted sixty feet apart marched in perfect rows, both straight and diagonal, as far as my eye could see. An Impressionist artist would probably love that swirling mist, the grassy vistas, and all those shades of gray and green.

But to those of us who know pecans, a grove in an autumn rain is a heartbreaking sight. One of the reasons Georgia grows more pecans than anywhere else in the world is because our autumns are mild and dry. The occasional rain that falls during harvest season is usually followed by a drying wind, so that in a day or two harvesting can proceed.

This season had been unusually wet, with two weeks of soaking rain. No matter how beautiful the grove looked in the mist, its beauty didn't make up for what I ought to be seeing.

Somewhere in that grove, mowers ought to be cutting the grass short between the trees. Where the mowers had finished, a mechanical shaker should have been grasping trees and shaking them gently, testing whether each variety was ripe enough to harvest. Where trees had been deemed ripe, another shaker should have been zipping along at a mind-boggling rate, grabbing and shaking a new tree every two minutes in a shower of nuts.

I loved watching those shakers, because clever little blowers on each wheel sent out a spurt of nuts whether they went forwards or backwards, saving every nut from being smashed. Two days behind the shakers, sweepers should have been moseying down the grassy medians "busting the middle"—clearing the middle of each row so limbs could be piled there, and brushing nuts that fell beneath the drip line back toward the trees. Crewmen should have been walking along behind of the sweepers, tossing fallen limbs and branches onto the grass, out of the way. Where that crew had been, more sweepers should have been moving up and down each row near the trunks, sweeping nuts into neat windrows on each side.

Behind the sweepers, I should be seeing Josiah's two green tractors pulling harvesters, which he fondly called "my eighty-thousand-dollar Hoovers." They vacuumed up the nuts and conveyed them by chain into the dump wagon pulled along behind. Through the dust the harvesters blew out, I should be seeing big peanut wagons, large enough to hold three dump wagon loads of nuts, moving to convenient stations around the grove to receive nuts from the dump wagons.

Harvesting is dusty work. Now that developers were building close to groves, in some areas the harvesters traveled in one direction only, to avoid smothering somebody's party in dust.

It is urgent to harvest before most of the machinery-clogging leaves start to fall, so at this time of year Josiah's grove ought to have been alive with clouds of dust and workers' shouts punctuating the mechanical din.

Instead, the grove stood silent and still. Pecans can't be harvested with wet leaves on the ground. A day of hard rain stops work for two or three days. Heaven only knew what two weeks of rain had done. Poor Edie. Poor Henry.

I didn't plan on turning in Edie's drive. It was past five, and the day had that smudged look it wears at dusk toward the end of autumn, when the year is tired and winding down. Joe Riddley was expecting me back so we could go eat the seafood buffet at the country club. But all of a sudden, as Whelans' drive was coming up on my left, I heard the honk of Canada geese. We don't see many geese in Hope County, and all my life I've stopped whatever I was doing to watch them fly over. I didn't like to stop on the road, so I pulled into the drive and rolled down my window. I ignored the drizzle blowing onto my face as I peered up at the sky. In less than a minute, a V of perhaps fifteen geese wheeled right over me, making for the pond down at the back of the grove. I watched until they disappeared.

The edges of the drive looked too muddy for turning, so I

decided to go around the circular drive at the side of the house. Edie was probably in Augusta with Josiah, anyway.

The house, set in the middle of the grove far down the gravel drive, appeared to sit in an enormous, shady lawn. Big, square, and plain, with a two-story columned porch, it had one quirky feature: the room Josiah had built when Edie was a teenager and wanted to sleep at the top of the house. For his only daughter, he had literally raised the roof—slicing off the top, installing three walls of windows four feet high, then setting the rooftop back down on the glass walls like a party hat. As I drove down the quarter mile of gravel that afternoon, I wondered if Edie still slept up there now that she was mistress of the whole place.

When I was small, I used to go to Whelans' with Daddy every fall to buy pecans, back when Josiah's daddy was a cotton farmer with a few pecan trees growing in damp bottomland. Josiah and his older brother, Edward, were young bachelors then. Edward, handsome and charming, had a new English degree from Emory and (so Mama said) preferred writing stories to plowing fields. Josiah—shorter, dumpy, and plain—was my favorite, because he'd tease me and chase me, shrieking with laughter, around the yard.

While Daddy and Mr. Whelan did business, Sally Whelan and I would sit in rockers out under a maple tree and Mary, her maid, would bring me a glass of buttermilk and cold corn bread to dunk in it. Mary had Pete when I was four, and I loved to play with him in his basket. I shocked Mama one day by declaring, "When I grow up, I'm gonna have chocolate babies. They're prettier than vanilla ones."

Had that baby really lived sixty years before he died? Days drip like raindrops. Years gush past like flash floods.

I slowed on the drive, wondering who would live at Whelans' next. It's tradition around here among some landed families for the older generation to pass the homeplace on to the eldest child. That previous August, Joe Riddley and I had moved out of the house his great-granddaddy built and deeded it to our older son, Ridd. But Edward Whelan, who was always a bit wild, drove too fast around a country curve one winter afternoon and died a bachelor. Josiah had only Edie. After she was gone, would Genna and Adney give up their pretentious new McMansion to move into this old place and grow pecans? If Genna was nervous in a house in town, she'd never last a night alone in the grove.

I was halfway around the circle before I saw a blue Honda parked under the carport Josiah had added behind his back porch. A broad black bottom was draped over one fender, its owner peering under the hood. I recognized Alex by the elegance of the black pants, the gold spike heels, and a jacket that looked like it had been lifted from a passing leopard. I rolled down my window. "Got a problem?"

Alex stood erect, brushing her hands to get rid of grease and dirt, and glowered at her engine. "You know anything about cars?" she called.

"Not enough to fix one. What's the matter?"

"It won't start. Goes 'click,' then nothing happens."

"Could be your battery. I think mine did something like that once."

She blew out frustration between her lips. "Wouldn't you know?" She twisted and peered down at her jacket. "And I've probably gotten grease on me, too. This thing is washable, but I'd like to look presentable. Natasha and I are on our way to visit Isaac's parents. I'd be halfway there by now, except I told Edie I'd drop off some files so she could work on that grant proposal tomorrow. She offered"—she reminded me, as if I'd said something—"and she's better at this than I am. I'd have given it all to her before she left to see her daddy, but I was still printing out the proposed budget. When we got here, I just turned the engine off long enough to get the stuff out of the trunk and run it up to that chair on the back porch." She jerked her head along a covered walkway between the carport and the back steps, and I saw the folders on the screened porch.

She peered around in dismay. "And now, while I've been fiddling with it, Natasha and Poe Boy have run off somewhere. That kid and her dog both need a place to run, but not right this minute. Tasha? Tasha! Where are you? Poe Boy? Come!"

All we heard was the gurgle of rain in the downspout. I shivered as rain blew into my open window, and I pushed the button to raise it most of the way. Alex slammed down her hood. "The two of them are probably halfway across the grove by now. They'll both be muddy, she'll have caught a cold—"

Because of something Isaac had let slip once, I knew that while Alex was in the army, in addition to getting her education, she had gotten pregnant and been abandoned by the baby's father. Isaac had said ruefully more than once, "Alex is smart, but she skipped class the day they passed out good sense. Look at how she worries about Natasha all the time. That woman needs to get herself a life." That didn't mean he wasn't crazy about his cousins. It was at his suggestion that Alex had applied for the library directorship three years before. But I saw what he meant about Natasha when Alex hurried haphazardly around the corner of the house. Spike heels aren't the best shoes in which to explore a spongy yard. "Natasha Penelope James! Where are you? You come back here right this minute!" She had a worried edge to her voice I couldn't ignore. Joe Riddley or no Joe Riddley, I couldn't drive away with a four-year-old missing.

Josiah had an equipment barn, a mechanical repair shop, and a big cleaning shed where a child could hide. Some of them held equipment that could hurt her. I parked and climbed out into the drizzle, holding my pocketbook over my head and glad tomorrow was my day for the beauty parlor. Avoiding the worst of the potholes—fast becoming mudholes—I headed toward the shop, where I saw a light through a half-open door. Men were probably working on equipment to wait out the rain. Whelan pets used to take refuge there when I was a child. "Natasha? Poe Boy?"

A bark answered my call, and a beagle trotted out, uttering yips of welcome. When I was thoroughly greeted, I gave him a push. "Find Tasha."

He headed not back to the shop but toward a small brick building I had forgotten was there. Little more than a large room with a chimney, tucked between the shop and the cleaning shed, it had been off-limits and locked when I was small. Today, smoke rose from its chimney and floated away to merge with the mist.

Poe Boy bayed as he bounded over thick, wet tufts of grass between the tractor ruts. He had inherited his mother's voice, and nobody can sound as insistent as a beagle. If Natasha was close by, she'd know he was looking for her. He stopped at the door and barked a command.

Henry Joyner stepped out, rolling down the sleeves of a bright orange coverall. He turned and said over one shoulder, "Somebody's looking for you." Poe Boy slithered between his legs and dashed, still barking, through the door.

"She's in here," Henry called to me. He used to be the bass soloist in the high school chorus, and still had one of the deepest voices I'd ever heard—something like a bullfrog crossed with a foghorn. It carried well across the space between us.

He held the door open, and a tiny girl in a pink sweat suit and a purple jacket darted out, oblivious of the drizzle. Poe Boy followed with a grin that said, "See? I found her."

Natasha was shrieking. As she got closer, I heard, "Here's Henry! Here's Henry!"—as if *he* were the one we had been looking for. "And look, Miss Me-Mama, I got a teera!" In one hand she waved a circle of metal. As she ran, pink barrettes on six braids bobbed like little butterflies circling her head.

A damp leopard in spike heels streaked around the back corner of the house, closing in on her prey. "What were you doing with that child in there? Tasha, did this man hurt you? What were you doing in there with him?"

I had never seen a large woman move so fast. She grabbed up the startled child and held her so tight I feared Natasha would be brain-damaged from lack of oxygen. All the time, Alex screamed at Henry—not in the cultured vocabulary she'd acquired at library school but in graphic language bred in Chicago's public housing and honed in the U.S. Army. It was odd to hear such language from one who looked like a model with raindrop diamonds on her shining curls.

Poe Boy enthusiastically added his dollar's worth. The misty grove echoed with bedlam.

Henry came closer. I read his name embroidered in white above his breast pocket and saw drops of water shining on his hair. He waited until Alex turned from him to the child in her arms, holding one arm up to shelter her from the rain. "I've told you and told you not to go anywhere with a stranger. How could you go running off—"

Then Henry held up one hand and stepped toward her. "She's all right. I didn't hurt her."

"How do I know that? How do I know—"

"Henry's my friend." Natasha reached out and patted Alex's cheek. She must be accustomed to her mother's temper, because it didn't seem to faze her. "Look, Mama, he gibbed me a teera." She held out a circle of metal.

"He's got no business giving you anything." Alex glowered at him.

I was getting soaked. Maybe it was time for me to intervene. "Don't antagonize him," I told her. "The man is a wizard at fixing things. Henry? Alex's car won't start. Would you take a look at it?"

He gave a disgusted snort, but strolled through the wet grass toward the Honda. He filled his orange coveralls nicely and walked with the easy stride of a man who knew it. The pretty little boy had grown into a handsome man, except for the sullen expression around his mouth. "What's the matter?" he muttered as he passed me.

"Sounds like the battery," I said, like I knew all about cars. I trotted along behind him, taking four steps to his every three. My poor shoes would never be the same. Poe Boy trotted at my heels—as much use at fixing cars as I am.

Henry went to the front of the Honda while Alex set Natasha on the backseat. He fiddled with something with his left hand and gestured with his right hand. "Try it now."

Alex glared in his direction, but slid behind the wheel and turned the key with her door open, obviously not expecting much. The car started like a new one.

"Nothing but a loose connection." Wiping his palms on his orange seat, he sounded like he was talking about more than the car.

He turned to go, but I stopped him. "Have you met Alexandra James, our library director? And this is Natasha."

"Natasha and I have met," he said shortly.

Natasha waved the circle of metal at me and called, "Look, Miss Me-Mama—"

"I told you not to call her that," Alex reminded her. "Her name is Miss MacLaren."

Natasha pouted. "Cricket says her name is Me-mama."

"Miss Me-mama is fine," I told Alex. "I've been called worse."

Natasha set the "tiara" on her head, but it slid down over one eye. She shoved it back. It slipped down again. Undismayed, she grabbed it in one hand and waved it about. "This one is too big, but Henry's gonna make me a real one with a diamond on it and a magic wand with a star on it and I'll be a fairy princess." She managed to say all that without pausing for breath.

Alex frowned, but all she said was, "How much do I owe you?"

"Nothing but a little respect." He turned on his heel and strode back to the shed.

"He's a real ray of sunshine." She peered into the back to make sure Poe Boy was in the car and Natasha was fastened into her seat belt.

"He's my friend," Natasha said firmly. Poe Boy yipped his agreement.

"He's a good mechanic," I added, "and you did get a bit wild back there."

Alex gave a rueful grunt. "I did, didn't I?" She lowered her voice. "But you don't think he messed with Tasha, do you?" I shook my head. "Isaac tells me I'm too protective, but she's all I've got." She twisted her lips into an embarrassed smile. "Thank the man for me next time you see him, will you?"

"I will." I waved as they headed up the drive.

As long as I was there and already soaking wet, I figured I might as well go on and thank Henry now.

❧ 5 ❧

The door was shut.

I knocked, and when Henry didn't answer, I pushed it open a crack.

The room was dim, lit only by a blazing fire in a hooded fireplace, but I could see that the walls were brick inside as well as out. Rain pattered on the tin roof. An anvil sat to one side, a blacker shadow among the gray.

Henry stood with his back to me, holding something in the blaze. With his light brown skin and orange coveralls he looked like a golden idol silhouetted against the flames.

I stepped inside to wait until he finished, and felt excitement rise within me. I hadn't seen a blacksmith's since childhood, when I used to creep into Granddaddy's blacksmith shed to watch him repair tools with a similar fire and anvil. Being allowed to work the bellows to keep the fire hot was a coveted privilege for his grandchildren. As his only granddaughter, I outranked the boys.

I heard a hum and saw that grandchildren and bellows had been replaced by an electric blower. Henry was so engrossed, I didn't want to interrupt, so I stood silent until he pulled something from the fire and turned to plunge a red-hot blade into a trough. White stinking smoke filled the shed. I doubled over coughing and turned toward the open door to catch my breath.

"Just a minute, Miss Mac," he said in a disgusted tone. "I can't stop right now."

I fanned the air in front of my face and peered at him through a watery haze. His eyes never left the blade. Within seconds, he pulled it out, and something viscous and gleaming streamed from the tip. He pulled up plastic goggles and wiped sweat from his forehead with his forearm, then opened the oven of an electric stove that stood incongruously to one side.

"What are you doing now?" I asked, curious.

"Making a machete." He stuck it into the oven and closed the door.

"I knew that. My granddaddy used to make and fix tools. But he never used a cookstove to temper his blades."

"It keeps an even temperature. I'm done now, for an hour or so." He pulled off a thick glove and wiped his forehead again. "What you want now?"

I gave him a long, level look. "Not the warmest welcome I ever got from somebody I gave lime suckers to most of his growing-up years."

He shrugged. "I'm busy here."

"We sell machetes pretty cheap these days."

"I prefer to make my own." He reached up to pull a cord that turned on a bulb above his head. It made a pool of light that didn't reach the corners.

I looked around and saw a couple of other handmade machetes hanging on the back wall.

"You prune with those?"

"Some, and the Mexican workers like them."

"What's that you used to harden the blade?" I went to peer into the trough. "My granddaddy used water."

"I prefer oil. It does make a stink, though." He propped his backside against a worktable, crossed his arms over his chest, and waited for me to explain why I was there.

I cleared the rest of the smoke from my lungs. "Alex asked me to thank you for getting her car started. She's not always—" I backed up and started over. "She tends to be very careful where Natasha is concerned."

He gave a disbelieving snort. "So careful she lets the kid wander off, open shut doors, and go into buildings all on her own? Where was her mother when she was roaming around?" He was very large and very angry.

Bothering him in the shed now seemed like an idea I should have thought about twice, but I resisted an urge to step back. "Trying to start her car. She thought Natasha and Poe Boy were going to stay nearby, and she didn't know anybody was around."

"In harvest season? There's folks all over this place— working on equipment, running the cleaning shed—" He stopped and exhaled a deep, disgusted breath. "Okay, you know all that, but maybe she didn't. Still, she oughta take better care of that kid."

"Well, she was sorry she jumped all over you, and she wanted me to tell you." That wasn't precisely what Alex said, but it was near enough.

He gave a sarcastic grunt. "I get to keep my library card?"

"Something like that."

"That's good. Never can tell when I might need it."

He pulled on his glove again, pulled down his goggles, and picked up a thin rod of metal with a pair of tongs. He thrust it into the flames and, when it was red-hot, carried it to the anvil and began to hammer it. Clearly he thought the interview was over. I ought to have left, but instead I stood watching while he reheated and folded the rod until a star with blunt points began to take shape. When the star was done, he took a second rod, eyed it, and sawed off a piece about twelve inches long. Then he heated both pieces and reached for his hammer. I stepped out of the way of sparks while he attached the star to one end of the rod. Finally, with a hiss of steam, he plunged the finished work into the oil. Again we were separated by a stinking cloud.

All that time he'd kept his back to me. He must have presumed I'd left, for he flinched when I coughed again. He recovered quickly, though, and held up the finished product with one hand while he turned off the blower with the other. "That look like a wand to you?"

I tried to match his careless tone. "Close enough for government work."

"Good. I didn't get her head measurement, so I can't do a tiara."

"I'll get it for you," I offered. "That's marvelous, Henry. And very kind."

I was the one being kind. His face was stony, and he seemed to have left all his manners and most of his conversation in South Carolina.

A dim memory stirred somewhere in the back of my mind. "You have a little girl, too, don't you?"

"I thought I did." He flipped a switch, and a belt moved rapidly, filling the small space with a shrill, angry whine. Henry's mouth looked like he'd been sucking on bitterness, and his gray eyes smoldered in the dimness like the dying coals behind him.

He strode toward me and raised one arm. I stepped back, breath caught in my throat.

He reached over my shoulder and seized one of the machetes from the wall.

Generations of fear rose inside me, branded into the fiber of my being by tales told woman to woman while snapping beans under the chinaberry trees of my childhood home. Would I follow my great-grandmother's bloody example? She was hacked to death by a field hand for the locket she wore.

I could not have moved if my life depended on it. For a second, I thought it did. Then Henry turned, carried the machete back to the sharpener, and lowered the blade to the belt. The room filled with metallic screams and a shower of sparks.

Hot with shame and pretending—as much to myself as to him—that I hadn't really been scared, I moved closer to watch, but out of range of the sparks. I didn't want holes in my pantsuit.

When he lifted the blade to examine it, I asked in the momentary quiet, "What happened to your little girl?"

He gave me a long stare. "You really want to know?"

I nodded. He lowered the blade again, and his voice was

brutal, striking me word by word as he punctuated the short sentences with the shrieks of metal against abrasive.

"I had a wife. *And* a little girl. For ten years. Until my wife got hooked on crack. Moved in with her dealer." He held up the machete and examined the edge, then pressed metal to belt again. Again shrieks filled the air.

When it looked like he was going to leave the story hanging there forever, I went close enough to yell, "Where is the child?"

He lifted the blade and spoke into the lull. "With her mother. When I told Janeen I wanted Latoya, she informed me Latoya isn't mine." Was it heat from the fire or his fury that made the air so thick and stifling?

He cut off the wheel, and all sound was sucked into silence.

The rain quickened overhead. He lifted the machete and swung it around his head again and again, filling the air with the *whoosh* of the blade.

"She knew the whole stinkin' time"—*whoosh*—"who that baby's daddy was"—*whoosh*—"but he wouldn't marry her"—*whoosh*—"and support the two of them"—*whoosh*.

I stepped away, having no desire to die even an accidental death in that shed.

Then he dropped his arm, and the machete fell with a thud to the table. "It was my own fault. I was too stupid and ashamed to take time for a paternity test before I said 'I do.'" He spoke toward the window and the deepening darkness.

"You were pretty young, too," I reminded him, wishing I had more in the way of comfort to offer.

He went on like I hadn't spoken. "Gave up a college scholarship, worked my tail off for ten years fixing cars to put bread on the table, and for what? Can you tell me that? For what?" He turned, picked up his hammer, and hit the anvil a blow that made my ears ring.

Tears stung behind my eyelids. No wonder he had changed. Who was it about whom someone wrote, "The iron entered his soul"? Knowing you have wasted years of your life, thrown away your best chances on somebody else's lie, can do that to a person.

Henry was talking to the fire now, spitting words into the flames. "I spoke to a lawyer. Thought maybe I could get custody. Janeen was an unfit mother, for sure. But the judge gave custody to Janeen's mother, on the grounds that Latoya wasn't mine. Wasn't *mine?*" He swung around and accidentally jerked the light cord. The shed went dark, except for the hellish fire. All I could see in its dim light were the whites of his eyes and his teeth—a mask of despair hanging in darkness. "Who was it changed her diapers, rocked her to sleep, fed her bottles, read her stories, helped with her homework, and covered for her mother all those nights she was out partying and didn't come home? If that didn't make her mine, what would?" He jerked the light cord so hard it broke off in his hand. He flung it into the fire.

I blinked, adjusting to the sudden light. "Where are they now? We might—"

He turned his back, and tears clogged his voice. "I don't have a clue. They left the place where we'd been staying, and Janeen told me not to try to find her, she wouldn't have me hanging around Latoya anymore. I did anyway, asked everybody she knew—even asked her bitch of a mother, and I'm not saying that lightly, Miss Mac. That woman raised Janeen, and I heard she gave Latoya back to Janeen as soon as the court stopped watching. But nobody would tell me anything. I've spent two years looking for my child. By now she's twelve. She's probably forgotten me. And I don't have any earthly idea where she is." The last sentence was wrung out from the whole cloth of grief.

He picked up the machete again and sliced the air, but it was a halfhearted effort. When it was over, he hung the blade back on its hook with a precision the act didn't warrant. The set of his shoulders warded off sympathy.

"So that's why you came home." I made my voice as matter-of-fact as I could.

"No. I came home because Daddy called, all upset. He

said there was something I needed to know and he wanted to tell me in person. I arranged with my boss to come the next weekend and stay a week, but before I got here Daddy died. Now Mama doesn't want to be alone, the damn crop needs harvesting, and at the rate it's raining I'll be here until kingdom come."

He picked up his hammer again, struck the anvil so hard that sparks fell in a shower around his feet. Hitting anvils was better than pounding people, I supposed, if you were that full of barbed wire and hate.

I wanted so desperately to say something that might help. "I'm sure Latoya will never forget you. No good we do to a child is ever forgotten."

He gave a grunt of pure derision. "You want me to make a magic wand for you? Think that can make fairy tales come true?"

"I don't believe in magic," I told him tartly. "Just miracles."

"Start working one on that librarian, then," he told me. "It would take a powerful miracle to make something human out of her." He bent to extinguish the fire.

Dismissed, I turned to go, then remembered two things. "What were you arguing with Edie about this morning?"

He frowned, as if trying to remember. "Oh, she wanted us to see if we could do some work in the grove, and I told her it's too wet. After tonight it's gonna be wetter."

"You haven't been playing practical jokes on her, have you? Putting her car seat back, or letting her cat out?"

"No." He tossed the word over his shoulder without looking around.

"Somebody has, and I wondered if it was you, teasing or something." It sounded pretty lame. I opened the door and let in the dusk, then I turned. "It was good to talk with you, Henry. Don't be a stranger. Stop by the store one day soon and I'll give you a green sucker."

He blew out an exasperated breath. "You're looking at an orange one."

❧6❧

High above the drive, Josiah had installed a halogen security light that had come on while I was with Henry. With rain falling around it, it seemed a giant shower spraying my car. I hurried toward it, pocketbook over my head, pants legs soaked, and shoes squishing with every step.

Because I was watching the ground for rocks and puddles, I didn't notice the approaching car until headlights blinded me. I dashed off the track into slick knee-high grass as a small white two-door swung around my Nissan and parked close to the back steps.

A black umbrella emerged, then a tall, pale somebody unfolded from the driver's door and bent to retrieve something from behind the seat. Long bright hair gleamed in the light.

"Hey," I called, still trembling from the scare she'd given me. "You must be Valerie."

She jerked erect. "Oh! I didn't know anybody was here."

I headed for the shelter of the carport. "That's my car." I pointed.

"Oh." She looked at the Nissan doubtfully, as if it had materialized. "I didn't see it." I didn't bother to remind her she had just driven around it.

She was tall, mostly legs encased in tight jeans. She wore a bulky white sweater over them and white running shoes. I couldn't determine the color of her eyes, but they were large and light, the best feature in a face that was long and strong,

with a large nose and wide chin. Odd shadows made one
cheek look purple and green. Her hair looked green, too, in
the halogen glow, falling from a center part straight to her
waist. It was so thick and strong, I had a sudden picture of it
swinging in one long braid from a castle window to haul up
a prince.

She heaved a loaded book bag over one shoulder as easily as if it were empty. "If you came to see Edie, I think she's,
like, gone." She peered around the grove, in case Edie should
appear from behind a tree.

"I was down visiting with Henry," I explained.

She gave the shed an incurious look. "Oh. Is he still
here?"

"Working on something."

"Oh." She stood swinging the book bag, not noticeably
skilled in the art of conversation.

"You must be Valerie," I repeated. "I'm Judge Yarbrough,
and I came down to—" At the moment I couldn't remember.
It seemed like I'd been there a week.

She waited, patient as a good child. "—see Henry?" she
suggested helpfully.

"Yes," I agreed, relieved. "And there's something on the
porch for Edie." I pointed. I didn't say I had brought it, but
then again, I didn't say I hadn't.

She glanced toward the screen. "Oh." She got more
mileage out of that word than anybody I'd ever met. "I'll take
it in. Do you want a cup of coffee or something? You look
real wet."

I *felt* wet. And cold. The damp air had a bite now that the
sun was down. A hot cup of coffee was the best offer I'd had
all day. So what if Joe Riddley went to dinner without me? I
would get there in time for dessert.

If she was surprised by my acceptance, she gave no sign,
just turned back to the car. "Oh. I nearly forgot my fabric."
She pulled out a white plastic bag. "I went up near Augusta
for it, after class. Won't it be great when that new store opens
and we can just run by for stuff?"

Fortunately, she didn't expect a reply. She strode along the covered walkway and onto the porch, fumbling in her book bag for her keys. I trotted behind like a Lilliputian following Gulliver. "I know they're in here," she lamented. "They have to be. I had them at lunch." Her hair fell in a shawl around her shoulders.

I wished I had hair long enough to warm my neck. "You drove home," I reminded her.

"Oh, yeah. So they must be here." She rummaged some more, while I stood there wishing I'd had the sense to wear my trench coat or at least bring an umbrella.

She pulled up the keys like a magician removing her first rabbit from a hat. "Oh! Here they are!" She dropped the book bag with a clunk and unlocked the dead bolt above the ancient knob. Her hands were large and strong, with long fingers.

"You play the keyboard, don't you?" I wanted to divert her from my chattering teeth.

She turned and looked down at me, obviously pleased. "Have you heard the band?"

"No, somebody told me. But you've got good hands for a keyboard."

She stretched her hands into two stars and considered them like she hadn't really noticed them before. "I guess. Come on in. I'll get some lights on."

She flipped a switch beside the door. The kitchen hadn't changed much in thirty years. Same brown cabinets with yellow countertops. Same cinnamon-toned appliances. Same table with a wood-toned Formica top and four country kitchen chairs. Same sunflower curtains framing the double window behind the sink.

Valerie locked the dead bolt behind us, then cruised the downstairs turning on enough lights to delight the power company. I took the keys she'd left on the table and retrieved Alex's files. Valerie and I returned at the same time. "Oh. I forgot all about those. Put them there." She pointed at the kitchen table toward which I was heading. "That way, Edie will see them as soon as she comes in. Be sure to lock the door, though. We're real careful about that."

Locking up seemed silly for the length of time it would take me to drink a cup of coffee, but I honored the request.

It wasn't until I turned back to hand her the keys and we stood face-to-face under the bright light, that I saw that the left side of her face still showed purple and green. She saw me staring and put up one hand to cover it. "I'm sorry. It looks awful, I know. I ran into a door."

Denial runs deep.

"That's what everybody says, honey, but you and I both know somebody did that to you, and whoever he is, he's not likely to quit."

"Oh, no, I ran into a door. Honest. I'm very clumsy." As a demonstration, she walked toward the cabinets and ran straight into the corner of the countertop. With Olive's accusations rattling around in my head, I remained skeptical.

I watched, puzzled, while Valerie took down two glasses, filled them with ice, and poured in iced tea. She handed me one. "Here you are."

I stood there shivering so hard the ice clinked in its glass, wondering what happened to that cup of hot coffee she'd offered.

She handed me the other glass. "Hold this and I'll turn up the thermostat. We turn it way back all day while we're not here." I had already figured that out. As soon as she left, I set the glasses on the table to prevent frostbite.

The heat came on with a click and a dull roar, but it would never be able to heat those high ceilings and big square rooms before I finished my glass of tea and left. Chilly wisps of air trailed down my neck and swirled around my ankles, reminding me that when the house was built, Georgians were more concerned about attracting breezes than keeping warm.

I started to pull out a kitchen chair. Valerie asked from the door, "Wouldn't you like me to make a fire in the living room? It's all laid and everything."

"That would be wonderful." I followed her through the

dining room, carrying both glasses and wishing I had grabbed a dish towel to put around them.

The dining room was filled with file-sized cartons stacked shoulder-high and neatly labeled with the names of Edie's various clubs. Papers covered the table and spilled onto the floor. Valerie looked around and explained, "Edie works in here, and she says you should never throw papers out. You never know when you might need them."

Across the hall I saw a big room empty except for several card tables and chairs. "That's where Edie's bridge club meets," my tour guide explained.

She led me to the living room, which was as cold as the others. With a wave of one arm, she asked, "Don't you love her bears?"

Edie's brocade couch, chairs, and grand piano were mixed in with Josiah's elderly recliner. On and around all of them were teddy bears. They sat on chairs, lined the mantelpiece, and nestled into the corners of the couch. An enormous bear wearing black tails, white shirt, and Wick's famous paisley bow tie sat on the bench of the old baby grand.

A family of Pilgrim bears sat in child-sized chairs at a small table before the fireplace. The table was covered by a pale orange cloth, decorated with short orange candles and dried flowers, and set with miniature china. When on earth did Edie find time to dress bears and decorate small tables, with everything else she had to do?

But a little girl lives and breathes in every grown woman. When I bent closer and saw that the tea set had two serving platters, a lidded serving bowl, and a gravy boat, I itched to pull up a chair and join them.

Valerie straightened Papa Bear's black construction-paper hat. "I helped make their clothes." Her voice was shy and proud. "Edie's teaching me to sew. The material I got today is for their Christmas outfits." She added, as if it were an afterthought, "I made Mama Bear's apron all by myself." She stepped back so I could admire it.

The orange apron was gathered onto a bib and tied at neck

and waist. Its stitches were almost straight, the gathers nearly even. "You did a great job," I congratulated her. "I'd never have guessed you were a beginner."

"I am, though. I never made anything by myself before." She stroked Mama Bear's shoulder as if to assure herself the apron was real.

The chill had reached my bones by then, and my hands and feet were beyond feeling. I set each glass on a coaster on the coffee table and rubbed my palms together. "Were you going to light a fire?" I'd have sat on the couch, but even the furniture looked cold, so I walked around, hoping to warm up. My perambulations took me over to the loveliest piece of furniture in the room—a rosewood curio cabinet with glass doors. It used to grace Edie's foyer.

"That's got a light," Valerie called from across the room. "Down on the right side."

I pushed a button and illuminated Wick's mother's prized set of American snuffboxes, so tiny and brightly colored they looked like jewels. "Those are Edie's boxes," Valerie informed me. "Folks used to carry chewing tobacco in them, or something."

Her voice was muffled. I turned to see her kneeling beside the fireplace, which was laid with wood, but no kindling and no paper. She had her head right down near the logs, peering at them as if waiting for them to reveal their secrets. "I guess I need a match—"

A blind man could have seen she had no idea how to light a fire. "Do you have any newspaper?"

She looked around. "I don't know if Edie got one today."

Next to the fireplace, an old copper bath held newspapers. A coal scuttle held kindling, and a china vase held long matches. I headed that way, but before I could reach them, Valerie grabbed a match. She struck it and tossed it into the fireplace. When nothing happened, she tried another. The third time she grabbed a fistful, lit them all, and flung them toward the logs. Several missed their target and bounced on the floor. Wisps of smoke curled from the carpet.

Valerie was still bent over peering at the cold logs. "It's not burning," she lamented.

I dashed across the room, shoved her aside, and stamped out embers, so busy looking for every wisp that I heard a motorcycle in the drive only to register that Henry must be going home.

Finally I reached for the lone match left in the vase. "Let me do it." I wadded paper under the logs, set kindling on top of the paper, and lit the fire.

"Ohhh." Valerie nodded as she watched flames catch the kindling. "I see."

I put the screen in front and pressed my hands against it, wondering if we'd need to amputate all my fingers or only a few. It took me a while to realize that the crinkly sound I heard was not the fire in front of me.

I looked around to see Mama Bear and her tablecloth blazing as merrily as the logs, with flames already slithering along the fabric to lick the back of the chair and the table legs.

I gasped. Valerie turned. "Oh, no!" She stood, mesmerized and useless.

I grabbed an afghan from the sofa and started to beat out the flames.

"Valerie?" a gruff voice demanded from the door. "What have you done *now?*"

A life-sized teddy bear, all black and gold, strode into the room, hoisted the blazing chair with one hand and the table with the other, and headed to the kitchen like a waiter bearing a flaming dessert. His heavy black boots squished as he walked. Mama Bear wobbled so in her chair, I followed to be sure she didn't fall. I reached the kitchen in time to see him tip her into the sink. A second later, the porch's screen door slammed shut.

Sunflower curtains dangled dangerously near the blaze, so I hurried over to turn on the water. Pain seared my right wrist as I reached for the tap and got too close to the flames. A hiss of steam filled the room. I choked as smoke filled my eyes and lungs.

My poor jacket was singed and my wrist burned like—well, fire. I was on my way to the fridge for ice when the gruff voice announced, "I beat out the fire, but the furniture's charred and some of the dishes got broke. Valerie?" he raised his voice. "You get in here, you hear me?"

The only answer was a whimper from the living room.

He called, unmoved. "Don't you cower in there like this ain't your fault. We all know it good and well is. You come on in here, now."

He stomped over to the sink and peered down at the bear. "Rest in peace, Mama."

While he examined the bear, I examined him. He was tall and stocky with a wiry red-gold beard and frizzy gold hair holding a glint of red. It was pulled back in a wet braid about a foot long, tied with a leather thong that matched those on his wrists. The rest of his hair was dry except for a few springy tendrils that were oddly soft against his heavy face. He was dressed all in black. Black jeans, slung low and drooping, soaked by the rain. Wide black belt dotted with huge silver studs. Black short-sleeved shirt to show off a tattoo of a golden sword with red flames all around it. Appropriate.

I didn't see Valerie until she gasped, "Oh! My apron got burnt up!" Forlorn, she peered down at the mess in the sink. "It's absolutely ruined." She lifted one charred orange scrap and held it to her cheek. Tears rolled past it and through it.

"The whole house nearly got burnt up." The man reached around Valerie and poked the bear with a wooden spoon from the dish drainer. "Poor Mama Bear is done for. What were you doing, Valerie?" His voice was both disgusted and puzzled.

"Lighting the fire."

He started toward the living room. "Omigod, the whole place'll be burning down."

She caught his arm. "It's okay. There's a screen in front of it."

He shook his head in dismay. "I've told you not to play with matches."

"I know, but I wanted her to get warm." She pointed my way. "She was shivering."

Her past tense was correct. There's nothing like a good fire to warm a body up.

The man turned to look at me good for the first time. With two blue-eyed golden giants standing before me and the sink sending up intermittent wisps of steam, I felt like I'd wandered into Valhalla. He'd have looked at home in a horned helmet, she in flowing robes holding a giant chalice of mead.

"Who are you?" he demanded. Or maybe, given his size, that was his normal way of asking for things. I suspected he usually got what he asked for.

"Judge Yarbrough." I emphasized the first word, although I seldom introduce myself that way. He was the person most likely to have given Valerie that bruised cheek, and I wanted him to know who and what he was dealing with. "I came to see Henry, and Valerie invited me in for—a glass of tea." No point in reminding Valerie she had offered hot coffee. The way her mind worked, she'd probably insist on making it right then. "When she tried to light the fire, a stray match must have landed in Mama Bear's lap."

He grabbed Valerie's arm and gave her a shake that would have felled a lesser woman. "She's sweet, but not wholly reliable around dangerous objects. Not real punctual, either. We need to get going, hon."

"Oh!" She clapped a hand to her mouth in dismay. "I need to change. I only got home a few minutes ago. And I'll need to cover—you know." Her hand reached toward her eye and poked her cheek. She winced.

"Go, then." He ignored the wince and pushed her toward the door.

As she ran up the stairs, I said, "I didn't catch your name."

"Maybe because we've been too busy for me to give it.

Frank. Frank Sparks." He gave a rumble of a laugh. "You've had enough sparks for one day, ain't you?"

I thought of Henry's fire in the shed and Valerie's in the house. "Just about."

I was feeling sick about Edie's house. The air was smoky, her carpet was pocked with burns, her little tableau was ruined, and I had no idea how much she valued the table, chair, dishes, or Mama Bear. If they were childhood heirlooms—

When I thought about her coming home from a long, wet drive and finding the place like that, I teared up.

Frank noticed, but he read me wrong. "We better let some of this smoke out." He reached across the sink and shoved up both windows at once. The wet air was clean, but frigid.

"Valerie don't mean any harm," he assured me, fanning with both thick hands. "She's a bit what you might call absentminded."

I'd be more likely to agree with Meriwether and call it flaky, but I've always found it wise to humor folks the size of small mountains.

I reached for my pocketbook, which was still on the table. "I guess I ought to be going."

"Us, too," he said amiably. "Valerie and me play in a band, and we're due to play for a wedding reception tonight, down near Sandersville."

"Shall I put out the fire in the living room before I go?"

"I'll do it." He tromped through the door, then called back over one huge shoulder, "I can't understand why she wanted a fire on a day like this, anyway. It's plenty warm."

Not with the rain-filled air pouring through two open windows, reminding me again that this was November and I was soaked. I wanted to get in my nice dry car, turn the heater on high, and find me some supper.

First, though, I gathered all my courage into one deep breath and said as he returned, "Don't hit her again. The courts don't look kindly—," His frown stopped me.

He looked as fierce as Hagar the Horrible, his bushy reddish eyebrows almost meeting over his nose. "Did she tell you I hit her? I never. She run into a door."

"That's what they all say," I said grimly.

He shook his head. "I wouldn't hit her. Even if I had a mind to, my mama would kill me if I ever hit a woman."

I tried to picture a mother who could threaten this man and get away with it, but my imagination boggled. Neither could I picture Valerie simply walking into a door. "Well, just remember what I said. Good night."

As I went out, I saw a black leather jacket and a shiny silver helmet slung across one of Edie's rockers like they were at home. A black-and-silver Harley was pulled to the far side of the carport, out of the wet. On the grass beyond the back steps, the small table and chair sat in the downpour with little dishes scattered about them.

I called from the porch, "Come help me clean up this mess before we leave."

Frank clumped out, carrying a tray. Together we sought dishes in the high grass under a glaring light that was as much hindrance as help. I was soaked and shaking so much my teeth sounded like castanets. He seemed oblivious to the wet and cold. His huge hands were awkward in picking up tiny dishes, but he combed the slick grass with his fingers to find every shard. He didn't say a word until we were finished, then he held up a handful of pieces.

"Some of it can't be fixed, but I think this here's all the pieces of the teapot and one of the bowls. I can glue them good as new."

If they were antiques, Edie would want them glued by an expert. "Let's leave them on the table. I'll write her a note," I suggested. "If she wants you to glue them, you can do it later."

When we'd set all the dishes on the kitchen table beside Alex's files, he muttered, "I'm real sorry I broke some of it. I was thinking more about the fire than the dishes."

"You saved her house," I reminded him. "I'll call her later to explain what happened."

"That's good. Like I said, we gotta play at a wedding reception near Sandersville, and we probably won't be back until Edie's asleep." Reminded, he turned his head and yelled, "Valerie? Get your tail down here. We gotta go, girl!"

I found a small pad near the telephone and left a note for Edie explaining the fire, taking equal blame and saying I'd be glad to ask Maynard Spence at Wainwright Antiques to arrange for repair or to look for another tea set, although I knew no tea set ever replaces the one you played with as a girl. By the time I finished, I'd written half a novel.

Frank had wandered to the foot of the stairs and was yelling for Valerie again, so I let myself out without saying another good-bye. Not until I reached the city limits did hazy unease congeal into thought.

I had locked that back door. So how did Frank get in?

⟨7⟩

I stopped by the house to change my clothes and barely made it to the country club before they stopped serving at eight. I was hurrying so fast that I barreled smack into Shep Faxon on the front steps. I personally find Shep's hearty depiction of a good ole Southern boy overdrawn and often offensive, so we use another lawyer, but he does the legal work for a lot of families in town. "You bettah hurry," he boomed in a thick country accent I know for a fact he did not grow up with. "They just set out the best desserts in Gawjah, and I know how fond you ah of good desserts." Chuckling at his own wit, he headed toward his white Cadillac. Shep drove only American.

Joe Riddley sat at a round table for six in the far corner of the dining room with our younger son, Walker, and his wife, Cindy. Seeing my husband across a room still gives my heart a lift. He's tall and lanky, like his Scottish grandfather, with high cheekbones, straight dark hair, and dark skin he inherited from his Cherokee grandmother. The tad of gray that's beginning to streak his hair makes him look more distinguished, and I cherish the lines in his face. I was there when every one of them was chiseled. He says I caused most of them, but just ignore him.

As I got closer, I gave a little huff of disgust. He had put on the brown slacks and brown-and-tan sweater I'd laid out, but substituted his favorite blue shirt for the tan one. Walker and Cindy, of course, looked like contestants in a Best Dressed in Hopemore pageant. Cindy's long brown vest and pants were particularly elegant, and exactly matched her hair.

Sitting with them, as if I hadn't already had enough of that family for one day, were Genna and Adney Harrison.

Adney saw me first, and lit my way across the room with a hundred-watt smile that said, "You are the very person we've been waiting for." No wonder the man was a good salesman. That combination of rugged face, smiling eyes, perfect white teeth, and well-shaped hands that moved expressively when he talked made it hard to resist anything he wanted you to buy, including Adney. As I neared the table— holding my right arm down at my side so nobody would notice the burn on my wrist—he half rose from his chair. "Here comes the Judge," he intoned.

Joe Riddley, who had his back to me, turned and gave me a considering look. "So you're still alive, are you? Since these folks saw me all by myself looking pitiful, and insisted I join 'em, I figured I'd go ahead and eat before I went down to the morgue to identify your body."

Genna gasped. She must not have been familiar with how Joe Riddley talks when he's been worried about me.

I clapped him lightly on one shoulder. "You can postpone that trip a while. You reckon these nice people will expect us to find another table now that I've arrived?"

"Don't be silly," Cindy said. She shifted her purse from the vacant chair between her and Joe Riddley. I carry a pocketbook, Cindy carries purses. That tells you something about the difference between us.

Walker gave me a considering look. "We might let you stay if you mind your manners. But remember, Mama, no talking with your mouth full and no elbows on the table." He got up to hold my chair, and bent down to kiss me.

When I put up my face, it was like looking in a mirror— same brown eyes, same honey-brown hair—until he wrinkled his nose. "Phew! You smell like a bonfire. You been burning evidence?"

Joe Riddley's head came up, sniffing, too.

I hurried into my seat and said, to distract everybody, "Don't sass your mama or I'll paddle you, even if you are on the board here." He was up for president the following term, which we thought was real good for somebody four years away from forty.

Of course, Walker and Cindy are country club to the bone. They and their children practically live there. Joe Riddley and I don't golf, don't play tennis, and—up until we moved into town—did all our swimming in our own pool. We joined the club when Ridd went to high school, so he could play golf. We've kept our membership because we enjoy the folks we run into there and Hopemore doesn't have a whole lot of places to entertain. Lately we'd started eating there every Friday because the new chef set out a weekly seafood buffet and a table full of desserts.

Walker motioned the waiter to bring me a glass of tea. "Coffee," I said firmly. "Hot."

As Walker resumed his seat, he asked Adney, "You think I can in good conscience accept the presidency of this club, considering how much money it loses each month on my folks?"

"What are you talking about?" I demanded. "We never eat as many meals in a given month as we have to pay for, under that new rule you all made."

"I don't know," Adney said solemnly. "You may not come as often as some folks, but I've been watching Joe Riddley here put away seafood, and from what Walker says about the number of desserts you work your way through—"

"You all be nice," Genna begged.

"I'm not paying them any attention," I assured her. Joe Riddley swore that God got so busy making Genna beautiful, he forgot to give her a funny bone.

She *was* beautiful. So beautiful that folks seldom remembered that her tousled red curls used to be a dishwater-blond ponytail, or that she'd headed to college with thin lips and a flat chest. Somewhere in the past fifteen years she'd learned to play up her big brown eyes and flawless skin and had acquired a set of full red lips and an impressive bosom. At thirty-three or so, she was a stunner. But she had never been an intellectual, and nowadays she seemed to have nothing weightier on her mind than pleasing Adney and finding the best places to eat lunch with friends. I frankly couldn't see what Adney saw in her.

On my way to fill my plate, though, I recalled that he was ten years older than she, and what had brought them together was discovering that her daddy's pharmacy was on his regular call list. Walker had said Adney had been taking care of Olive since they were kids. Maybe he just liked taking care of women.

I'd barely settled in my chair again before Joe Riddley asked, too low for the others to hear, "So why were you so late?" He was eating the last pile on his plate, something involving crab, cream sauce, and noodles. He is very systematic about the way he approaches those buffets, filling a plate with one category of seafood at a time and eating all of one dish before he tackles the next. That was the end of his crab. With luck, I could stall him until he was ready to go for shrimp.

"Oh, you know, traffic court goes on and on." I applied butter to my roll as carefully as if I were going to be graded on the project.

Joe Riddley was a magistrate for thirty years before he retired and I took his place, so he has presided over his share of traffic courts. He actually enjoyed it, keeping a private tally of the number of trees that jumped in front of people, invisible speed limit signs, and red lights that looked green.

Right that minute, he was looking at me the same way he used to look at people who insisted the radar had been wrong. "Court didn't run late." He swabbed up the last bit of cream sauce with a bite of roll. "I called down there around five, and they said you'd left soon after four." He pushed back his chair and growled, "I'm going for shrimp. Cindy, you and Genna better help Little Bit here concoct a good story while I'm gone, or I'm gonna start looking for the fellow."

Genna looked so worried, I said, "Stop teasing. You're upsetting people."

Joe Riddley peered down at me like a tall dark stork. "I'm not teasing. I've read those women's magazines you leave lying around. They say when your spouse starts coming home late and lying about where he's been, there's bound to be somebody else. That goes two ways, so you better come up with a believable story, Little Bit, or I'm gonna oil my shotgun."

The others laughed, but Genna still looked anxiously from one of us to the other. She obviously expected imminent divorce.

Walker was also looking at me, but he had a speculative spark in his eye. They were going to find out eventually what I'd been up to—secrets don't last long in a small town—so I decided to make a story out of it. Southerners love stories. We learn as children that if you can make your story funny enough and long enough, annoyed adults may forget the reason they asked you to tell it.

So, as soon as Joe Riddley set his shrimp-filled plate next to mine, I started telling them about the geese in the sky, Alex's loose battery connection, Henry making machetes and a fairy wand, being offered hot coffee and given iced tea in a freezing house, and Valerie's attempt to make a fire without paper or kindling.

I neglected to mention what Henry had told me about his daughter and the part about Alex yelling at him for what he might have done to hers.

Folks were having a good old time, laughter flowing as freely as sweet tea, and I was well into describing Mama Bear engulfed in flames when it dawned on me that Genna might not want to hear we'd almost burned down her stepmama's house, so I skipped to the Black Knight riding in on his Harley to save the day—omitting the fact that he'd materialized through a locked door.

I'd barely finished when Genna said in a tight voice, "Olive says Edie needs to get rid of that girl. She— But Edie won't talk about it, and sleeping at the top of the house like she does— Besides, she never did want to be bothered with inconvenient details." She stopped short, maybe because she'd remembered inconvenient details of her own that Edie hadn't wanted to be bothered with.

Adney touched her arm lightly. "Let it go, honey. You know Olive is more annoyed about that bridge tournament right now than about Valerie."

Not for the first time, I wondered about a gene pool that could produce both Adney and Olive. He must have snatched all the looks and charm from their mother's womb five years before his sister was born. I got so distracted, picturing an unborn child grabbing everything he could get, that I didn't tune in to the conversation until Adney was saying, ". . . and Genna wants Edie to sell that big old place, invest her money, and move into something smaller in town. Edie won't, though, and I keep telling Genna, 'Honey, we can't make her do anything she doesn't want to do.' I guess the kind thing would be for us to sell our place and move out there with her, but I sure hate to move again so soon."

Again I suspected he'd also be reluctant to trade his elegant house on the golf course for Edie's in the pecan grove. Besides, that gravel drive would be real hard on Genna's Mercedes.

"What does she need all that space for?" Genna looked around at each of us, daring us to come up with a good answer and conveniently forgetting she and Adney had nearly twice as many square feet. "A town house would be easier to keep, and she'd be so much safer." Genna sounded like security was a major worry in Hope County.

"It's real peaceful out in the country," Joe Riddley opined. He forked in his last bite of shrimp scampi and shoved back his chair. "Be right back." He loped toward the buffet and came back with a plate loaded with catfish, always his last course.

We'd talked of other things while he was gone, and I'd thought we were finally finished discussing Edie until Genna turned to Cindy. "Edie's getting real forgetful, too. I'm worried about her. Last week she left her door unlocked all night. Burglars could have walked right in!"

Walker, who is an insurance agent, reassured her. "The actual chances of anybody showing up at that particular back door on that given night were slight. However"—he gave me a stern look—"I do recommend locking doors." I have been known to be a bit lax in that department. Then he leaned over and said to Genna in a whisper anybody could hear, "Everybody gets a little forgetful when they get old. Take Mama here—"

I opened my mouth to slap him upside the head with a few well-chosen words, but Adney looked around to make sure we weren't being overheard, lowered his voice, and said, "You all want in on a good deal? This isn't public knowledge yet, but next month a decision's gonna be made to finally four-lane Whelan Grove Road as far as I-20. A buddy of mine has a friend in the Georgia Department of Transportation, and he's already looking to buy land around the corner from the superstore. He says that whole area will eventually go subdivisions and commercial, because a fast road to I-20 will make this a practical drive for folks working in Augusta. My buddy says to buy quick, though, before the county commission messes things up with zoning regulations like the city council did inside the city limits several years ago."

Since Joe Riddley had worked like the dickens to get the city council to zone Hopemore, I expected him to say something. Instead, he sat there chewing catfish with a thoughtful expression. I hoped he wasn't planning to invest our life savings in real estate.

Adney was off and running now. "Edie can make a killing if she holds on to the land right at the road and sells the rest for housing. Think about it. Lots with huge pecan trees in the yards? People would kill to get one. They could build gorgeous places out there."

"You interested in developing it?" Joe Riddley asked mildly.

Adney held up both hands. "Not me. I'm a traveling salesman, not a land developer."

Joe Riddley chewed some more. Was he planning to become a real estate developer, without knowing the first thing about it?

Genna pouted. "If you owned your own business, you could stay home more." Then she sighed. "But Edie isn't going to sell the grove. She'll live in that old house until it falls down around her ears, and you'll be on the road forever."

Adney laughed. "Poor Genna, she keeps dreaming of the perfect marriage with a husband who comes home every night. Unfortunately, sweetie, you married a man with restless feet. You know I'd get bored if I wasn't on the road. Besides"—he leaned over and nuzzled her neck until she smiled and blushed—"it keeps the spice in our marriage." He shoved back his chair. "Who wants dessert?"

Walker shoved back, too. "We'd better hurry before Mama Locust descends on the table."

I drove home behind Joe Riddley, thinking I'd gotten off pretty light and glad we'd had people to distract him. While I fed Lulu, he went out to fetch Bo, his scarlet macaw, who lives on a small back porch behind the kitchen. If it was up to me, I'd leave that bird outside all the time. We had paid a fortune to enclose, heat, and air-condition his porch. However, Joe Riddley and Bo like to watch television together, Joe Riddley in his recliner and Bo on his shoulder.

I headed to the bedroom to exchange shoes for slippers, then took my favorite corner of the couch with Lulu beside me, her warm doggy head on my lap.

Joe Riddley pushed the "mute" button on the remote. "Okay, tell me what you were really up to down at Edie's, and this time skip the fairy wands and teddy bears."

I stroked Lulu as I told him about Alex's call that morning, how worried Edie was, and what Olive thought was going on, then I recapped my afternoon, with all the pieces this time. After I finished, Joe Riddley scratched his cheek like he was coming up with a brilliant idea. "You know, you don't really have to save the whole world. Parts of it can get along without your help."

"I know that," I said hotly. "I hadn't planned on going down there. I told you, it was because I wanted to drive by the superstore, but then I heard geese—"

"—and if you hadn't heard geese, you'd have seen something else that made you need to turn in. We both know you are itching to convince Alex that Edie doesn't have Alzheimer's, and you think the best way to do that is to find out who else left the door unlocked and moved her car seat."

There are definite disadvantages to marrying a man who has known you since he was six and you were four.

He wasn't finished. "You were most likely correct in what you told Alex. Edie is under a lot of stress right now, and that's probably why she's forgetting a few things." He reached for the remote. "But tell me, would you say you alleviated any stress by burning down her house?"

Bo, who always takes Joe Riddley's side, fixed me with a cold white eye. "Little Bit? Little Bit!" he scolded in Joe Riddley's most exasperated tone.

At least Lulu reached up and licked my chin. She always knows when I need a friend.

When Joe Riddley got engrossed in his programs, I went to the phone to make some calls. First I called Alex and had her measure Natasha's head. Then I called Henry and, since he was out, left the measurement with his mother, Daisy. Finally I called Edie. I felt I owed her a personal explanation in addition to the note, and I wanted to offer to look for a replacement tea set. Of course, if anything else odd had happened and she happened to want to talk about it . . .

She answered on the second ring. "I hope I didn't wake you," I apologized. "I know it's late—"

"I just came in from a card game," she assured me with a laugh that sounded more like the old Edie.

"Did you win?"

"What do you think? Can I help you?"

"I wanted to tell you why your house smells like smoke."

Our mamas raised us both right, so when I apologized for the fire Edie chimed right in assuring me no real damage had been done.

I was careful not to lay the blame on Valerie, so I was a bit vague about how the fire got started. Edie was too polite to ask for details.

I lamented profusely that her tea set got broken, and she claimed, "That's all right. I can glue the teapot together."

I jumped in with, "No, let me ask Maynard Spence to look for a new set," and she won that round by saying, "It's not an heirloom, MacLaren. I got it at a flea market a few years ago."

I moved on to the next playing field. "Your little table and chairs are ruined."

"Not at all. I'll sand them down and paint them, and they'll be as good as new."

"Well, poor Mama Bear—"

"Mama Bear was getting pretty scruffy anyway."

It was my turn to win, and we both knew it. "I insist on replacing her. That would make me feel a little better about all this."

"Okay, you can buy me a bear, but you aren't taking the blame. I know it had to be Valerie who let that match loose in the house. That girl is a walking disaster." She seemed to find that funny.

"I met Frank," I said, letting my voice trail off.

Edie laughed again. "Doesn't he look scary? But you wouldn't believe how handy he can be. He's fixed a lot of things around here since Valerie started bringing him home—my computer, a stopped-up sink, a running toilet. He even went up on the roof and replaced some shingles."

"Considering the height of your roof, that was downright

considerate. They said they were going to perform at some wedding reception tonight."

"Yeah, people seem to like their music. They do wedding receptions or play in clubs almost every week. I've been meaning to go hear them sometime, but I haven't. Seems like by the time I get home, I don't want to go back out."

"I can understand that." I could hardly wait for us to be done so I could sit on my couch with my feet up and watch Joe Riddley watching television.

"You think they're getting serious?" I was moving onto ground I had no claim to, and Edie had a right to get cross, but she laughed again.

"Heavens, no. Valerie's engaged to a man in the Navy. He's away on his six-months' whatever-it-is, but he'll be back a few weeks after Christmas."

After that we wound down, with me promising to buy her another bear and bring it by the library, and her telling me not to hurry, with everything else I had to do. "It's not urgent," she assured me. "Anytime in the next hundred years."

"Maybe even in the next fifty," I offered.

Death stalks us all our lives, and we never know when his breath is on our heels.

On Thanksgiving, we went to Ridd and Martha's for dinner, since they now had the big house. We had strong instructions to "come casual," but I like to fix up a little for special occasions, so I wore a new fall floral skirt with a yellow cotton sweater. I also persuaded Joe Riddley to change out of jeans and a tan work shirt into khaki slacks with a plaid shirt. It goes without saying that right up until we sat down, he wore his red cap with "Yarbrough's" stitched above the bill. He wears that cap so much, the boys swear they'll bury it with him.

The old Yarbrough place is half a mile down a gravel road. We were almost there when Joe Riddley looked in his rearview window and asked, "Is that Adney behind us? The way that SUV is mincing along, he must be afraid he'll get it dirty."

I turned. "I can't tell if it's Adney or Olive. They both drive gray Nissan Xterras, although Adney uses a Maxima for work." As a Nissan owner myself, I thought they had good taste.

When they climbed out I was glad I'd dressed up. Genna must have missed the "dress casual" bit, because she wore a beige silk slack suit with a creamy silk blouse that shrieked, "Spill cranberry sauce down me!"

Edie climbed out wearing a long khaki skirt with an orange sweater. She even wore pumpkin socks with her clogs, in honor of the holiday. The socks were a lot cheerier than her face, though. She looked like she hadn't slept all week. I nearly quipped, "Did somebody steal your beds?" until I remembered that this was her first Thanksgiving without Josiah or Wick. I was glad Martha had thought to invite them, and reached out to give her a hug. "Still winning at cards?"

She gave a funny choking sound. "Yes, there is still that." She grabbed onto me like she'd never let go, then stepped back with an embarrassed laugh. Edie and I weren't hugging friends.

Olive was in black and gray, of course. I wondered if she'd read some fashion advice that black was appropriate for all occasions.

"Welcome!" Ridd's daughter, Bethany, and her best friend, Hollis Stanton, called from the porch in unison. Bethany added, "You all come on in. Dinner's almost ready."

Hollis and Bethany had been best friends since third grade. Hollis's family had recently moved away, so she was living with Ridd and Martha for her senior year.* Bethany was tall and slender like her daddy and granddaddy, with their dark hair and eyes. Hollis was short and stocky, with a face full of freckles, a saucy grin, and a cloud of the liveliest red hair I'd ever seen. In certain lights it held glints of green, purple, and gold. The fact that Hollis had a lovely soprano voice always startled me, for she didn't look anything like my idea of a soprano.

I kept wishing I was at the children's table during dinner. The day was warm enough for Martha to serve them out on the screened side porch, and they had a lot more hilarity.

In addition to our four grandchildren and Hollis, Martha had invited two other teens, Smitty Smith and Tyrone Noland, whom she and Ridd had recently taken under their wings. Tyrone had been a favorite of mine since he was in el-

*Who Let That Killer in the House?

ementary school, a pudgy child with soft brown hair and eyes
like chips of sky who would stop by the store to ask, "You
want I should sweep your store, Miss Mac?" Because I knew
his mother struggled to make ends meet working in the produce department at the Bi-Lo, I usually found something for
him to do to earn spending money. He'd grown into an enormous young man, and had gone through a phase when he'd
dyed his hair black and worn nothing but black clothes. He
now looked like a German shepherd, his hair dark brown
with black tips. Today he had on a maroon shirt. I considered
that progress.

Smitty, on the other hand, I still had trouble tolerating. He
was shorter than Tyrone by a good five inches and probably
weighed a hundred pounds less, but every ounce of Smitty
was tight, angry muscle. Granted, since he'd started hanging
around Ridd and Martha's, he had shaved the long hank of
bleached hair that formerly grew out of his shaved scalp. He
now shaved his whole head. But he still wore all black,
sported cruel dragons tattooed on both arms, and wore more
earrings on various parts of his body than I owned. He had
the long, wary face of a predator and the cold gray eyes of an
eagle, and he regarded the world with an expression that was
hooded and watchful, like he was biding his time, waiting to
swoop in for a kill.

I went to refill the mashed potato bowl once and peeked
out to see what the children were finding so funny. Tyrone
and Hollis were cutting up, as usual. Only Smitty wasn't
laughing.

At the grown-ups' table, the men had two thoughts:
shovel down all the food they could, then stagger to the den
to watch football. From their analysis of various players'
strengths and weaknesses, you'd have thought the coaches
would be calling them later for tips on how to win.

Olive complained across the table to me about problems
she was having fixing up her place. "I bought a new couch,
but I know it isn't the one I sat on in the store. That one was
firm, and this one is so soft you sink down in it. My back

won't be able to stand that. But they insist it's the same one, and they won't come take it back." Considering that the furniture store she'd used was up in North Augusta, a good hour and a quarter away, I could understand their reluctance to make the trip. I made what I hoped were appropriate responses, bucking the ebb and flow of the men's football talk.

Genna and Cindy did try to draw the men into other conversations, but I could have told them they were doomed. Even Adney didn't have much luck trying to pump Walker for insurance rate estimates for some chain of sports complexes a friend of his wanted to build in small towns across Georgia. Walker never gives rates until he does research, but Adney kept insisting, "Just ballpark. Give me a ballpark figure. He wants to put in a rock-climbing wall, in-line skating, and a place for skateboarding. I told him I'd ask you what you thought you could insure him for. This could be big, Walker. You could make big bucks." Sounded to me more likely Walker could pay out a lot of claims, but that was his business.

Down at the other end of the table, Martha tried to draw Edie out, but Edie scarcely said a word. She looked so wretched and ate so little, I wondered if she was missing Wick or if Josiah had taken a turn for the worse.

After dinner the kids ringed themselves around our table, and Ridd said, "It's a Thanksgiving tradition in our family to name things we are thankful for. Bethany, you want to start?"

"Family, friends, and health," she said promptly.

"No fair. That's three," Cricket objected from near his mother's chair.

Martha reached out and pulled him close. "What are you thankful for, honey?"

"You," he said in a gruff whisper, rubbing his head against her shoulder.

The other children named standard things like pets and friends, but Smitty surprised me. "Second chances." His gaze slid to Ridd, then away.

"I'm thankful we're all here and safe," Cindy contributed.

Walker squeezed her hand. "I'm thankful for the best wife in the world. With apologies to the rest of you wives, of course."

Olive waved for Ridd to go next. He lifted his glass toward me. "I'm thankful for my parents—who are both still with us in spite of Mama's best efforts this year."

Some people thought that funny.

Joe Riddley put in freedom to worship as we choose, and I added thanks for a country where we're still free to speak our minds most of the time. Then things came to a halt.

"How about you, Adney?" Walker prodded.

Adney lifted his hands with a grin. "You all have covered the bases, seems to me. Genna? How about you?"

She tried to smile, failed, then burst out, "I'm sorry. I just miss Daddy so much." She pressed her napkin to her nose, jumped up, and left the room. Adney went after her.

"Olive?" Ridd asked.

She sighed. "I'll pass this year. Like I've been telling Mac, the furniture store sent me the wrong couch and I've been on the phone all week trying to get the decorator who is supposed to paint my apartment, so I know when he's coming and what color paint to buy. And now Edie told me on the way down here that our vacation schedules were posted yesterday, and I only get two days off at Christmas." She raised her hands in surrender. "Too many things are going wrong right now for me to try and think of things to be thankful for."

That certainly let the yeast out of everybody's rolls.

"Why don't we go let our dinner settle, then come back for dessert?" Martha suggested.

We all helped carry food and dishes to the kitchen. I nearly had a heart attack when I saw Smitty carrying in a stack of Martha's china with a glass balanced on top. Tyrone brought up the rear with six more glasses, but they both looked more expert at carrying dishes than I would have expected. They must have been eating at Martha's a lot lately.

"Hey," I greeted them. "What you all been up to?"

I expected "Nuthin' much," but Tyrone's big face lit up.

"We're taking sword fighting. What's it called again, Smitty?"

"Kenjutsu." To hear that word roll off Smitty's tongue, you'd have thought he'd been speaking Japanese all his life.

"We're having our first demonstration next Saturday afternoon. Not this one, but the next one," Tyrone added, in case I didn't remember the difference between "this Saturday" and "next Saturday." "Could you come? We're gettin' pretty good."

The thought of somebody turning Tyrone and Smitty loose with swords froze my gizzard, but I nodded. If somebody got killed, I could be a reliable witness. If I weren't the corpse.

"Now, you and Edie get out of here," Martha told me. "We've got plenty of help."

I could tell Edie was of two minds about whether to stay or go, but I've never needed more than one invitation to leave a kitchen. I suggested we take a walk.

We ambled along without talking, enjoying the warm autumn sunshine and content to leave the conversation to a forest full of birds settling in for winter. Behind us we could hear my three youngest grandchildren calling and laughing as they flung a Frisbee.

"Kids are so sweet," Edie said wistfully. "Do you ever wish they'd never grow up?"

"Heavens, no." But something in her tone made me ask, "Is it Valerie giving you trouble, or Genna?"

She rubbed her mouth with one hand, as if wiping away something sour. "Both. Genna said you gave Ridd and Martha your house."

I swatted away a late fly. "Sort of. We swapped with them, then used the money from the sale of their house to help buy the one we're living in. It's been a tradition since the house was built to give it and the five acres around it to the oldest child. Walker will get an equivalent amount from our estate—if I haven't spent it all first."

"But what about your old age? How do you know there'll

be enough? I mean, people live so long now, and health costs are going up so fast." She bent to pick up a stick and started swishing weeds by the roadside. I'd never seen her so pent up. She looked like she'd rather be hitting some*body* instead of goldenrod.

She didn't want to know what plans Joe Riddley and I had for our old age. She was worried about her own, about the very real questions that plague all of us who are aging. *What if I get incapacitated and need expensive care? What if I live longer than the money holds out? Will my children take care of me? Will they be financially able to, even if they want to?*

Those shadows hover around a lot of other conversations. We eye one another wondering, *How could he afford early retirement? Are they crazy, spending all that on a cruise, or do they have better investments than we do?*

I considered carefully what I ought to say. "I heard Genna suggesting that you sell your daddy's house—"

Edie blew her lips out in a puff of disgust. "Genna keeps forgetting that the house and grove still belong to Daddy until—" She paused, then burst out, "Oh, Mac, I don't want to lose him! But to see him lying there day after day is almost more than I can bear." She turned away to stare across our neighbor's watermelon field. I moseyed on slowly to give her time to collect herself and catch up.

When she came up alongside me, she asked abruptly, "Do you forget things a lot?"

"I don't know. I can't remember." That fell flat, so I admitted, "Of course I forget things, sometimes. I figure my hard drive is getting full, and wish somebody would invent a program to erase temporary files from the human brain, like they have for computers, to release some capacity. But it doesn't bother me much. Are you still worrying about that?"

"Some." She took the top off a goldenrod with one neat slice.

"Is it affecting your card playing?" I'd always wondered how she kept track of who had already played what, anyway.

She shook her head and said in a pleased voice, as if surprised by the discovery, "No! No, it's not. I play as well as ever. It's just at home that I keep coming across silly little things I don't remember doing." She gave a snort intended for a laugh. "Maybe I can start a bridge club in the Alzheimer's center."

"If that was a joke, buy a book and practice," I told her. "But stop thinking like that. You're only fifty. That's young these days. You're just under an enormous amount of strain."

"But what if I wind up like Grandmama? Doesn't it terrify you to think about getting older and being unable to take care of yourself?" She kicked a pebble far down the road.

No, but I had Joe Riddley, Ridd, Walker, and their families, all of whom would be kind to elderly ancestors. Edie had Genna, Adney, and Olive, none of whom I'd trust with my old age. What people ought to be told at twenty is, "Don't just invest your money, invest your life. Invest yourself in an extended family or a broad community of support that will take care of you when you get old." I didn't know what to say to Edie, impoverished as she was.

She may have been having some of the same thoughts, for she was quiet the rest of our stroll to the highway. Halfway back, I pointed to a stand of pines Joe Riddley had planted several years before. "That's our old-age pension. They ought to be ready for cutting about the time we get old. My daddy used to say God made pines the same nice green as money."

She stopped to take a rock from her shoe. "The grove takes care of all Daddy's expenses. We never thought it would come to that, but it pays his bills." Finally I heard her familiar chuckle. "The nuts take care of Daddy, and my salary takes care of this nut. Alex said she told you that Wick—well, he left me in a mess, is what he did. I used to get so mad I wanted to break things, but now I find I enjoy my job."

I was struck by how relieved and at ease she seemed now that she had somebody to listen. People were never meant to carry their burdens alone.

We headed home, talking about upcoming changes at the library and some ideas she had if they could get funding.

I should have remembered, though, one of Joe Riddley's wisest observations: People usually wait until the very end of a conversation to bring up what's closest to their hearts. As we turned into the drive, Edie asked, out of the blue, "Do you think Valerie is getting too involved with Frank? You saw them together a couple of weeks ago."

"They seemed close—" I began.

"Too close?" Edie kicked another piece of gravel up ahead. "Valerie is engaged to somebody in the Navy. Did she mention that?"

"No, but you told me."

"He's away on six-month deployment, and she talks about him less and less. Meanwhile, Frank practically lives at our place, and Olive and Genna—" She paused to take a deep breath. "They think Valerie is letting him spend the night."

Now we'd gotten to where the peanut butter met the bread. Edie had always lived what she believed, and she didn't tolerate single people sleeping together under her roof. She and Genna had had several run-ins about that while Genna was in college.

"I don't believe it," she added, a shade too fast to be convincing. "I told Valerie how I feel about that before she moved in, and I trust her. I like Frank, too, though some people find him a tad peculiar. But since she started hanging out with him, Valerie has changed."

"Changed how?" I was picking my way through that conversation like a cat walking on a sticky floor.

"A lot of little things." She trailed her stick along Ridd's newly cut lawn. "She got her belly button pierced a couple of weeks ago. She says she's fixing to get a butterfly tattooed on her ankle, and she's talking about piercing her tongue."

I winced. "Yuck! But Walker showed up from college one weekend with his hair in a Mohawk. I guess every generation has to shock its elders before it *becomes* the elders."

Edie wasn't interested in pop psychology. "But her *tongue?* The possibilities for infection are enormous!"

"I know. But you know what bothers me most? That we grown-ups have permitted the world to get so outrageous that kids have to go to dangerous lengths to be shocking. Seems to me we should have stepped in and called a halt somewhere back there, but I've never figured out where or when we failed."

"I refuse to take the blame for pierced tongues. Besides, how can Valerie sing with something in her mouth that makes her lisp?"

"I don't have a clue. The only comfort I can offer is that in fifteen years all these tattooed, pierced kids with pink and blue hair will probably look—well, like Genna, or my kids."

"I never looked like that in my life!"

We jumped. Neither of us had noticed Genna coming toward us. It's hard to walk on gravel without making a sound, so she must have walked on the grass. Was she deliberately trying to hear our conversation? I gave her the benefit of the doubt and decided she'd been protecting her expensive shoes.

She frowned at Edie, then turned to me. "Did she tell you Valerie is letting Frank stay overnight?"

"You don't know that!" Edie clenched her stick so hard it cracked.

Genna stood her ground, one hand on her hip. "Adney and I both know somebody is deliberately terrorizing you. Who else could it be?"

"Terrorizing?" I repeated blankly.

Edie slung the pieces of her stick across the yard. "I am not terrorized, I am confused."

Genna spoke to me, ticking off items on her fingers. "First her car seat is back when she doesn't remember leaving it that way. Then her door is unlocked and the cat is in when he's supposed to stay out."

I nodded. "I heard about all that."

"Then she finds one of her blouses in the laundry hamper

when she knows she ironed it the day before. It's got a stain on the front, too."

Edie lifted one hand, but Genna was only to finger four. "She finds her dishwasher full of clean dishes she didn't put there, and"—her right pointer hovered over her left thumb— "there was something about magazines. What was it?"

Edie shrugged. "I thought I'd left a bag of magazines on the backseat of my car to take to the nursing home, but I'd left it on the back porch. This is ridiculous. I'm forgetting a few things, that's all. I'm not forgetting to pay my bills, or go to work, or how to play cards," she finished on a triumphant note.

"But you're wearing yourself out taking care of that big place, trying to oversee the harvest, going to see Granddaddy Jo, playing cards all the time, and working. You can't do it all, Edie. You can't!" Genna's face was flushed and damp, and red curls stuck to her forehead. "If you'd listen to other people for once, you'd put that grove on the market and get—"

"A nice little town house?" Edie's face was so pink she looked more likely to die of a stroke than Alzheimer's.

For once, I was glad to see Olive heading our way. She must have known what Genna had come out to say, because she demanded before she reached us, "Did you mention the keys? Or the pornography?"

Genna turned my way. "Talk some sense into her, Mac. She could be living in a lovely, safe, convenient town house if she weren't so stubborn." She stomped back to the house.

Olive watched her go. "I just came out to tell you Martha said dessert is ready." She also hurried back to the house.

"Don't say a word," Edie warned, "if you plan to 'talk sense into me.'" Her tone mimicked Genna's exactly.

"I wouldn't have the nerve. But have all those other things happened since we last talked?"

She nodded. Now I understood why she looked so ravaged.

"What was that about keys?"

Her hand trembled as she reached out to strip dead leaves from a hydrangea bush near the walk. "I found a set of keys in my purse that don't belong to me. I cannot for the life of me figure out how they got there. I don't leave my purse lying around."

I mulled that over as we climbed the front porch steps. "Is there any identification on the ring? A car dealer's name or something like that?"

"Nothing but a brass tag with one word engraved on it. I looked it up on the Internet . . ."

"And?" I prodded when it began to look like that word would hang in the air for eternity and we would never get dessert.

She gave me an embarrassed grimace. "It led to a soft-porn Web site. Adney thought that was hilarious. But now my e-mail is full of pornographic messages. Filthy, stupid stuff."

"Not to mention boring and repetitive," I added. "I was similarly afflicted after one of our teenage helpers got access to my office computer. You can clean it up, but it will take time."

"Adney's coming over Sunday afternoon to work on it."

Olive spoke fiercely through the screened door. "We have a bridge game at your place Sunday afternoon, in case you've forgotten that, too. And it's a waste of time for Adney to clean up the thing. Valerie and Frank will just use it again to look up more porn sites."

"You don't know that!" Edie's voice was low and trembling.

Olive gave a little snort. "You know as well as I do you wouldn't get that much filth from visiting the home page of one Web site. So where else could it come from? Unless Henry's getting in and using the computer when the house is empty."

Edie went rigid, and her voice was like ice. The last time I'd heard her speak like that was when the chair of the county commission suggested we do away with the bookmobile to rural areas. "Stay out of my business, do you hear me? All of you. I'm sick and tired of it. I can take care of myself."

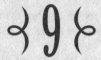

On my way to work Friday, I drove two miles out of my way to see if lightning had made an isolated strike and burned down the superstore before its grand opening at nine. The big gray box still squatted in its new parking lot, festive flags flying and balloons tugging at their tethers.

Trying to make myself feel better, I went on the Internet and ordered a new Mama Bear. A confirmation e-mail informed me it would arrive Tuesday or Wednesday.

Joe Riddley came in around eleven, hung his cap on its hook by the window, and reported, "I ran by and had a look at the new place. Their poinsettias are two dollars cheaper than ours, they are running a loss leader on pine straw for a dollar a bale, and they had a line at the garden center checkout register. But you know who's running the garden department? Buck Johnson."

Buck used to work for us, but we'd had to let him go because he was so ignorant about the nursery business, he couldn't remember which were annuals and which were perennials. Seeing my face lighten up a bit, Joe Riddley added, "I chatted with the store manager a little, and he said they were delighted to get Buck, but he knew we'd been sorry to lose our manager."

I knew why he was making me laugh. He hoped to distract my attention away from that bulging plastic bag he carried. I eyed it and got a sheepish look in reply. "I bought some socks as long as I was there, and they had shirts and work pants at a real good price—"

"Traitor," I muttered.

He dropped the bag beside his desk. "You'd come back with a bag, too, Little Bit. There's something mighty enticing about so much merchandise under one roof. It reminds you of all sorts of things you've been meaning to get."

"I've been meaning to get busy on this payroll," I snapped. "So if you will pardon me—" Then I immediately felt bad, because it wasn't his fault. I knew he was hurting as bad as I was. He was just a nicer person.

He dropped a hand to my shoulder. "Don't get your dander up, honey. We're going to be all right. This is nothing but one more change. By the time folks get as old as we are, we're bound to know that adapting to change is part of life. It keeps things interesting." He gave me a little squeeze and reached for his cap. "I'm going down to the tree lot for a while. You ought to see the dried-out things they have in their parking lot. Must have been sitting in a closed truck for weeks. I didn't see a single one being sold, and our lot has been hopping all morning."

Back when the boys were little, Joe Riddley had the bright idea to plant Christmas trees behind our nursery. Folks came from all around to choose and cut their own live trees, and we always threw in extra greenery. He strode out the door whistling.

He never knew I was watching out the window when he got in his car. I saw his shoulders slump. It's hard to lose a business. It's harder when three generations before you have succeeded so well. But he had a point about adapting.

Old Joe Yarbrough, Joe Riddley's great-granddaddy, was running a small sawmill when General Sherman lit through Hope County in late 1864. Riding the wave of a sudden demand for reconstruction lumber, Old Joe built his sawmill into Yarbrough's Lumber Company. Almost any tour of late-Victorian homes in Middle Georgia includes houses built with Yarbrough lumber. That's what enabled Old Joe to buy a thousand acres of farmland and build the big blue house Ridd now owns.

A few decades later, Old Joe's oldest son noticed agriculture was making a comeback, so he branched out into Yarbrough's Feed and Seed, selling fertilizer, pesticides, bulk seed, animal feed, and orchard trees. The family survived the Depression by selling off the lumberyard and planting a number of their acres in vegetables, which they ate, sold at reasonable prices, and gave away. That built a lot of goodwill.

After World War II, Joe Riddley's daddy, J.R., was smart enough to see that soldiers coming home would want to fix up their houses and yards to affirm that life was starting over, so he added a line of lawn mowers and small power tools, and turned some of his acreage into a nursery to carry ornamental trees and shrubs, perennials, bedding plants, and supplies for lawns and home gardens. He was also the first in Hope County to believe that pecans could be grown as a cash crop, and he convinced Josiah Whelan back in the fifties to plant his grove.

About the time Joe Riddley got out of college and went to work with his folks, subdivisions started springing up all over the region, so he and his parents decided to sell the hardware and equipment side of the business and develop the sizeable nursery we now had outside the city limits, to supply developers and large landscaping firms.

In one form or another, Yarbroughs had prospered and supplied the needs of several counties for nearly a hundred and fifty years. But none of the former generations had had to face a mammoth company with financial resources to undercut prices until we had to quit. I wished we had sold out years ago. I could be basking on a Tahiti beach instead of figuring another payroll and wondering how long we'd be able to meet it.

Lest our employees were wondering the same thing, Joe Riddley gathered them together Friday afternoon and told them, "Don't worry, we aren't letting anybody go unless we absolutely have to. We're going to keep on providing excellent service and decent prices. I think folks will come back."

I wondered if he knew they all headed to the superstore when they got off work.

That same weekend several other things happened that I only heard about later.

Adney went down to Edie's late Friday afternoon to clean out her computer, since he couldn't do it Sunday, and found Frank loading Edie's stereo into Valerie's car. Frank claimed Edie had sold it to him, but Adney called the sheriff's department, who sent a deputy to check it out.

From an upstairs window, Valerie saw Frank spread-eagled against his cruiser and called 911. "Come quick! Somebody's hurting my boyfriend!" Then she called Edie.

About the time the first deputy was explaining to the second deputy what was going on, Edie screeched to a stop in her driveway. She blistered Adney and apologized to both deputies, informing them that she *had* sold Frank the stereo, since she never used it. Adney got so hot under the collar with Edie that he went home without looking at her computer.

We heard about that when the sheriff came over Friday night to share leftover turkey Martha had sent home with us. He told the story of Frank's near arrest and concluded, "The deputies thought she was making it all up to protect Sparks, but they couldn't charge him with theft when the person being stolen from claims she sold it to him." He finished chewing his turkey sandwich, then asked aloud what I was thinking. "If Edie didn't sell him the stereo, and lets him get away with this, who knows what he'll be 'buying' next?"

Sunday, we invited Walker and Cindy to go with us to a fish camp down by the river for an early supper. The country club was closed for the weekend, so we'd missed the Friday seafood buffet, and there's a limit to how many times in a row Joe Riddley is willing to eat turkey. It seemed funny to

have only four of us, but Martha, Ridd, and their kids had
gone down to see her family for the day, and Cindy's parents
had invited their kids up to Thomson for the weekend and
would return them later that night.

As we followed the waitress toward our table, I watched
Cindy's chic rear in a long rayon skirt and wondered if I
ought to get me a long skirt or two. Joe Riddley bent to mutter, "No, Little Bit. You wouldn't look like that. You'd look
like a mushroom."

"When your husband starts reading your thoughts, you've
been married too long," I muttered.

"Stop bickering, you two," Walker said, pulling out a
chair for me, "or we'll ask them to seat you at a children's
table."

Everybody ordered fried catfish. Cindy and I agreed to
meet for coffee Thursday morning to double-check our
Christmas lists, and then, to make conversation while we
waited for our order to come, I asked Cindy if she'd heard
from Genna about what happened Friday. "I sure did," she
said. "Wasn't that awful? Genna knows good and well Edie
never sold Frank that stereo. Why would she?"

"Maybe she needed the money," I suggested, to see what
Cindy would say.

She laughed. "Yeah, right. But did you hear what happened yesterday? It was worse!"

She scarcely waited for me to shake my head. "Adney
went down again while Edie was at work, to see what he
could do with her computer, and found Henry Joyner, bold as
brass, sitting at her kitchen table eating his lunch."

"How'd he get in?" Joe Riddley asked for the rest of us.

"Adney asked him. Henry said his daddy and Josiah always ate lunch there together, and he'd just kept it up—that
he used his daddy's key. Can you imagine?" Cindy never
gave her maid a key. Whenever they went out of town, I had
to go over and let the maid in.

"Clarinda has our key," I pointed out, reaching over to

smack Joe Riddley's hand. He was working his way through the basket of hush puppies intended for the four of us.

Joe Riddley moved the basket of hush puppies so I couldn't reach it, took the last two, set it beside Cindy, and added, "And Mary, Pete's mother, cooked for Josiah's mother, so Pete and Henry were both raised in that house."

"Henry should have turned in the key." Cindy reached for a hush puppy, looked puzzled, and handed the basket to Walker. "Can you get more of these?" She continued as if she hadn't interrupted herself. "Genna never imagined he had one. She said Adney asked Henry to give it back, but Henry said he works for Edie and she'll have to ask him herself if she wants it. When Adney warned him he was going to tell Edie he had it, he said the look Henry gave him would have peeled paint." She looked up and exclaimed, "Why, there's Olive!"

Olive came in wearing her usual cheerful combination of black and gray, but today she also wore an unusually big smile. "Congratulate me," she commanded as she stopped by our table. "I just came from Edie's bridge party, and I won!" She pointed the fingers of one hand toward her chest and did an affected little dance. "That means I'm in the lead for the January tournament."

"Congratulations," I told her, since it was expected.

"You must have gotten all the good cards," Joe Riddley suggested.

•Olive smirked. "It's skill, not cards. Of course, Edie did seem a bit distracted. Who could blame her, with all that's been going on?" She pulled up a chair and proceeded to fill us in on what we already knew.

Monday afternoon, I took Cricket to return library books and found Alex staffing the desk. She was dressed for the holiday in her trademark black pants, a silky red blouse, and a tapestry jacket covered all over with candy canes and sprigs of holly. More candy canes dangled from her ears. "You look too gorgeous to be working the desk," I greeted her. "Besides, I thought you didn't do overdue books."

She gave me a disgusted grunt. "I don't, as a rule, but we're shorthanded. I have two folks down with flu. Olive worked this morning and is to come back this evening, but she had a dentist appointment this afternoon. Donna's needed at the children's desk after school. And Edie, who was supposed to work this afternoon, called around noon real upset and said she had to go see her daddy right away and doesn't know when she'll get back."

"Go see Miss Donna," I instructed Cricket, giving him a little push. He skipped happily away. I turned back to Alex. "Is Josiah worse?"

Alex rested her arms on the desk so our eyes were level and spoke softly so other patrons couldn't hear. "I asked that, first thing, but she said he's fine, she just needed to ask him about something important. Now, how does she expect that man to answer her?"

"Not easily," I agreed, also speaking softly. "But Edie was upset? And didn't say why?"

"No, but she was in a hurry and not real coherent. I'm telling you, Mac, something is going on down there. Maybe it has to do with that fellow we saw the other day."

"Henry?" I was so startled I spoke too loud. Several people looked our way, so I lowered my voice. "Why should you think that?"

Alex spoke softer. "Saturday afternoon, I was out front here after a visiting-author event, and Edie was on the desk. She took a call and talked real angry, so after the author left, I spoke to her about it. That's not like Edie. She usually keeps her cool and never forgets her manners. But I can't have patrons hearing my staff talking like that, no matter how upset a staff member gets. Edie apologized and admitted she got carried away. She said it was Adney calling, saying Henry had a key to her house and wouldn't return it unless Edie asked for it back. The funny thing was, she wasn't mad at

Henry, she was mad at Adney for upsetting Henry. Can you imagine? That man has no reason to have Edie's key!"

"My cook has our key. And Henry grew up on the place. His family has probably always had keys."

The look Alex gave me said real clear that is not the way people act in Chicago. "I cannot think of any reason why he needs to be in her house when she's not there." She stood up straight and arched her back to stretch it. "Don't you get tired of looking at things from way down there?"

"Just when I get a crick in my neck from looking up at the rest of you."

"Speaking of looking up—" She nodded to where Cricket stood at my elbow, proudly holding up four books. Donna Linse stood smiling behind him.

"Look, Me-Mama, I picked four books, and I can read one of them all by myself, can't I, Miss Donna? 'Cause *Elephant Buttons* doesn't have any words." He was prancing in his excitement. When did I lose that delight in learning something new?

I examined the books he'd chosen and promised we would read them to each other as soon as we got back to the store, then sent him off to look in the display cases while I checked out the books.

When he was out of earshot, Donna asked in her sweet, soft voice, "Were you all talking about Edie and Henry Joyner?" When we nodded, she said, "I didn't mean to listen in, but Edie did ask for her key back Saturday. I heard her, because we were both on the desk right then. She called and told Henry that with her daddy away, she'd rather not have keys in the community."

"What did he say?" Alex asked the question before I could.

"He hung up on her."

I felt sorry for Henry right then. "I guess he was hurt."

Alex snorted. "He's got no reason being hurt. A woman's house is her house. No man's entitled to have a key to her house unless she gives it to him."

There was that word again. "Entitled." Since the super-store had opened, the word had been stuck in my craw. I knew what it felt like to have something I felt entitled to taken away. There are some things you *deserve* to have, dang it! Like life, liberty, and the pursuit of your own business without somebody coming in from outside and taking away everything you've worked for all your life. Or the key to a house where your grandmother cooked and cleaned and your own parents cared for a demented old woman, so you can eat lunch at a table.

"People are entitled to respect from the folks they work for," I insisted.

Donna nodded. "He had to feel like she didn't trust him anymore. Well, I have to get back to my desk." She drifted back to the children's section.

"It has nothing to do with respect or trust. It has to do with safety," Alex insisted.

My funny bone suddenly got a jolt. "Does this argument seem odd to you? I mean, here are two white women worry-ing that a black man didn't get enough respect from a white family and a black woman arguing that he was out of line."

"It's not about black and white," Alex said firmly. "It's about women being safe."

I shifted my pocketbook on my arm and hefted Cricket's books. "You're probably right. And the fact that the issue *is* women and men rather than black and white may be progress, but this whole conversation still feels strange."

Alex shook her head. "Lotsa things are strange around here right now, girlfriend. I don't trust anybody except you and me, and I'm not always sure about you."

ꝰ 10 ꝰ

The replacement bear arrived Tuesday morning. Dressed in a pink tutu and ballet slippers, she looked more like a four-year-old dancer than a Mama Bear. I introduced her around the store, and she created a diversion we all badly needed, for we had no customers.

The bear was soft and dark brown, with two bright brown glass eyes and a pink flower on an elastic band circling her head. I was tempted to keep her. She'd look real cute in the wing chair, and she'd be somebody to cuddle when Joe Riddley got grumpy. He was real grumpy at the moment, because he'd ordered more poinsettias than I'd advised him to buy, and they weren't moving.

I was forced to change my mind, though, when a deputy came in while I had the bear on my lap. The look he gave me reminded me that a judge needs to act like a judge.

I wrapped the bear in Christmas paper and took her with me when I went home for dinner. Joe Riddley came in a few minutes later, and we ate Clarinda's chicken and dumplings in such glum silence that she told us, hands on her ample hips, "I'm gonna go look for me a job with *pleasant* people. Why don't you all go get yourself nighttime jobs diggin' *graves?*"

I called later to be sure Edie was working. She was, so I headed to the library again. The gorgeous weather was still holding, so I walked, glad of a chance to get out and see

Oglethorpe Street and the courthouse square. Downtown looked real festive, even without customers.

When I got to the desk, I scarcely recognized Edie. She'd shrunk, or maybe she looked that way because of the way her shoulders slumped under a gray wool suit and white blouse that looked more appropriate for chairing a board than for checking out books. Her face seemed to have wrinkled overnight. Dark half-moons connected her cheeks to her eyes. What was worse was the expression looking out of those eyes: fear, anger, despair, and a sort of fierce determination to hold it all together when her world was clearly falling apart.

"I brought you a present," I told her, handing over the bulky package.

"Thanks." She started to drop it behind the counter, unopened.

"Don't you want to see what it is?"

When she saw the tutu, she exclaimed, "Oh!" She tweaked the pink flower, then clutched Mama Bear to her chest.

"That's how she makes me feel, too," I admitted. "It took all the willpower I have not to keep her. You think Papa Bear will like her?"

"He'd better." Edie buried her face in the fuzzy spot between the bear's soft ears, then sighed and propped the bear on the counter against the computer monitor. "Poor Papa Bear. He's still lying on the couch in his Pilgrim costume, not a stitch of Christmas clothes to his name."

"Valerie said she bought material to make him some."

Edie turned so I couldn't see her face. "Valerie has other things on her mind."

You'd have to be a braver woman than I to ask questions after that tone of voice. Edie bent to retrieve returned books from the bin beneath the counter, and I turned to go. "Thanks," she called softly after me, with a pitiful attempt at a smile.

Before I had gone five steps, Genna passed me, heading

toward the counter with such purpose that she nearly ran me down. She looked pretty in khaki pants and a sweater the color of eggplant. Her hair was fluffy, her makeup perfect. I wondered how early I'd have to start to look that good by noon.

As she caught my eye, she flushed. She carried a white poinsettia in a pot wrapped in green paper, when we both knew Yarbrough's poinsettias were wrapped in red.

In spite of what Joe Riddley may tell you, I did not pause at the bulletin board to eavesdrop. I stopped to read a poster about free breast cancer screenings, because my mammogram was overdue. It was pure coincidence that I overheard what went on next.

Genna set the poinsettia on the desk. Then she touched Mama Bear and smiled. "Cute." She leaned on the counter and said, "I came to say I'm sorry for what Adney said Saturday and what I said at your place last night." It didn't take much detecting skill to guess Adney was out of town again and Genna had spent the night at Edie's.

Edie shifted the flower over to one side, out of the way of people returning or checking out books. "Sorry isn't enough."

"I was upset."

Then Genna must have realized an apology is not the time to defend your position, because she added, in a meeker voice, "I tried to call early this morning, but you had gone. I left messages both here and at your house, but you didn't return my call."

Edie started processing the books she'd retrieved. "I've been busy. I haven't listened to messages." Genna started to reach out toward her, but when Edie added, "I just got here," Genna froze with one hand half extended, like a child flung away in a game of statues.

"Where were you?" Her voice was breathless, almost frightened. When Edie didn't answer, Genna stood on tiptoe and pulled herself up so she was lying across the counter. "Did you go see Shep? Was it about changing your will?"

Edie turned so her back was to the counter. "That's none of your business."

Genna's hot reply could be heard by anybody in the room. "It is, too, my business."

"Shhh!" Edie commanded.

Genna looked around, embarrassed, and lowered her voice, but not enough. I could still hear every furious word. "You got everything my daddy had. He didn't even leave me the snuffboxes, until after you—" She broke off, with the decency to be embarrassed.

"Come and get them anytime. But they are all you're likely to get."

"You don't mean that. You wouldn't really do that. You're just trying to upset me."

Edie whirled to face her, and although she kept her voice low, it had such force it easily reached me where I stood. "You've already upset *me*. And Valerie. And Henry. I guess it wasn't enough to be rude. I presume you also listened in on my private call last night. Now get off the counter."

Genna slid to a standing position. Both hands were clenched at her side, and her voice was shaking. "Okay, I picked up the phone to call Adney, and you were talking. And yes, when I heard it was Shep, I did listen. It does concern me—you know it does. I've already said I'm sorry about what I said to Valerie and what Adney said to Henry, and I am. But you—Adney and I are both worried about you. You are so isolated out there. Why won't you come closer to where we are?"

Her voice rang with what sounded like genuine concern. Maybe that touched Edie, for she took a deep breath of her own before saying, in a gruff voice, "I'm all right. I'll be fine."

If Genna had been smarter, she'd have left it at that. Instead, she had to add, "Not as long as Valerie is there and hanging out with Frank. Who knows what he might do?"

"They're gone, thanks to you." Edie's voice had the bitter ring I'd heard earlier when I'd mentioned Valerie. "Valerie moved out this morning. If you were so worried about my being *isolated*"—she said the word with heavy emphasis—"you shouldn't have driven her away. And don't look so surprised. After last night, what did you expect?"

Genna's nostrils flared. "What I expect is that she's moved in with Frank."

"She has not!" Edie blazed. "She went back to her aunt's, which she absolutely hates and which means she'll have to drive over an hour each way to class and work."

Genna drew in a hissing breath. "She's not the little innocent you think she is. And if you have left her my daddy's money, so help me, I'll . . ."

"Get out of here!" Edie picked up the flowerpot and hurled it to the floor. Dirt and fragments of flower spattered everything, including Genna's neat slacks. She stepped back as Edie's hot words erupted over her. "Did you hear me? Get!" Edie swept one arm toward the door. Startled patrons began to gather from the edges of the library as her shrill voice rose to the rafters. "My life is my life! My house is my house! You've driven away Valerie, and I had to go down on my knees to Henry to keep him from quitting. I'll thank you to leave me alone!"

"You won't see—" Genna began.

Edie picked up Mama Bear by both legs and started pounding her head against the counter. The pink flower flapped helplessly. "Stop telling me what to see. Stop telling me what to do! I'm sick of everybody telling me what to do. I'm sick of everything and everybody! Do you hear me? Sick of you all!"

She hurled poor Mama Bear blindly through the air and caught our oldest resident, who had turned ninety-four his last birthday, square in the chest. He took a startled step back and would have fallen if someone hadn't steadied him. Edie never noticed.

She pounded her fists against the countertop, shouting over and over, "I can't stand any more. It's too much! Too much! Too much!" She collapsed across the counter, her shoulders heaving with sobs.

Genna reached out a hand toward her, then drew it back. Anybody could see that touching Edie right then was a risky business. You could put out a hand and draw back a nub.

A small crowd collected near the counter. Donna Linse ran quickly from the children's section and through the door marked EMPLOYEES ONLY. In an instant Alex strode through the door.

"Edie?" She rested one big hand on the back of Edie's neck, and her voice sounded like she'd stepped into a normal world. All those years of military training, I suppose. "I need you to help me in the back. Donna will take over the desk." Like a grown-up dealing with an overwrought child, she led Edie away.

Genna stood stricken, one hand pressed to her mouth, until the door closed behind them. Then she turned and fled. Her mascara, I noted, was not as waterproof as the advertisers claimed. It ran down her cheeks with her tears.

⧙ 11 ⧘

I called the library Wednesday to see how Edie was. Olive informed me briskly that she was taking a few days off, and hung up.

Wednesday afternoon, Clarinda left us a chocolate cake. Eyeing the size of piece Joe Riddley ate after we got home from church dinner that night, I said, "I think I'll run some of this down to Edie. It won't do the damage to her clothes budget it could do to ours."

I couldn't figure out where Clarinda had put our plastic containers—she'd been reorganizing the kitchen ever since we moved into our new house three months ago—so I put a couple of slices on a paper plate and wrapped them securely with foil. Then, just as I turned to fetch my shoes, a deputy called and asked if I could come to the sheriff's detention center for a hearing. By the time I got one of the county's most frequent guests admitted to a cell for yet another night, it was too late to go anywhere. I left the cake in my car so I could run it by Edie's in the morning on my way to work.

Thursday showed up gray and sullen, the kind of day when clouds grumble, the sky glowers, and birds dart out only when necessary. The wind was so cold, I grabbed my coat as I left. The sun was merely a faint brightening in the sky. With the clouds that thick, I figured old Sol would sneak over Georgia without ever showing his face. I wondered if Edie would be sleeping in, since she wasn't working. If I didn't see signs of life I would leave the cake on her porch and call her later to say it was there.

Her crews were already working. I glimpsed Henry's orange jumpsuit down near a peanut wagon and slowed a little later to watch a shaker do its funny jig with an enormous tree.

Edie's blue Saab was parked under the carport, so I figured she must be there.

I grabbed the cake, started for the back steps, then stopped. The kitchen door stood open. A splash of broken glass littered the porch floor. "Edie?" I called, then louder, "Edie?"

No answer.

I shivered in spite of my coat. Except for the distant harvesting machines, I didn't hear or see a soul. We'd lived out in the country for nearly forty years, but we'd had a pen of dogs and a good neighbor across a pasture and a watermelon patch. Whelans' place felt as isolated as an island.

I knew as well as anybody that I should set the cake on the hood of my car and call 911. The operator would dispatch a sheriff's deputy to check things out.

But what if Edie had broken the door pane? What if she was muddling around making coffee and fixing to call somebody to come repair it? In the state she'd been in Tuesday, she'd never forgive me if I brought the sheriff down there over nothing and she had to greet him in her bathrobe. "Nosy" and "interfering" were words that came readily to mind.

I set the cake on the same porch rocker Alex used for her files and tiptoed into the kitchen, careful to step around the glass. "Edie?" I called.

No answer. The house felt empty and cold. She hadn't turned the heat up yet.

I tiptoed through to the hall, peering into the dim living room, dining room, and den. I even opened the door to what must have been Josiah's bedroom. "Edie?"

Nothing.

Since I'd come so far and hadn't been barreled over by a

robber, I might as well make sure she was all right. I climbed the stairs, stopping every three or four steps to call. "Edie? Edie!"

By the second-floor landing, I was real sorry I hadn't called 911 downstairs. I stopped at the foot of the third-floor stairs and retrieved the phone from my bag. I nearly punched in the three simple numbers, but I'd come this far. I might as well do the thing thoroughly. Genna said Edie couldn't hear a thing from her upstairs room. She could still be sleeping.

I tiptoed up the stairs, my knees protesting at all this activity so early in the morning. "Edie?" I called quietly.

The door to her room was closed. I eased it open and peered in.

Edie lay sprawled on her back on the bed, surrounded by blood. Her head lolled at an improbable angle, and it didn't take a genius to see her throat had been slashed. Her eyes stared at the ceiling as if wondering how blood could have splattered all the way up there.

I could only look for a second before backing out. "Dear God." I slumped against the wall of the staircase, pressing my hand to my mouth and trying to remember how to breathe. Blood rushed to my head, making me dizzy. My ears roared, and my knees threatened to buckle. I will never know how I made it all the way down to the second-floor landing without pitching headfirst down those dark, steep stairs.

I punched in 911 and could hardly speak coherently to explain where I was and what was needed. When the operator told me a deputy would be right out, I blurted, "Please don't tell Joe Riddley where I am." I felt like a fool. "He gets real worried," I babbled, "and I don't want him to know I found—I mean, he doesn't need to be bothered—" I was making things worse, but I couldn't seem to stop.

"I understand, Judge. But listen to me. Whoever did that could still be in the house."

That was a real cheering thought. I froze, not even daring to look around the dim upstairs hall.

The operator's soothing voice continued, "You stay on the

phone, now, while you go back outside to your car. I'll be right here until you assure me you are safe. You hear me?"

I went real fast down the stairs for somebody who felt a hundred and five.

"I'm okay now," I told the operator.

"Are you in your car?"

"Not yet, but I'm outside." I couldn't talk any longer. I simply didn't have the strength.

"Somebody will be right there." She hung up with a click.

The porch rocker was as far as I could get. I tottered over and sat down—squarely on the cake. I got up and retrieved the pitiful squashed thing, but it wasn't going to do anybody any good now, and just the sight of it made me realize that my stomach was fixing to return my breakfast. I dropped the cake to the floor and dashed down the porch steps to the grass just in time.

Back on the porch I brushed my rear, hoping I hadn't gotten chocolate on my good beige slacks and hating myself for thinking about such a trivial thing at a time like that. Then I sat down and rocked, wondering how Edie could be dead. Funny, practical, wise, smart Edie. Who would run the literacy council and the bridge club? Who would run the Episcopal church?

I tried to pray, but could only manage what the Bible calls "groans too deep for words."

The world began a long, slow spin. I dropped my head to my lap and rocked in sorrow, bafflement, and pain. I'd been told by Alex, Olive, and Genna that something was going on down at Edie's, but I hadn't believed them. If I had—?

After almost any death, somebody is sure to ask, "Could I have done anything more?" But when death arrives prematurely, summoned by violence, those around the victim are forced to ask, "Could I have done anything to prevent this?" It is a terrible, unanswerable, and eternal wondering. I sat there shaking like Middle Georgia had been whisked to deepest Antarctica. I clutched my coat closer around me, but I was cold from the inside out.

I knew I ought to get up and go sit in my car where it was warmer, but my head couldn't get through to my feet. The log says the deputies arrived five minutes after my call. I'd have estimated it was about fifty years before a police cruiser came screaming down the drive and stopped with a spurt of gravel.

Why had 911 sent the city police instead of the sheriff? At that point I didn't care.

Two officers jumped out. One called, "You got trouble down here, Judge?"

I had to test my voice a couple of times before I got it to work. "I don't, but Edie Whelan does. She's in the room at the top of the house, and she's been brutally murdered."

I sat for another freezing century while they ran up the stairs at a rate that made my knees tremble. Eventually one of them came back down, clutching his phone in a way that let me know he'd already sent for reinforcements.

His face was ashen, his eyes shocked and staring. "You see all that?"

I nodded, but couldn't speak. His face had reminded me of exactly what I had seen. I pressed my hand against my mouth to keep what remained of my breakfast down where it belonged.

He shook his head. "I wish you hadn't. She was a friend of yours, right?" I could barely manage a nod. "I'm gonna call the Judge—I mean Joe Riddley—to come get you. Then we'll get to work on this right away."

That got me thinking a little more clearly. "Don't bother Joe Riddley. I've got my car. I can get home."

He dragged over another rocker, sat down facing me, and took my hands in his. He worked for his dad's construction company in off-duty hours, and I could feel callouses on his palms. They soothed me. People with calloused palms were people I knew and could understand. Unlike people who chopped somebody else to death.

I shuddered.

"Are you all right?" He must be worried I was heading into shock.

"Sort of. But I never want to see a sight like that again."

He started rubbing my cold hands between his warm ones. "You've had a rough year." His voice was gentle. "What's this—the third body you've found since June?"

"I don't go looking for them. I just came down today to bring Edie some cake."

"Cake?" He looked around, maybe wondering if I'd eaten it while I waited for them.

I bent down and handed him the remains. "I sat on it."

That's when I started to cry. I cried for the cake. I cried for Edie. I cried for the senselessness of what had happened in that house, and that nobody had been there to prevent it. I cried because I was mad I couldn't stop crying. Finally I managed to pull myself together enough to blubber, "Get me some tissues from my car."

When I had mopped my face and brushed the damp hair away from my forehead, he offered, "You can go on home now. We'll come by and get a statement from you later."

I couldn't go home. Clarinda would want to talk and talk about all this, and I couldn't bear that yet. "I'll be at my office," I told him.

I drove away into a gloomy day perfectly coordinated with my mood.

At the store I managed to run the gamut of cheery good mornings without breaking down, but a perceptive clerk hurried to the pot for steaming coffee. "Go sit down, Judge. You look plumb awful."

I fell into my desk chair and took the mug gratefully. The burn of the first swallow reminded me that I was alive. "Come in and shut the door," I told her. "I want to tell you what's happened. Then you can tell the others."

Cindy called a few minutes later. "Mac? I can't have coffee this morning."

I had completely forgotten our date.

Her voice sounded as shaky as I felt. She must have gone too far too fast on her morning run. Cindy and Genna were both devoted runners.

Genna. Had the police been to tell her yet? I'd plumb forgotten her.

Cindy answered that question. "I'm fine, but Genna—Edie—she's—" Cindy gulped and gave a little whimper of pain. "Oh, Mac, Edie was murdered at her house last night!"

I might have blurted out "I found her" if Cindy hadn't continued to pour out her own part of the story. "I'm over at Genna's right now. She called me right after the police came, because Adney's over in Birmingham and she doesn't know the name of his motel. She can't reach him until he wakes up. He turns his cell phone off to sleep, and he likes to sleep until eight. She's asked me to stay with her until she can reach him and he can get home."

"I'm glad you're there. Thank God Genna didn't sleep at Edie's last night."

Cindy lowered her voice. "That's what I told her, but she got hysterical. She thinks it's her fault—that if she'd insisted on staying down there, maybe this wouldn't have happened."

"More likely she'd be dead, too."

I could hear voices in the background. "Are the police still there?"

"Chief Muggins. He got here right after I did, and he's asking her an awful lot of questions. You'd think he thought she did it! He keeps asking over and over where she was last night and this morning."

"He's just doing his job." It took every ounce of charity I possessed to say that. Our police chief heads the list of people I don't like, and if I weren't a magistrate, I might not care who knew it. "You do what you need to, honey. We can have coffee another day." I figured we ought to get off the phone before Chief Muggins realized she was talking to me. Having found the body would make me the prime suspect in his book. I'm not on his Favorite People list either.

I couldn't work, of course. After a few futile attempts, I

laid my head down on my desk and felt miserable until our door opened. I knew who it was before I opened my eyes. Joe Riddley had been working in the boxwoods, and he carried their musky scent on his clothes.

He came straight to me and laid his big hand on my head. "You already heard?"

I nodded. "Cindy called. She's over at Genna's. How'd you find out?"

He stroked my hair. "I met Officer James in his cruiser on my way back from the nursery. He flagged me down to tell me." He cupped my head in his hand and held it tenderly. "It's a terrible thing."

I reached for a tissue to mop my face. "It sure is."

If you think I was being deliberately devious, not telling him I'd found Edie, you are right. Joe Riddley has never been real fond of what he calls my "meddling in murder." I keep telling him I don't go looking for bodies, but if I come across one, I can't just pretend it wasn't there. He keeps telling me we pay our taxes to hire police to investigate crime, and neither they nor he wants me involved. So far neither of us has convinced the other.

He gave my scalp a quick squeeze, then sank into his own chair across the way from mine and hung up his cap. We were quiet for a while together.

Our office has the standard modern technology needed to run a business these days, but the beaded board walls, wide unfinished floorboards, and oak rolltop desks are exactly like they were in Joe Riddley's grandparents' day. We've kept them that way because we like them, and that old office is a mighty comforting place to be. It's seen a lot of grief in the fourteen decades Yarbroughs have worked there. When I get upset, it invariably reminds me that life does go on.

After a while Joe Riddley said, "Lord, we don't understand this, but we ask you to receive Edie into your presence."

I swallowed tears. "And help us catch whoever did it."

"Help the officers of the law catch whoever did it," Joe

Riddley amended my prayer, "and give Little Bit here sense enough to stay out of the whole mess."

"You aren't supposed to pray that way." I grabbed another tissue and blew my nose.

"Been praying that way for years. God would think it odd if I stopped now." He stood and reached for his cap. "I was on my way over here in the first place to tell you we got the landscape contract for that new subdivision going up over in Burke County."

"That's wonderful, honey." I reached for another tissue and blew my nose. To tell the truth, I didn't feel at all wonderful, although that job would pay a lot of bills.

He sighed and echoed my thoughts. "It was wonderful news back when I heard it. Doesn't seem to matter much right now." He put his cap back on his head and looked downright morose.

I caught his hand to keep him from leaving quite yet. "Why are the police dealing with this instead of the sheriff?"

"Sheriff Gibbons and all his deputies are working a crash up this side of I-20—the other end of Whelan Grove Road, in fact. Two tractor trailers collided, and three other cars were involved, with fatalities."

He paused to give me time to absorb this further tragedy. Whenever I hear of something like that, I am astonished that such a dreadful thing could happen without the rest of us feeling at least a tremor in the air.

"They should have widened that road years ago." I sniffed. "It gets far too much traffic."

"Too many accidents, too. Officer James said this one has blocked both lanes and will take a while to sort out. That's why the 911 operator routed the call to Chief Muggins."

"Did Officer James say if they have any idea who killed Edie?"

"No, but he did say they found the weapon in her bathroom. A machete, apparently."

I clutched my throat. "Machete?" My teeth started playing a lively tune. A joke ran through my mind: "Why did the

Siberian buy a refrigerator? So he could keep warm in the winter." Why did a Hopemore magistrate think of jokes when her friend had been hacked to death? Because she couldn't bear to think about who used machetes.

"Henry—" I could hardly get the word out. "He makes machetes."

Joe Riddley crumpled back into his chair like the straw man of Oz with the stuffing knocked out of him. "Don't speak out of turn, Little Bit. Lots of people use machetes. Maybe one of Edie's migrant workers broke in to rob her, not knowing she was in the house."

"Henry was making a machete when I was there."

"Lots of folks use machetes," he repeated stubbornly.

We might have gone around in that circle longer, but he leaned toward me and said angrily, "You stay out of this, you hear me? Whoever did this is somebody you don't need to be aggravating."

"Don't you point your finger at me, Joe Riddley Yarbrough."

"I'll hook it in your collar and hang you on that hook over there if you take one step toward getting involved in this."

"I ought to at least tell Isaac I saw Henry making a machete."

"You don't need to tell Isaac a bloomin' thing, you hear me?"

I drifted off into thinking that anybody who knew us would realize how upset we were, because we were calling the assistant police chief "Isaac." When Joe Riddley was first appointed magistrate, over thirty years before, he'd decided we would give law enforcement officers the respect of their titles outside our home, no matter how well we knew them. He even called Buster "Sheriff Gibbons," although they'd been best friends since kindergarten.

I came out of that thought just as he was saying, ". . . help Isaac needs from you is to go tell Alex. He said he's not up to that right now and asked if you'd do it. I said you'd be glad to."

I winced at his choice of words. "I will not be glad to. Why me?"

"Because he's busy. Besides you know Alex, you knew Edie, and Officer James thinks it would come easier from you than from a stranger." He checked his watch. "You need to get going, too."

I sniffed and reached for another tissue. "Somebody ought to tell Josiah, too."

"I told him I'd do that." The way he was cupping his chin in one hand, rubbing one cheek with his fingers, he dreaded the job. I felt a stab of anger at Isaac for putting that on him. Still, nobody could do it better.

"You reckon he'll have any notion what you're saying?"

Joe Riddley slammed his fist on my desk. "How the Sam Hill do I know? But I said I'd do it, and I will, just like you'll go tell Alex. It's the least we can do."

He almost never roars at me, so I didn't take offense. He wasn't mad at *me*. I wanted to pound something, too. Or balance on a roof ridge somewhere and howl like a dog. We'd had a number of murders lately, and each one of them had been dreadful, but for a woman to be hacked to death in her own home—

"Things like this shouldn't happen in Hopemore," I muttered.

"Things like this shouldn't happen, period." Joe Riddley jerked open the door. "I'm off to see Josiah."

"Honey?" I called him back. "If you'll come help tell Alex, I'll go with you to Josiah."

He considered, then gave a short nod. "I'd be glad of your company. But let's get going. We don't want Alex hearing this from somebody else."

"Speak for yourself," I muttered as I reached for my pocketbook. "I'll give half my estate to anybody who steps up and volunteers to tell her."

⊰ 12 ⊱

Alex and Natasha lived in a second-floor apartment in a new brick complex with white trim, black shutters, and brass door knockers on shiny black front doors. Yarbrough's had provided the landscaping. As we pulled into a vacant parking place, as upset as I was, I couldn't help thinking that the plants and grounds still looked real nice.

"You want to go in by yourself?" Joe Riddley suggested, his voice hopeful. "She might prefer to hear it from you alone."

"You just don't want to see a woman cry. Come on. I need your support."

Even without makeup, Alex was stunning in a floor-length black silk robe and gold wedge slippers that showed off dark red toenails, but when she saw us, she rubbed one hand over her face like she hoped lipstick and mascara would magically appear. I could tell she wondered why we were there so early.

"Can we come in?" I asked. She stepped back to let us enter. "Your place is beautiful," I told her, astonished that she managed to keep a white velvet couch and chair so clean with a four-year-old in the house. She must vacuum pretty often, too, to keep that dark blue carpet free of lint. And don't tell me I shouldn't have been thinking of carpets and couches at such a time. You do the best you can.

She waved us toward the couch, apologizing that the mahogany dining table at the other side of the room was buried in files. "I've been working on another grant proposal," she told us. "Edie does them faster, but I can't keep asking her to do them in her spare time." She sat down in a chair across from us and smoothed the robe over her knees. "I may hire somebody else to replace her at the desk and let her spend more time raising money. She's got the knack."

"Ummm." I hadn't said a word and still felt like a liar.

Alex clasped her hands before her. Her nails this week were Christmas red with silver balls. "So, what brings you out so early in the morning? You want a cup of tea?"

"No, thank you." I felt tears starting up again. "Edie's dead, Alex." My voice stopped.

Alex started wheezing. She jumped up and dashed from the room. In a couple of seconds she was back with an inhaler. "Asthma," she gasped. "I'll be all right."

After a few more deep breaths she said in an unsteady voice, "I was scared of something like that. You knew Valerie moved out?" She didn't wait for my nod. "I hated the idea of her down there all by herself. Just hated it. But—" She couldn't hold back her tears any longer.

I handed her a tissue and cried into another. Joe Riddley shifted uneasily in his seat.

Alex sniffed and swallowed. "How did she do it, do you know?"

I was too startled to answer. It was Joe Riddley who leaned forward and said, "She didn't." He added, as gently as you can say those three brutal words, "She was murdered."

Alex flung up her head and her mouth flew open. I had not known until that moment that a black person can turn pale. "What you say? Murdered? She didn't kill herself?" She read the answer in our faces. "What happened? How'd you find out?"

I ran to fetch her a glass of water, leaving Joe Riddley to answer. "I saw Isaac on the highway, coming from her place. He asked if we'd come tell you."

"Isaac sent you here?" She gave a little grunt of disgust.

"Can't blame him, I guess. Last time he brought me this kind of news, after Mama got herself shot and killed, I hauled off and hit him. But with Edie, you'd think he'd have the decency—"

The doorbell rang.

She strode to the door and flung it open, probably expecting her cousin. From the kitchen I saw it was Donna Linse, her small face bloodless in the hood of a bright purple parka.

"Edie's been hacked to pieces!" She clutched her thin chest like she was holding herself together to prevent a similar fate. "Somebody broke into her house and cut her to bits!"

Joe Riddley spoke up quickly. "Hold up, Donna. That's not what Officer James told me. He said she was possibly killed by one blow of a machete, but he didn't say a word about hacked to bits. Let's don't go spreading stories like that."

All his life he's had the gift of calming frantic people. Donna relaxed a little and stepped inside, but Alex clutched her throat, her eyes wide with horror. "A machete?"

"That's what Isaac said," Joe Riddley confirmed. "They found one that may be the murder weapon, but they don't know yet."

Alex grabbed Donna's shoulder and shoved her into the chair she'd vacated. "Here. Sit down." She came toward me, and dragged over the armchair from the dining room. Planting it beside Donna, she sat down and ordered, "Catch your breath, then tell us what you heard."

The chair wobbled beneath her, so while Donna recovered a little, Alex brought it back and grabbed another, muttering to me, "I gotta get that thing fixed before it falls down with somebody. Now, Donna, what do you know?" She sat heavily in her chair.

Donna's voice shook. "I went to the Bi-Lo for a few groceries and ran into the wife of a deputy. He was the one who answered the 911 call after Mac—" She looked up and saw me for the first time. "You tell them! Edie was hacked to pieces, and there was blood everywhere!" She collapsed in a storm of weeping.

Alex whirled to me. "You found her? Why didn't you tell me?" Her voice was terrible.

I licked my lips. "I was working up to it." I was also avoiding Joe Riddley's eye.

"Working up to it? You find my best friend hacked to death, and you were working up to tell me?" She leaped to her feet and prowled like a panther. "I told you! I told you something was going on down there. I told you and Isaac both, and nobody did diddly-squat about it."

"Edie didn't believe—"

"You don't see somebody heading for a cliff, Mac, and do nothing to help them because they don't believe the cliff is there." Betrayal was in her voice and the set of her mouth.

Joe Riddley held up his hand again, to stall her. "No call to shout at MacLaren here."

His quiet common sense pierced her anger, and grief flooded out. She dropped her face to her hands and sobbed huge sobs. Donna fetched her a wet washrag to wipe her face. Finally she blubbered, "Go on home, Mac. We'll talk later. Let me know if you find out about arrangements."

I dreaded that walk to the car, but Joe Riddley didn't say a word. He kept a hand on my shoulder, even opened the car door for me, which he doesn't often do anymore. He lowered himself into his seat and sat there without turning the key.

"You found her," he finally said.

I shut my eyes tight and nodded. I couldn't speak.

"You saw her like that?"

I took a deep breath to try and control the tears, but the arctic cold had come into my bones again. When I nodded, I started to shiver and shake.

He reached behind him and got a blanket we always carry. It was awkward to unfold it behind the wheel, but he managed, and he wrapped it around my shoulders. Then he leaned over and held me like he used to when we were courting teenagers. "Oh, Little Bit, Little Bit."

I cried my heart out on his shoulder, surrounded by sixty years of love.

He handed me a box of tissues from the backseat. "You should have told me."

"I just went to take her the cake. The back door was open—" I couldn't go on.

"You still want to ride to Augusta?"

"A bargain is a bargain."

He reached out and touched my cheek. "There's nowhere I'd rather have you right now."

"There's nowhere I'd rather be."

We drove the long way around to avoid the accident near I-20, which meant following several timber trucks on two-lane roads. Joe Riddley's not a speedy driver even on empty roads, so by the time we pulled into the Golden Years parking lot, it was well past eleven.

A stocky brunette shoved a visitor's book our way with a pen. I noticed that Joe Riddley signed in without asking for the room number and headed for hall C. "Have you been to see him before?" I asked, trotting to keep up with his long legs.

"A time or two," he acknowledged, "when I happened to be up this way."

To have done a good deed and never mentioned it was typical of my husband.

When we got to the room, though, I thought Joe Riddley had made a mistake. Josiah Whelan was stout, with thick hair that sandy color that slides into gray. The bed was occupied by a shrunken old man with lifeless white hair and a face that had fallen in on itself. Then I saw his eyes—Edie's eyes, which made something extraordinary out of ordinary faces. I also saw a plastic container beside his bed holding false teeth.

He lifted his right hand from the covers in greeting, but I couldn't tell if he recognized us or was simply glad to see anybody at all.

Joe Riddley went over and clasped his good right hand. "Hey, buddy."

Josiah squeezed his hand and grimaced in what I guessed was a smile.

Joe Riddley squeezed back. "MacLaren came to see you, too."

I went to the other side of the bed and took his left hand. It was whispery and dry, a dead weight in mine. A believable smile was more than I could manage, so I bent and gave him a kiss on his forehead.

"Watch it, Josiah," Joe Riddley warned. "Don't you mess with my wife, you hear me?"

Josiah opened his mouth and made some noises accompanied by a vigorous nodding of his head. I couldn't make out a single word in the sounds, but thought he was laughing. Josiah always liked a good laugh.

"Well, lookee who's got comp'ny," said a cheerful voice behind us. "You all sit down and visit a spell." A large nurse in an aqua smock and white pants went to open the blinds so the sun warmed the room. Her short, untidy hair was an improbable blond, and her lipstick blurred around the edges of her thick mouth, but her touch was kind as she rested a hand on Josiah's pillow. "You all have a good visit now." She bustled out.

Josiah still clung to Joe Riddley's hand like it was the edge of a life raft. With his other hand, Joe Riddley pulled up a chair close to the bed. I sat in a straight chair down at the bottom, where Josiah could see me if he cared to look.

The room was peaceful. Edie had tried to make it homey by putting pictures on the wall, including one of the Whelan homeplace and pecan grove. A Thanksgiving cactus spilled fuchsia blooms down a brass pot on the tiled windowsill, and a pothos in a whimsical frog pot curled down from the top of a built-in wardrobe. Still, the room had that smell of urine and age that is so hard to conceal in a home where incontinent people live and windows are never opened.

"Would you like some water?" Joe Riddley asked. When

Josiah nodded, he gently steered a straw to the dry, cracked lips. When water dribbled down Josiah's chin and onto his shirt, his lower lip quivered like he was about to cry.

"Don't drown him," I said crossly, getting up to fetch a white towel from a small stand beside the bed. As I dabbed Josiah's damp chest, I pure-T *hated* to see an old friend like that. I hated worse feeling like a hypocrite, acting cheerful when we'd come with awful news. He was so pathetically glad to see us. I knew now why Edie made that two-hour drive every day. Not just because she needed to see him, but because of how much he enjoyed having her come.

I got up. "I want to see the nurse a minute." I gave Joe Riddley a look that meant, "You tell him while I'm gone." I never can tell how well he has read a look, but he nodded, so I hurried out. The aqua smock was disappearing into a room down the hall.

I propped against the wall and waited for her to come out.

"We aren't here on a happy errand," I informed her when she appeared. "Mr. Whelan's daughter was killed last night, and the police asked us to let him know."

"Oh, no!" Her hand flew to cover her mouth. No manicures for Mary O'Connell—the name on her badge. Her nails were bare, her fingers beginning to curve with arthritis. "Was it a car wreck? When she didn't come yesterday, we wondered what had happened. She was so faithful to come every day."

I shook my head. "It wasn't a wreck. She died at home, we heard." I couldn't go through the story again. She was sure to hear it on the evening news. "The reason I'm telling you is that Mr. Whelan will need some special attention these next few days."

"Of course. Poor thing. It don't seem fair, does it?" I thought she meant it was unfair for Edie to die before her daddy, but I'd underestimated her single-minded devotion to her patients. "He looked forward to her visits so much." She sighed. "Of course, people are born to die, 'n' I oughta be used to it by now, but you don't ever get what I'd call real used to it. I'll do what I can to lessen his pain." She trudged down the hall, her heels rolling out and her pants tight over her ample hips.

Angels aren't always thin and beautiful.

As I headed back to the room, a hoarse cry from Josiah's room was followed by inarticulate shouts. Ms. O'Connell hurried down the hall on soundless feet, followed by two other members of the staff. She explained to them over one shoulder as they went, "His daughter died, and he's all tore up about it."

I went more slowly and found Josiah surrounded by people far more competent to help him than I. Joe Riddley slumped in his chair, wrung out and grieving at having hurt his friend. I went to stand behind him and put a hand on his shoulder. He covered it with one of his.

Josiah writhed and moaned on the bed, shaking the side rail with his one good hand, grief ensnared within his damaged body.

"Get a posy," Ms. O'Connell ordered. Somebody else left the room at a brisk trot. I couldn't for the life of me understand how a flower would help, until she returned with a white strait-jacket affair. Quickly they got Josiah into it and restrained him from harming himself.

Only his eyes moved now, wild and angry. I had the feeling he knew he was trapped in his useless body, understood everything that was happening, and raged at his own helplessness.

"I'll bring him a sedative." Ms. O'Connell hurried out, calm and efficient.

Joe Riddley bent over to touch Josiah's shoulder. "I'm so sorry we had to bring you this bad news. We're leaving now, but I'll come back later in the week."

Josiah tossed his head on the pillow. "Hey," he said urgently. "Hey."

"Hey," I said softly, touching his arm.

He rolled his head from side to side. "Hey! Eh—pee—eh—pee."

"Edie?" I hazarded a guess. "You want to know what plans are being made for her? We'll come back and tell you when we know."

His head rolled frantically now. Furious eyes begged us to understand. "Pee. Pee. Pee!"

"Here." An aide reached for the urinal and held it over his bed.

He knocked it from her hand and sent it flying across the room. "Oh! Pee. Hey! Hey!" He grew more and more agitated.

"Maybe you all ought to leave now and let us get him settled down." Coming in with a needle, Mary O'Connell spoke pleasantly, but it was more than a suggestion.

As we started for the door, tears streamed down Josiah's wrinkled cheeks and pooled in the sunken places where his teeth were gone. "Hey," he moaned, pleading for us to understand. "Hey. Hey."

We could still hear him grieving when we reached the front door.

❧ 13 ❧

If you have been keeping track of the time—which I hadn't—you will realize we were in serious trouble. When Joe Riddley and I aren't going to be home for dinner at noon, we let Clarinda know. If we're running late, we call ahead to say so. By now, we were already three minutes from late, we'd be lucky to get home by one, and I'd let my cell phone battery run down.

I wanted to pull off the road and call her, but Joe Riddley refused to stop. "We'll only be a little late," he assured me. *He* didn't have to worry. Clarinda thinks *he* walks on water.

As he proceeded at his usual decorous pace while everybody passed us, I remembered that Edie ought to be alive on this gloomy, cold day, and I felt I owed it to her to enjoy it. Eventually, however, questions began to float between me and the view. *Who killed her? Why? Was it a stranger, or someone she knew? Was it quick, or did she suffer? Was there one single thing I or Alex or anybody else could have done to prevent this?*

By the time we pulled into our garage, my stomach was tied in knots. I doubted the forthcoming discussion with Clarinda was going to untangle them. As I reached for my door handle, I told Joe Riddley, "You need to know that I'll probably spend Christmas in the hospital with bleeding ulcers from all this stress."

"Ulcers aren't caused by stress. They're caused by bacteria or something." Dr. Yarbrough pushed the button to lower the garage door and headed to the house. That man has no nerves.

Then I remembered the months after he'd been shot,* when his nerves were raw, and I winged a prayer of thanks for the way he naturally is: slow, calm, and only occasionally ornery.

We found Clarinda snoring in Joe Riddley's recliner with my mother's afghan over her lap and Lulu dozing on the rug at her feet. When Lulu gave a welcome yip, Clarinda levered the chair to sit up and gave a grunt of utter disgust. "Hunh. I thought that was the sheriff coming to tell me you'd died on the highway."

"Were you and Joe Riddley raised by the same mother?" I inquired. "You both constantly expect disaster whenever somebody's late." Not to mention Lulu, who was hopping around like I'd returned from the grave—but that's the nature of beagles.

"Being around you does that to people." Clarinda climbed out of the recliner and stomped to the kitchen, surrounded by waves of aggravation. "You can have your dinner, but what isn't burnt is already cold." She jerked two plates from the cupboard and served them with scalloped potatoes, slices of baked ham topped with pineapple slices, and green beans. It looked fine to me, but she carried the plates to the dining room and set them down with thumps that shook the table.

"Mind the crockery," Joe Riddley said mildly. He hung his cap by the kitchen door and went to wash his hands.

I looked around for any sign of salad. Having worked for me long enough to read my mind far too often, Clarinda gave a short nod toward the refrigerator. "Got congealed salad. Good thing, too. Lettuce and tomatoes would have rotted, waitin' for you to get here."

"We had a good reason." I slid the salad from the refrigerator and saw it was one of my favorites, full of grated car-

But Why Shoot the Magistrate?

rots and crushed pineapple. Joe Riddley's not real fond of stuff in his gelatin, so Clarinda only makes it occasionally, for me. The salad hadn't been cut, either, which meant she hadn't eaten. No wonder she was cranky. She and I both have a hard time being nice when we're hungry. She was pouring two glasses of tea like she wished it was poison.

Feeling bad that we'd been late when she'd gone to extra trouble for me, I said, "I didn't mean to tell you until after dinner, but we had to go tell Josiah Whelan that Edie died."

She whipped her head around. "What happened to her? A car wreck?"

"You've got car wrecks on the brain. Watch out! You're pouring tea all over the counter."

About that time it reached the edge and her stomach, soaking her to the skin. She jumped and clutched her middle, then grabbed a sponge and started mopping the countertop. I cut three squares of salad and set each on a bed of lettuce with a dab of mayonnaise and a maraschino cherry on top. Mama used to fix them like that, but I generally spooned the salad into small bowls. Why was I going to so much trouble? To postpone telling Clarinda about Edie.

Clarinda finished the countertop and wrung out the sponge like she'd rather be wringing somebody's neck. She didn't say a word while she got out the mop and dried the floor, but then she propped her backside against the lower cabinets, folded her arms over her sizeable chest, and glowered. "It's something bad, ain't it? Something you oughta called and tole me."

I turned too fast, annoyed with her and the rest of the world. My elbow caught the cherries and sent them flying. When the jar hit the floor, it shattered. I would never have believed one little jar could hold so much juice. It splashed all over everything in sight, including me.

Clarinda howled. "All over my kitchen. An' I give it a good cleaning just this morning."

I grabbed Lulu and carried her out to the backyard, which we'd recently fenced. She complained about staying in the cold, but she'd gotten shot the same night Joe Riddley did, and a three-legged beagle has enough problems without glass in her paws.

Clarinda was still glaring at the floor and the juice-speckled lower cabinets. I grabbed a paper towel and dabbed my shoes, stockings, and the hem of my best beige pants—which now had pink polka dots and, possibly, chocolate cake on the seat. Then I took her arm and steered her toward the living room. "Let's leave this mess a minute. It's not going anywhere, and neither of us is gonna be good for anything until we talk."

She headed to a chair and I sank to the couch. "Edie was murdered sometime last night."

"Murdered? How? By who? How come you didn't call me as soon as you found out?" Her forehead was a field of furrows. Her lower lip jutted out like a shelf.

"We don't know who did it. The police are investigating."

"The po-lice? You mean the sheriff. Whelans live out beyond the city limits." Clarinda knows law enforcement procedures as well as we do. Maybe better.

I explained about the wreck near the interstate, then added, "Isaac James asked us to go tell Edie's boss and Josiah. I'm sorry I didn't call here, but my cell phone battery is dead."

Clarinda rocked back and forth, holding her face in her hands and moaning, "Jesus, oh, Jesus. Poor Miss Edie. And poor Daisy, too. This will like to kill her."

Something floated to the surface of my memory. "Aren't you related to Henry's mama?"

"Daisy's mama's daddy was my mama's first cousin." That made Daisy something like Clarinda's first cousin thrice removed, but you'd have thought Daisy was her sister, the way she propped her hands on her lap, leaned forward with a gimlet stare, and demanded, "You're not fixing to tell me Daisy and Henry got anything to do with this, are you?"

"Probably not," I hedged, "but Isaac found a machete that

may be the murder weapon, and I saw Henry making a machete last week."

She gave one of her "that don't mean a thing" grunts. "Sure he makes machetes. Henry can make anything. But he'd never kill Miss Edie. What cause would he have? The Joyners been working for Whelans since Elijah took off in the heavenly chariot. Some folks say—but never mind that. Just keep in mind that Henry gave up a good job to stay and work the harvest after Mr. Josiah's stroke. He'd have no cause to kill Miss Edie, if he was the killin' kind—which he ain't. Henry's sweet, underneath that thick skin he developed married to That Woman." I could see capitals as she spoke the last two words.

She frowned, but it was her thinking frown, not the you-better-watch-out one. "Wonder what'll happen to the grove now? I sure hope poor Henry hasn't lost himself a job."

"My guess is, it still belongs to Josiah, but I don't know who'll administer it for him."

She leaned on her hands again and heaved herself to her feet. "You was busy. I can see that." It was the closest she would ever come to forgiveness. "But you oughta told somebody to call tell me. What if somebody had called axin' about the murder, 'cause I work for the judge, and I don't know a *thing?* You be thinking about that next time."

"I hope there won't be a next time." I went to wash my hands, wishing I could wash the day's events down the drain.

⊰ 14 ⊱

That awful day wasn't over yet.

Cindy dragged herself into my office sometime after four, looking like she was trudging through thick, wet mud and about to fall facedown in it. Her makeup hadn't been renewed for hours, and when she took off her long jacket, I saw that her tan jeans were wrinkled and her brown cardigan was crooked over a pale yellow turtleneck. I'd never seen my elegant daughter-in-law so rumpled.

I'd also never seen her look so weary. She slouched as she crossed the office and sank into the wing chair. Cindy never slouched. Her posture was one of the things I'd admired about her in the years before I started liking her.

I turned gladly from the computer, where I'd been pretending to work on inventory. We still had too many poinsettias. Too much of everything, since that blasted superstore opened. "Have you been over at Genna's all day?"

She nodded as if that simple act took too much energy. I was touched that she'd chosen to creep into my office to recover. "You were real sweet to stay with her."

She massaged her temples with both hands, then shoved back her hair, which was so well cut it was still sleek as mink. "I ought to get home. The kids are with friends, but they've probably got homework, and I should—" Her voice trembled. "But I can't. I can't!" She pitched forward onto her knees, taking great gasping breaths.

I touched her gently on the top of that shining hair, stuck tissues in her hand, and headed for two mugs of coffee to let her grieve in peace. When I got back, she was sitting upright in the chair again, but with her nose red and her eyes wet, she looked a lot younger than thirty-five.

She smiled when I handed her one of the steaming mugs. "Thanks. I'm frozen." She took a long, grateful sip and exhaled stress in a sigh.

"You are plumb worn out, honey. You didn't need to stay over there all this time." I took a swallow of coffee myself, enjoying the warmth running down my throat. I was wearing an extra cardigan I keep at work, and I still hadn't felt warm enough all day.

She took another sip, followed it with another sigh. "There wasn't anybody else, not even Olive. She was over in Augusta today doing something about a couch and didn't hear about Edie until the twelve o'clock news, coming home."

Cindy stretched out her legs and slid down on her tailbone. "I thought I could leave when she finally got there, but she talked on and on about some trouble she was having with her decorator, until Genna sent her home. Genna said after she left that it's bad enough that Olive expects Adney to help her pay for all the expensive stuff she wants, without having to listen to her complain about it. She—Genna, I mean— begged me to stay with her until Adney got home from Birmingham." The way she sighed, I got the feeling Cindy had been a reluctant Samaritan. "It took ages to find him, then hours for him to get here." She shoved back her hair again and massaged her scalp with long fingers.

"Find him? Doesn't he have a cell phone?"

"He woke up late and forgot to turn it on. Genna finally called his boss to see which hospital he was visiting first. By then he was in a meeting, and she got one of those women who exist to make other people's lives difficult. You know the kind? Said she couldn't possibly bother Adney, but she'd give him a message when the meeting was done."

"That's not just women, honey, it's the tyranny of petty

power. If you give some people even a little power, they feel entitled to club folks with it every chance they get." There was that word "entitled" again. I hadn't used it for years, and now it kept cropping up.

Cindy was going wearily on with the story. "Well, that woman at the hospital nearly made Genna crazy. Wouldn't call Adney. Wouldn't even listen to what Genna was trying to tell her. Of course, Genna was crying so hard by then, she wasn't easy to understand. I finally grabbed the phone and said, 'We have a crisis here and we need Adney Harrison right this minute. If you can't arrange to put him on the line, Judge Yarbrough will call your sheriff.' " Cindy laughed, and I was glad to see her finally relaxing. "She had Adney on the phone in one minute flat."

"Good for you, honey." I didn't bother to point out I have no authority in Alabama. I was honored to have figured so prominently in her plans.

"Maybe," she said dubiously. Now that the deed was done, I suspected her Southern mama's credo, *Be sweet, now,* was dumping dollops of guilt on her conscience.

She repeated her sip-and-sigh routine—sort of like a "breathe in the good air, breathe out the bad air" therapy, with the addition of sugar and caffeine. I sipped my own coffee and waited for her to go on. She obviously needed to talk.

"Adney didn't help much when he did come to the phone. His first words to Genna were, 'Honey, I've told you not to bother me when I'm with a client.' She started apologizing, then blubbering, so I took the phone again to explain what had happened. Adney was real sorry then, of course. He said she's always calling him with little things that have gone wrong in the house, and he figured she'd overdrawn their bank account or dented her car. He said he'd go check out of the motel right away, but it was already ten, so he couldn't get get here until four. I left as soon as he arrived, and as terrible as it sounds, I was never so glad to leave a place in my life."

She set her empty mug on the floor with a *thunk.* "Bless her heart, Genna is helpless without him. She couldn't decide if she wanted to eat or not, couldn't think of anybody she wanted to call to tell about Edie, and she sure couldn't handle the police. They have hounded her to death, asking the same questions over and over. Did Edie have any enemies? Had she mentioned being frightened of anybody? Genna told them about Valerie and Frank—how she and Olive think they were playing tricks to worry Edie—and the officers said they'd look into that, but then they started asking again where Genna was last night, and if she could prove it. How can you prove you were alone and asleep?" Cindy's voice rose in indignation. "I told her to call Shep and refuse to say a word until he got there, but Genna said Adney would call him on his way home. I think Shep is coming over a little later today."

Cindy shifted uneasily in her chair. "I probably shouldn't say this, but Genna is worried that Edie may have left some of her money to Valerie. Genna knows Edie talked to Shep last week. If Edie did something dumb like that, could Genna contest the will?"

"You can always contest a will. Whether she won or not would depend on what she could prove." I didn't think Edie had been incompetent to handle her affairs. Overwrought and stressed out, but not incompetent. "If Edie *was* revising her will this week, though, it's unlikely she got it signed before she died. And if Valerie and Frank were the beneficiaries, they'd be foolish to kill her before she signed it. I'd advise Genna to stop making suggestions like that. It could backfire. After all, if a new will wasn't signed yet, the person with the best motive would be Genna."

Cindy lifted one hand and pressed her lips. "Maybe that's why the police came back the last time. Adney hadn't been home fifteen minutes when I left, but the police were pulling in again as I drove away. Do you reckon they know something about the will already?"

"I doubt it. They probably only wanted to talk to him."

"It's all so awful!" Cindy laid her head back against the wing chair and closed her eyes. "I keep thinking about poor Edie, dying out there all alone, and I can't stand it. Thanks for being here. I couldn't bear to face the kids without this breather."

"Come anytime." Why had it taken me fourteen years to learn to appreciate this woman?

She stood. "I feel like I've been rode hard and put up wet." We both grinned at that old saw. Then she winced. "A machete. I cannot bear to think about it, and I can't seem to think about anything else. They have to find out who did this, or nobody will feel safe in this town."

She paused at the door. "Will you stop by Genna's sometime tonight?"

"I hadn't planned to. I scarcely know them, except as friends of yours."

"I wish you would, if you can bear it. Nobody else is going over there. They don't have many friends."

I could take care of that. As soon as Cindy left, I called a member of our church who was active in several clubs Genna belonged to and also coordinator of a group in the church that takes meals to families in case of sickness or death. I hung up with the comforting knowledge that Genna and Adney would have enough food-bearing visitors to know the community cared.

When I left work for the day, I stopped at Bi-Lo for some fruit, swung by the house for a pretty basket, and tied a jaunty red bow on its handle. Armed with a condolence gift, I headed to High Mortgage Lane.

The subdivision had been built six years before, one of the clones springing up all over America. Genna and Adney's house was gray stucco with a high arched window in front and steep gables that looked like a roofer's nightmare. Their lawn, I was glad to see, was thick, green, and weed-free. Yarbrough's lawn service keeps a pretty yard, if I do say so myself.

I noticed, however, that Genna had set two terra-cotta pots of pansies in the shade when I had specifically told her they needed sun, and she'd planted camellias right in front of her low dining room windows when I'd warned her they would grow ten feet tall. However, they probably wouldn't live long enough to obscure her view. The short hours of December sun wouldn't harm them, but by August the western sun would burn them up. Why don't people find out how big a bush will get before they plant it, and plant it where it gets the proper light?

On the other hand, I could hear Joe Riddley reminding me, "Replacing bushes puts bread on your table, Little Bit. Let them plant where they want to."

I tried the brass knocker with "Harrison" engraved on it, but nobody came. Shivering in the wind, I waited a decent interval, then punched the doorbell. It rang a full Westminster chime, so they had to know somebody was there. By the time I heard feet running down the stairs, I was wishing I'd brought hot coffee instead of heavy fruit.

When Adney opened the door, I got a whiff of aftershave and saw that his hair was damp and he was barefoot. I hoped I hadn't dragged him out of the shower. Poor thing, his eyes were red and bloodshot, like he'd cried all the way home, and he had bags under them as big as kiwis.

"Genna's dressing." He leaned against the doorjamb and made no move to invite me in, in spite of the cold wind. "Shep Faxon's coming over in a few minutes to talk. We'd have gotten dressed sooner, but you wouldn't believe the string of nosy people we've had by here in the past hour, bringing food like we were invalids or something." He caught sight of my basket and had the grace to turn pink.

"Here's one more," I joked, thrusting it at him. "You can eat this or give it away."

"Oh, no, we like fruit. That's great. I didn't mean—" He set it inside the front door.

I cut short his misery. "Folks are just trying to say how sorry we are about all this."

He ran one palm over his hair and down the back of his neck. "I know, and I do appreciate it, really. It's unbelievable, isn't it? I keep thinking I'm having a nightmare. Edie—" His voice broke. He gave a little cough and said, "Edie was a special lady. I loved her very much." His mouth creased in the

familiar warm grin, but the bloodshot eyes above it did not
smile. "That may sound corny, but I don't have any family
except Olive, and since Genna and I moved here, I think I'd
gotten closer to Edie than Genna had." He exhaled a huge
sigh. "I keep thinking that maybe if I'd been in town, or if
we'd persuaded her to move into a safer place—"

"Don't beat up on yourself," I warned him. "You can't
bring her back that way, and you'll only feel worse."

He nodded. "I know." He reached out and gave me a bear
hug. "Thanks for coming."

I hugged him back, then stepped away. "I won't keep you.
I just wanted to say how sorry Joe Riddley and I both are."

"You folks are great." He smoothed his hair back again. "I
don't know what Genna would have done without Cindy."
He shook his head. "I know I'm repeating myself, but it's unbelievable, isn't it? One week you're having Thanksgiving
dinner together, and the next—" He shook his head.

"I'm sure the police will soon find out who did it."

Adney went from sorrowful to sarcastic in one second
flat. "They think they already have. They think it was Genna.
Or me. Or both of us taking turns, maybe. Aside from the fact
that I loved Edie, they keep forgetting I was in a meeting in
Birmingham—six hours away—last night until eight, and
got a wake-up call at eight this morning. And I have to log in
the odometer reading every time I get in or out of my car, so
I can get reimbursed. Genna—" He gave a short laugh.
"Anybody who knows Genna knows she couldn't do something like that. Even if she could or would, she wouldn't do
it at night. She's scared of her own shadow after dark. She
actually locks herself in our bedroom when I'm gone, if she's
not staying over—" He broke off, pinched his nose, and took
a deep breath through his mouth. "I'm sorry, Mac. I still can't
believe Edie's gone." He squeezed his eyes shut to hold back
the tears, but a couple escaped to spill over onto his cheeks.
"I hope they fry whoever did this!"

"They have to find them first," I reminded him.

❧ 15 ❧

I spent Friday alone in my office, catching up on work I had neglected lately and refusing to let myself dwell on Edie's death. The only people I talked to all day were an Augusta television station and the weekly *Hopemore Statesman,* both wanting to interview me about finding the body. I turned them down. Joe Riddley said he didn't feel like seafood that night, and I was glad not to have to talk to people at the club about Edie. I scrambled some eggs, and we watched television, then we went to bed early.

I felt better when I woke Saturday. I was still brokenhearted, but I felt like I could get up and go on. Joe Riddley had men's cleanup morning at the church, getting ready for the Christmas decorating committee, so I decided to walk to the store.

With the general capriciousness of Georgia weather, this was a gorgeous day, though still cold. You'd never have known Thursday was bitter, windy, and gray. Today's sky was blue, with faint wisps of clouds over to the west. Bundled in my coat and a corduroy suit, I enjoyed the cold air on my face and took deep breaths when I caught a whiff of somebody burning leaves—although I hoped they were outside the city limits, or I could be seeing them soon in front of my bench. A sudden breeze picked up a small pile of leaves at my feet and spun a miniature tornado down the sidewalk ahead of me. The air seemed alive with sound—the yips of two puppies on a porch playing I-dare-you-to-jump, music somebody was sharing from a car radio, and the buzz of chain saws as men in a cherry picker trimmed trees down the block. As I waved at two old codgers in Yarbrough caps leaning against their pickups, my eyes blurred. I'd remembered that Edie ought to be alive to enjoy all this. Josiah, too. Shut up in that airless room, he was as dead as she to this gorgeous world. I sent up a prayer for each of them as I walked, aware of the sheer blessedness of being able to feel a cold wind on my cheeks and hear birdsong in the treetops. It was the same feeling I get after visiting somebody in jail.

At the office, my day didn't start going downhill until just before ten, when Sheriff Gibbons knocked and stuck his head in. "I need to talk to you." He tramped in like he was carrying thirty pounds of extra lead in his britches, sank into my wing chair, crossed one ankle over the other leg, and sat slapping his hat against his boot.

"Put down that hat," I ordered. "You're driving me crazier than I already am."

He set it on the floor by his chair. After that, conversation came to an unprecedented halt. Bailey Gibbons and I have known each other since we were playground kids. Never had we run out of things to say. Today, though, he peered around the office and finally asked, "Joe Riddley down at the nursery?"

"Supposed to be over at the church for the men's workday. Of course, he could be gallivanting with some floozy."

Even that didn't get a smile. He was slouched so deep in my chair, I figured I might have to call for a hydraulic jack to extract him. That same jack might be needed to get words out of him.

"Is something wrong? Something more than Edie's murder, I mean."

He chewed his lower lip. "Clarinda's a cousin of Daisy Joyner, right?" He barely gave me time to nod. "In the next week or so, I may need a preliminary hearing for Henry's arrest."

I held up both hands in protest. "*I* can't hold that hearing. Clarinda would never forgive me. You'll have to ask one of the other magistrates."

He nodded. "I figured that, but thought you ought to know."

"Know what?" Neither of us had noticed Clarinda sticking her head in the office door. I'd failed to teach her to knock for nearly forty years, so it wasn't worth mentioning now.

She came in shedding layers: two cardigans under her jacket and a scarf over her head. As soon as the weather dips below forty, Clarinda bundles up like we live in the Yukon. Once it tops eighty, she complains she's "gonna die of heat prostration." I keep threatening to fly a flag on days she's satisfied with the temperature, to let the weather angels know.

"It's tryin' to rain out there." She nodded toward the window.

All I saw were a few white clouds. "It's a nice day," I disagreed.

"You wait," she predicted. "It's gonna come down bucketfuls. I hope you brought your umbrella from the car when you walked over. You'll need it, if you plan on goin' out for dinner."

Sheriff Gibbons picked up his hat and offered her his chair. "I was just fixing to leave."

She shook her head. "No, you sit back down. I'll take this chair, here." In Joe Riddley's big leather chair, her feet dangled several inches off the floor.

"Know what?" she repeated to the sheriff. "What does she need to know?"

She annoyed me so much, butting in like that, that I decided to tell her. "Know that he may have to arrest Henry for Edie's murder. If his machete turns out to be the murder weapon—"

"Pshaw." She interrupted with a snort of disgust. "He ain't gonna arrest Henry for that. Anybody could have used that thing. Did you find his fingerprints on it?"

Sheriff Gibbons sat back down, perched on the front of the chair like a man hoping to make a quick escape. "Whoever did this was real careful and clean."

"Henry's real careful and clean, but he didn't do this thing," Clarinda assured him. "Was she—raped?" She said the word bravely, but we both stopped breathing until he answered.

"No, we think it was a robbery gone wrong. A valuable collection—at least Ms. Harrison assures me they were valuable—of snuffboxes was taken from a cabinet in the living room, and all Ms. Burkett's jewelry and her watch. Her diamond, too. And a couple of pieces of silver from the dining room sideboard."

Clarinda screwed up her mouth, which she does when she's thinking. Then she pontificated. "She probably heard whoever it was and went down to investigate, then whoever it was chased her up the stairs and killed her."

"Now why the Sam Hill would anybody run up two flights of stairs when she could run out the door and through the grove?" I demanded. "You haven't seen those stairs. They nearly did me in, *walking* up them."

"You ain't in shape like Miss Edie was."

The sheriff spoke quickly. "We may never know exactly what happened, but we do know a couple of things. First, while it looked at first like the back door was opened by somebody breaking the windowpane in the door and turning the lock, there's a dead bolt that has to have a key on both sides, and the glass was broken from the inside, so somebody opened the door with a key, then tried to make it look like a break-in."

"That means it had to be somebody who *had* a key." Clarinda's powers of deduction can be amazing. She sounded so satisfied, I hated to burst her bubble.

"Which only leaves Genna, Valerie, Henry, and maybe Adney. But Valerie moved out last Tuesday. Did she take her key with her?" I asked the sheriff.

"We haven't talked to her yet. She's staying with her aunt, down near Waynesboro. We'll see her today or Monday."

Clarinda was still back a few paces. "Henry? Henry's got a key?"

"He did. Donna Linse, over at the library, said Edie asked him to give it back last Saturday. Maybe he did."

The sheriff shook his head. "It was still on his ring when I talked to him yesterday."

"What about an alibi?" Clarinda demanded, like she knew more than the sheriff about police procedure. "Where does Henry say he was?"

Poor sheriff, he looked like he wished he could dash for the door. "Same place everybody else says they were. Fast asleep. She died sometime after midnight. But whoever it was needed not just a key to the back door, but also one to the shed where the machete was kept. In his first interview, Henry claimed he has the only key to the shed and said he's careful about locking it, because he's not familiar with the men on this year's crew and doesn't want to put temptation in their way. In a later interview, he said maybe he forgot to lock it Wednesday afternoon. But that's a pretty odd coincidence—him leaving the shed unlocked on the very night somebody else wants a machete."

"Coincidences do happen," Clarinda maintained. "Maybe whoever it was went looking for Henry, found the shed open, and decided to use a machete to kill her."

Actually, she had a point. "Or the shed could even have been left open another day," I added. "Henry kept the machetes hanging behind the door. Maybe one was taken several days before, and he hadn't missed it."

"Maybe." The sheriff didn't sound real convinced.

Clarinda slid to her feet and started gathering up her sweaters, jacket, and scarf. "You can't arrest a man because he thinks he has the only key to a shed." Satisfied she'd put a spoke in the sheriff's wheel, she turned to me. "The reason I came by was, I went by your place and put my wash in." We'd offered several times to buy her a washer, but she pre-

ferred to do her wash over at our place. Occasionally she
didn't get around to it during the week, and stopped by to do
it on Saturdays. This wasn't the first time she'd asked—or,
rather, commanded, "Put it in the dryer when you go home.
Don't you let Mr. Joe Riddley do it, now. I don't want him
handling my unmentionables." By which she meant her out-
sized bras. She headed for the door, then added, "I'll get it
Monday."

"Yes, ma'am," I murmured.

She slammed the door as she left.

I looked up at the sheriff, who had politely stood when
Clarinda did. "The machete isn't all you have on Henry, is
it?"

He sat back down and gently fanned his hat back and forth
between his knees. "No. We found a pair of orange coveralls
under some bushes down at Whelans' yesterday evening.
They've got Henry's name on them and are smeared with
what looks like blood. We've sent them up to the state crime
lab in De Kalb County and asked for a rush, but even so we
probably won't hear for a week."

It took me a couple of minutes to recover from that. For
one thing, I kept seeing Henry in his overalls, looking real
good, the day he fixed Alex's car. I also had to swallow a
couple of times to keep down the picture of Edie spurting
blood all over the coveralls. Then I remembered something
else. "But he was wearing them in the grove Thursday morning. I saw him when I was driving down to Edie's."

"He claims he has three pairs. He was wearing one when
we talked, and at first he said the others were home in the
wash. When we asked him again a little later if he was sure
where they were, he suddenly 'remembered' "—the sheriff's
hands sketched quotes around the word—"that one pair was
missing. Said he'd left them hanging on the shed door Sunday afternoon because he'd only worn them half a day and
figured he'd wear them Monday. But they were missing
Monday, so he had to go back home for a fresh pair. He

couldn't offer any explanation for how they could be missing if he had the only key to the shed."

I thought that over. "Maybe whoever took the machete also borrowed them—which would argue for an earlier theft."

The sheriff's face has been compared to that of a bloodhound in more than one article. Today he looked particularly mournful. "The forensic specialist who looked them over before taking them to the lab didn't find any hairs except a couple of Henry's on the collar. It would be almost impossible to wear them without leaving at least one hair." He slapped his hat on his knee. "We're pretty sure it's him, Judge. We'll go slow, of course. There's one puzzling thing. The blood on the coveralls looks more like smears than spurts, and she certainly spurted. Sorry," he said quickly when he saw my face. "I didn't mean to tell you that. I mostly came by to verify that I need to request another magistrate and to ask if you'll send Clarinda over to be with Daisy when the time comes."

"Why don't you ask me to wrestle a couple of pit bulls instead? Or to spend a morning in the den of some hungry lions?"

He settled his hat on his head and touched the brim in a salute. "I'll keep you in mind if either of those opportunities comes up."

I won't lie and tell you I got a speck of meaningful work done the rest of the morning. I kept seeing Henry as a winsome little imp and could not believe he had killed Edie Burkett. But I respected our sheriff. He was a good and meticulous lawman. I also remembered that afternoon in the shed. The more I thought about it, the more I was convinced that Henry had intended to frighten me. What frightened me more was the possibility that whatever had happened between him and his wife might have left him with a deep need to terrorize women he felt had wronged him. Donna had said he'd hung up on Edie when she asked for her key back.

To further spoil my morning, Clarinda's predicted rain set in before noon, coming down like all the angels in heaven were weeping. I felt more like stomping around screaming, myself. As if it weren't enough that Edie was dead and Henry likely to be accused, we might as well close up and go home. Business had already been slow. With the rain, it didn't take brains to figure out shoppers would prefer one of Augusta's malls or the big, dry superstore to a string of downtown stores joined by a streaming sidewalk. Through the glass pane at the top of my office door, I saw a sea of red poinsettias. Other people might see waves of holiday cheer. All I saw was money down the drain.

I kept putting off going to lunch, hoping Joe Riddley would show up with his umbrella. Mine, of course, was back home in my car. Besides, I didn't relish eating alone. I was leaning toward taking one of the business trucks and going home to forage—followed by a nap—when the phone rang.

"Miss Mac? This is Tyrone. I called to remind you about our sword-fighting demonstration. You said you'd like to come, and it starts in thirty minutes."

That was a perfect ending to the morning.

❧ 16 ❧

I slit one side of a big trash bag and pulled it around me like a cape while I dashed to the nearest truck, which happened to be one of our largest ones. Climbing into a high truck in a straight skirt is a feat that deserves a medal, and I hate backing those things in a crowded parking lot. Today our parking lot was so empty I didn't have to worry about modesty or hitting anything. There wasn't a soul around to hand me a medal, either.

On my way over, I drove through Hardee's to pick up a hamburger. Since you can get almost anywhere in Hopemore in ten minutes, I had time to gulp down lunch in the parking lot before going to my first—and possibly last—sword-fighting demonstration.

The event was in the old Hopemore elementary school. Joe Riddley and I went there and so did our sons, but after the new school was built, the old one became school administrative offices, then stood vacant for years. Jed DuBose had recently persuaded his grandmother to buy the building and turn it into an endowed community center in memory of his father, who died in Vietnam. I smiled at the yellow sign: ZACHARY'S PLACE. Zach DuBose would have loved that sign, and would have been pleased, I think, to know his old school was now filled with children and adults studying everything from art, music, and drama to karate and sword fighting.

Tyrone was waiting for me at the door, peering anxiously

through the downpour. He didn't recognize me under my black bag. I almost didn't recognize him, either, in white cotton pants and a white jacket-shirt with three-quarter sleeves.

"What did you do with your shoes?" I demanded, shaking my bag and leaving it with the umbrellas in the foyer. "It's December, remember."

"We fight barefoot. Come on in. It's down this hall." I followed him down halls I knew better than he. As we reached the old cafeteria, a tall, stocky figure came toward us. The light was in my eyes, so at first all I could see was a white cotton shirt, a floor-length black skirt, and long white toes peeping out. I was racking my brain for any woman that big in Hopemore when a husky voice called, "Tyrone, you're supposed to be inside."

It was Frank Sparks, Valerie's friend. He turned and entered the cafeteria by another door.

"Is he studying sword fighting, too?" I asked as Tyrone ushered me in the main door.

"Oh, no, ma'am. He's our sensei." Tyrone uttered the word with a glow of pride.

"What's a 'sin-say'?" I was beginning to have a bad feeling about this.

"The master. He studied at a dojo in Macon, and he's really good. He and his friend will do a demonstration at the end of the day."

Across the room, Frank was talking to another man wearing a white shirt and black skirt. Each held long golden scabbards that I presumed held long, sharp swords.

I faltered, thinking of Edie being killed by someone with a sharp blade. If Frank had killed her, though, would he coolly demonstrate his blade skills today? While I watched, he went to speak to an agitated knot of young men and boys, all dressed like Tyrone, in white cotton shirts and pants. At his words, they all looked more hopeful. It reminded me of that instant after a chaplain prays with a football team before a championship game.

This group of fellows, however, also reminded me of

something else. A year before, Smitty was the head of a size-able gang of young thugs. He ruled by being the meanest dude around. I eyed the pack across the cafeteria and was not surprised to pick out five or six members of his former gang. Was Hopemore about to have a resurgence of that particular group, now trained to fight? The idea of a sword-brandishing high school gang almost made my heart stop.

"You coming?" Tyrone had picked up a folding chair from a cart by the door and was carrying it toward red mats in the middle of the room. I approved of the red mats. They'd be easy to fall on and would hide any blood.

"Just getting some brochures." I grabbed a yellow and a green one to make it true.

As we reached the small semicircle of chairs around the mats—no more than twenty in all—I saw the back of one familiar head. "I'll sit by Ridd," I told Tyrone.

"Here's your mama," Tyrone told Ridd in the tone of one delivering a package. He unfolded my chair, then lumbered across the room to join his friends and await the starting bell, whistle, or whatever.

Ridd grinned up at me. "Didn't expect to see you here."

"I promised Tyrone. And I know your daddy says I'm prone to think I have to take care of the world, but I wouldn't have missed the look on his face when I showed up."

Ridd looked around. "Unlike his mama, or Smitty's. But I do see somebody I know. Be right back."

I settled onto one of the most uncomfortable folding chairs I'd ever encountered, and I've met a few. This one had a list to the right, which meant I had to lean to the left to stay balanced.

Once I'd gotten the hang of that, I took time to look around. I had no idea what we were in for—whether they would fight two by two, in lines facing each other, or in a general melee. I made sure I knew where the exits were, in case somebody got too rambunctious with his sword.

While I waited, I read the brochures. The yellow one de-scribed upcoming programs at the DuBose Center. They were offering classes in oils and watercolors, starting up a community chorus, had a quilting society meeting there on Tuesday mornings, had a puppet theater class for children on Saturdays, and a writing workshop scheduled for January. I could even take "Self-Defense for Seniors." That might come in handy if Joe Riddley got obstreperous. A new chamber music group was holding a Christmas concert that sounded interesting.

As Ridd sat back down by me, I asked, "You interested in trying out for the new Hopemore Thespians' performance of *Arsenic and Old Lace?* You used to be real good in drama."

He laughed. "In high school. But who knows? I might give it a whirl." He took the brochure and started reading.

I turned to the green brochure, which offered specifics about the Hopemore Budokan. It informed me that budo meant "the Way of the Warrior." I looked over at Frank, Smitty, and Smitty's friends, and shuddered. But it also said that the student of budo aimed not for trophies but to better understand the world and oneself—mind, body, and heart. That sounded like a good, if improbable, aim for those particular teens to pursue. I also learned that students began with jodo, which was the art of using a fifty-inch staff, and then progressed to kenjutsu, or sword fighting. I wondered how far Smitty and Tyrone had come. I'd enjoy the afternoon better if I didn't have to worry about one of them cutting off somebody else's arm.

I nearly dropped my brochure when a gong sounded. My first impulse was to fall to the floor and cover my head, but two young men walked out onto the mat, bowed, and began to fight with long bamboo sticks. I didn't understand much of what was going on, but they used careful, practiced maneuvers, almost like a dance. At the end of their fight—if that's what it was—they again bowed. Several grown-ups across from us clapped with pride.

After the first couple of rounds, watching a sword-fighting demonstration where I only knew two performers got to be as exciting as attending my grandchildren's annual piano recital, where I only knew three pianists. I started watching Frank instead of the folks in the middle.

He sat cross-legged near the far wall, hands resting lightly on his thighs, and looked away from the action only occasionally to scan the crowd. I wondered if he was disappointed in the turnout. He certainly wasn't disappointed in his pupils. Several times I saw his face brighten and guessed somebody had done something right.

His companion sat beside him, also watching, but his face was impassive.

Two teams were changing places when I heard the door open and a breathy whisper. "Oh, good! I didn't miss it all!" That was followed by the sound of a falling chair.

I turned and saw Valerie Allen, her face as rosy as her sweater, righting a chair and carrying it toward us. She tiptoed with her shoulders hunched, as if she hoped stooping would make her less visible. Why should she want to be less visible? She was lovely and feminine in her fuzzy pink sweater and slim black jeans.

When she saw me, she smiled and carried her chair over on the other side of mine. She more fell into it than sat, and I noticed that Frank held up the action until she was done.

"I had to finish a paper," she whispered as two more combatants moved onto the mat and bowed. "But I told Frank I'd come if I could."

He didn't smile at her, but he sat up straighter, if that was possible, as he turned to watch the current performers.

When the duo I'd been waiting for came to the mat, I was astonished at the pride I felt as they bowed to one another. Tyrone still looked like a big, bumbling boy trying to be dignified, but Smitty was calm and controlled. His bare head looked appropriate with that outfit, and as he bent his slender body toward Tyrone's, he looked more natural than I'd ever seen him.

Ridd leaned over and muttered, "If Smitty had been born in an earlier era, he could have become a warrior hero."

I nodded. "Too bad our current society doesn't have a place for swashbucklers."

The two were new at the art, and it showed, but the whole time they fought I kept wishing I'd brought my video camera and the whole family. I don't think I felt any more pride back when Walker carried a football sixty yards for a touchdown or when Ridd made the winning putt in a high-school golf tournament. When Smitty and Tyrone gave each other a solemn formal bow and left the mat, I clapped so hard my palms stung.

After them, fellows with real swords started demonstrating how they could slice a bundle of bamboo with one blow. Every time a sword split the air, I thought of Edie, though, and it took all the self-discipline I possessed not to run from the room. Valerie may have had similar thoughts, because she kept one fist pressed to her mouth, and her eyes were wide and frightened.

Finally Frank and the other man rose and approached the mat. Each carried a sword. As they turned and bowed, the sun came out and streamed through the western windows, edging the men in gold. Valerie leaned forward in her seat and clasped her hands so tightly in her lap that the ends of her fingers turned pink. The men raised their swords and began to fight.

With the first clash of swords, my whole world went dark except for the glint of sunlight off the flashing blades. My ears roared. Sweat broke out on my forehead and ran down my back. I took deep breaths, willing myself not to faint, and my hamburger churned within me. Again and again the blades rose, clashed, rose, and clashed. By the time the two men finished and bowed to each other, I could not have left my chair if my life had depended on it. I felt like I'd been soaked in water and wrung out hard. I fought to control myself so Ridd wouldn't notice anything was wrong.

Watching Frank had not affected Valerie as it had me. "Weren't they great?" she said, bouncing up and down in her chair. The way her eyes followed him as he spoke to the boys again, I felt a pang for her sailor out at sea, but at that moment I didn't care about Valerie's love life. I only hoped she'd survive if it turned out Frank had killed Edie.

As she turned, I saw a bruise on her chin. She saw me looking at it, and put up long fingers to hide it. "I bumped my head on a desk, leaning down to pick up a pencil."

This was a conversation we'd had before, with similar results. "That's a creative explanation," I told her. "I never heard that one before."

"It's true!" She drew away from me. "I know people don't believe me, but I'm real clumsy."

"Well, you know where I am if you need me."

"Okay." She didn't sound like she planned to come.

"Are you doing okay since Edie's death?"

The little light that was left in her face disappeared. "Not very. I can forget for a little while, but then I remember again, and I feel like I'm drowning. That's the worst thing that ever happened in my whole life."

The worst that ever happened in Edie's, too, but I didn't mention that. I was looking for words to console her when Tyrone spoke above us, his voice cracking with excitement. "What did you think? Did you like it?"

Smitty stood at his elbow, not saying a word, but watching Ridd and me with those cold gray eyes, waiting for something. I wished I knew what.

I smiled at both of them. "You did great. I was real proud to know you."

Tyrone, ever aware of unhappiness around him, turned to Valerie. "Didn't you like it?"

"Oh, yes," she told him. "But I got sad afterwards, thinking about my friend Edie and her poor old lonesome daddy. She died, you know, and I used to live with her. But you all did great."

"Poor old daddy, nothing," Smitty muttered with a scowl. "Got what was coming to him."

"You don't have to worry about that murder getting solved," Tyrone assured Valerie. "The judge here will take care of that. She's real good at finding out stuff. Folks can't hide *anything* from her."

Tyrone beamed. Smitty smirked. Ridd frowned.

Valerie cried, "Oh, no!" She jumped to her feet, knocked over her chair, and stumbled toward the door.

❧ 17 ❧

When we got outside, the sun shone on waterlogged streets. Ridd looked at his watch. "Looks like I'll have time to get my car serviced before I pick up Cricket. He's been over at Natasha's all afternoon. Alex closed the library until Monday."

"Let me pick him up," I offered. "I have to go to the beauty parlor, and Alex's is on my way home. We'll feed Cricket supper, then bring him home." Only later did I remember that Alex had kicked me out two days ago. I hoped she'd at least welcome me long enough to pick up Cricket.

Never underestimate the reconciliation powers of two exuberant prekindergartners. They greeted me jumping up and down and yelling, "Look what we got! Look what we got!" Poe Boy joined in enthusiastically, leaping and barking.

Cricket waved a familiar wand with a star on one end, now painted gold. A circlet of gold metal adorned with a silver diamond shape perched on Natasha's head. "Henry brought 'em! And the teera fits, too. Look!" She felt to make sure the "diamond" was properly situated in front.

"I see it does. You are a real princess."

"'N' this is a real magic wand, Me-Mama, so don't go waving it around without thinking," Cricket warned.

"I won't. I hate to break this up, but I came to pick you up, Cricket."

Two lower lips poked out and two little faces fell. "I could

visit with Natasha's mama a while first," I offered, hoping
Alex wouldn't evict me right away.

Natasha's pearly little teeth flashed. "She's in the dinin'
room, talkin' to Henry."

That was certainly worth seeing. I let them lead me to the
dining room table, where Alex sat turned sideways toward
her small kitchen. Today she wore a cherry-red velour jog-
ging suit with Santa on the front. Her feet were bare, her toenails silver. The armchair of her dining room chairs rested
upside down on top of the table, but I didn't see Henry.

"Miss Me-Mama came to talk to you," Natasha announced, conveniently forgetting my original errand—or
maybe hoping I would. "Come on, Cricket. Let's go back to
our kingdom."

"Why, hello." Alex was still wan, but she seemed to have
forgotten our last parting.

"Hello, yourself," I greeted her. "You planning on serving
that chair for dinner?"

"No, Henry fixed it." You'd have thought he'd solved the
Mideast crisis, she sounded so impressed. "That thing's been
wobbling since I bought this set at an estate sale, but he just
took some glue and a couple of screws—" She flicked one
hand to complete the sentence. "He swears it will be good as
new when the glue dries. Of course, he's gonna have to sit in
it first, to make sure it works." Her voice was low and teasing.

That's when I noticed Henry's orange coveralls, a splash
of color on her white kitchen floor. He lay on his back with
his head under her sink.

He slid out enough to look up at me. "Afternoon, Miss
Mac."

"Afternoon, Henry. Looks like Alex has you working."

His gray gaze slid her way. "That woman is high mainte-
nance."

"I had a leak in the hot water pipe," she explained. "Every
morning I've been putting a bucket under it and every
lunchtime I've had to hurry home to empty the bucket and

put it back. I even had to set my clock to get up in the night to empty the thing. And my electric and water bills this month were out of sight. Henry said he had stuff in his truck that would fix it, but so far he's just made a bigger mess." She waved to plumbing parts lying around him.

"You better hush, woman, or I'll leave it like this and you'll be taking cold baths." But he reached for a tube of glue and slid back under the sink.

Alex watched him with a happy glow I hadn't seen on her in a while. I joined her at the table, and the three of us chatted about trivial things until Henry finally said, "Well, that's fixed," and slid out. He stood up and ran water. I looked at him and wished I didn't keep wondering if he'd killed Edie Burkett.

Alex bent to peer under the sink. "Looks like it. What do you like to drink?" She waved to a small bar in a corner of the dining room.

He shook his head. "I can't drink and drive with a judge sitting right here."

"Well, what about—?" She opened the refrigerator and pointed to an array of soft drinks and juices. Henry pointed to white grape juice.

Alex turned to me. "Mac?"

"Make that two," I told her.

"Juice! Juice!" two voices clamored, dashing in from the back. Poe Boy followed, his tail wagging with hope.

"Who said anything about juice?" Alex demanded, hands on her hips. But her eyes were laughing. "Have you all ever noticed," she asked us grown-ups, "how kids can hear a refrigerator door open half a mile away, but never hear you calling them to take their baths?"

Natasha and Cricket giggled and accepted the plastic cups of juice she poured them. "Sit down to drink it," she ordered, and they obediently went to a corner of the kitchen and plopped down on the floor. Poe Boy took a few laps from his water bowl, then flopped beside them.

Henry had been returning his equipment to a big gray

toolbox. "They obey real good," he said with approval. "The way you carried on the other day, I expected you'd spoiled her rotten."

"Humph!" Alex snorted. "I got better sense than that. Here's your juice. You can sit at the table if you don't spill."

"Thank you, ma'am," he said meekly.

She pulled out a cheese ball from the refrigerator and got some crackers, and we sat and partied a while. I hated to think that by next week this time Henry could be behind bars. If only someone else could have gotten to that machete.

That reminded me of another possible weapon. "Did either of you know we have a class in Japanese sword fighting in town? I've just come from a demonstration. Smitty Smith and Tyrone Noland are in the class. Isn't that scary?"

From the way Alex and Henry both grew still, I knew they had made the connection with Edie's death.

"I wanna study sword fighting," Cricket informed me from his corner.

"You'll have to wait a few years," I told him. Then I added, for the grown-ups, "You'll never guess who teaches the class."

"Frank Sparks," Henry said promptly. "He told me one day when I was working at the forge. Said he'd like to learn to make his own swords and asked if I'd teach him."

Alex no longer glowed. "Excuse me a minute. I need to collect Cricket's things." She hurried out of the room, calling, "Cricket? Natasha? Let's find Cricket's things."

"I wish I hadn't said anything," I muttered. "But while she's gone, did you teach Frank what he wanted to know?"

He shook his head. "I'm not skilled enough to make swords."

"But he was in your shed? He knew the machetes were there?"

He nodded. "Sure." He lowered his voice. "But if you're thinking Frank might have killed Edie, the sheriff will have to figure out how he got back in the shed when it was locked."

I looked at him steadily. "You'd do well to call a lawyer, Henry. Just in case."

He set his glass on the table with a thump. "The sheriff's got nothing on me."

"He might. If you won't do it for yourself, do it for your mother. Call a lawyer. You might be needing one."

He stood up and carried his glass to the sink. "Anybody who wants me knows where to find me. I've got a harvest to get in. Mr. Josiah needs the money, and I aim to make sure he gets all he can." His voice was rough and angry. He strode out the door and slammed it behind him.

Poe Boy came barking, with Alex right on his heels. "Where's Henry?"

"I made him mad," I admitted. "But he'll be back eventually. He forgot his tools."

❦ 18 ❧

Late Sunday afternoon I called Martha and suggested we go down to Myrtle's for a piece of pie. Myrtle makes the best chocolate pie in Georgia. It has three-inch meringue with little sugar beads on it, and it always gives my spirits a lift. So does Martha, who is one of my favorite people. Talking to Martha is one of the things that keeps me sane.

"I'll come, but I'll have to bring Cricket," she warned me. I assured her that was no hardship for his grandmother. He was good about coloring his place mat and letting us talk.

We'd no sooner gotten seated in a booth than Alex and Natasha came in. Alex looked dashing in a tapestry jacket with her black slacks, and Natasha looked splendid in a red velvet dress edged with lace, sporting her golden tiara and carrying her wand.

"Here we are!" Natasha exclaimed when she saw us. "We came for ice cream. We coulda come sooner, but Mama was talking to Henry."

Cricket climbed down from beside me, grabbed her around the neck, and they hugged and rocked like they hadn't seen each other in months, until they fell on the floor giggling.

"Get up off that floor!" Alex commanded. "You've got on your new Christmas dress."

Myrtle's floor was no place for anybody. I kept telling her somebody was going to break their neck on her pitted old tiles and sue, but she kept sighing and telling me she couldn't afford a new floor right yet. That was in a league with "I can't afford to pay my help any better," and would have been more believable if she didn't manage a new car and a fancy cruise each year. Still, she did make the best pie in Hopemore.

Natasha retrieved her fallen tiara and climbed to her feet. "You want ice cream?"

Cricket nodded. "Chocolate!"

Since Myrtle's wasn't real busy on that cold winter Sunday, I suggested, "Why don't you join us, Alex, and we can let the children eat and color in the next booth?" In just a few minutes Myrtle had supplied them with place mats, crayons, and chocolate ice cream, and the ladies with pie and coffee. The kids sat behind Martha and Alex. I said I'd keep an eye on them.

I ate the tip off my chocolate pie and gave Alex a considering look. "Now what was Natasha saying about Mama talking to Henry again today? You all sure were having a good old time yesterday before I drove him away."

A laugh rumbled low in her throat. "He came back for his tools and stayed around long enough to eat dinner with us." Seeing my look, she added, a bit defensively, "I thought it was the least I could offer after he fixed my chair and that leaky sink."

I hated to let the air out of her tires, but she needed to know. "You do realize he's the chief suspect for killing Edie, right?"

"Henry never killed anybody!" She had spoken too loudly, and looked over her shoulder to be sure the children were still coloring.

They weren't paying any visible attention, but Cricket had big ears. I lowered my voice. "Maybe not, but you ought to go slow until the sheriff makes a decision about that."

She gave a sour little grunt and leaned across the table to say softly, "Girlfriend, I already made one mistake. I got Natasha out of it, which was a lot more than I deserved, but I don't aim to go down that road a second time. I go so slow

where men are concerned, snails leave me in the dust." She
sat back up and took a bite of her pecan pie. "Mmmm, this is
good." She grew serious again. "I wish I could do something
to help find whoever it was. Don't you? Seems like we ought
to have seen or heard something that would help, but I don't
know when I've felt so useless."

"Don't try to involve Mac in any detecting," Martha advised Alex. "Last time, she nearly got herself and Clarinda
both killed. Pop's made her promise on a stack of Bibles she
won't go looking for trouble again. But speaking of trouble,
it just came in the door."

I turned and saw Olive Harrison. Nobody invited her over,
or even looked her way after that one glance, but the next
thing we knew she was sliding in beside me. Her mahogany
hair clashed with the big red poinsettia she set on the table. It
was wrapped in the green paper our new superstore must be
buying by the truckload.

"Isn't that pretty? I thought I'd take it over to Adney and
Genna." She wriggled and settled herself in like she planned
to stay a while. "Poor things, they didn't deserve all this
mess."

"They're not poor," Cricket said from the next booth.
Olive looked startled, and no wonder. The children weren't
visible over the back of the booth.

"It's not goblins," Alex told Olive. "It's Cricket and
Natasha, coloring."

"I'm making a monster," Cricket called, "and it eats people, so you better watch out."

"You better watch out, too," his mother warned. Cricket
was prone to speak whatever he was thinking, and he had
never liked Olive much.

"It just eats people with green hair," Cricket assured her.

Olive gave a high little laugh. "Well, that's the best news
I've heard all week." She leaned across the table and confided in an I'm-telling-tales-out-of-school voice, "Genna's fit
to be tied. Shep Faxon came over Thursday and told her Edie

left her everything she owned except for a couple of little bequests to friends—"

That made me choke on my coffee, remembering Edie's cute sweater and how she'd joked that she'd will it to me. I wished she had—I'd wear it with joy. But that was just the way we teased back and forth with each other.

Olive was rattling on, as usual. ". . . but Adney talked to him today, and Shep insists there isn't any money—just the Saab—which Genna doesn't need—and the snuffboxes and jewelry that got stolen. Genna knows good and well there's money and investments somewhere. Edie sold the pharmacy plus her house after Wick died, and it didn't cost her much to live with her daddy. So where's the money? That's what we all want to know." She looked around to make sure Myrtle's other patrons weren't hanging on to her every word, but seemed disappointed none of them seemed to know we were there. "I'm still convinced Edie gave it to Valerie. Or maybe to Henry. He's been mooching around her place a lot this fall, and he drives a sporty little Honda."

Alex was about to say something she might regret, so I hurried to remind Olive, "Henry works for Edie, and he used to work for a car dealer. That's probably where he got his car."

"Whatever." She shrugged. "He certainly didn't need a key to her house to harvest nuts. Adney's going to talk to him and make sure that key is returned, and he's going to see if he can't find out what happened to Wick's money. Wick didn't leave Genna a thing when he died. He left every penny to Edie."

The way Alex was clenching her fists, I suspected she was provoked enough to tell Olive exactly what Wick had left Edie, but I shook my head with a frown. If Edie hadn't told her, Olive didn't need to know.

Thank goodness, she had already headed in another direction. "As if all that weren't bad enough, I still haven't gotten that couch mess straightened out, and I went over to the new store last Wednesday night to buy the paint for my dining room, and it's way too dark—not the right color at all—but they won't take it back." She'd started out talking to me, but wound up looking at Martha.

It was hard for me to visualize a scale of troubles long enough to contain Edie's murder and Olive's dining room paint, but Martha's nicer than I am. She said, without a trace of sarcasm, "I'm so sorry. Could you add white to it or something?"

"I doubt it." Olive didn't want solutions; she wanted sympathy and shared indignation. "It was supposed to be ivory, and it's more like taupe. Even lighter, it wouldn't be the right color. And I stood right there while the man mixed it, asking if he was sure he was putting in the right colors. I was practically dead on my feet, it was so late, and I might as well not have bothered. After work I'd rented a truck and gotten the two men next door to carry my couch out, and I drove it back to North Augusta myself, to show the store it wasn't the one I'd ordered, but after all that trouble, they close at six on Wednesdays. It was past ten when I got back, and I wanted to run by Edie's to see if she was all right before I went to the store for the paint—"

"You went by Edie's Wednesday night?" Alex asked fiercely.

Olive nodded. "I hadn't seen her since"—she looked over her shoulder toward the children—"you know, what happened Tuesday. I wanted to make sure she was all right. I'd hoped to go in for a minute. It wasn't but ten thirty when I got there, but all her lights were out and her car was there, so I figured she'd already gone to bed. I saw Genna leaving as I pulled in. I didn't stop to talk, though, because I still had to get that paint, and the store closes at eleven. Can you believe I stood right there while the man mixed all three gallons, and he still didn't get it right?"

What I couldn't believe was that she'd had the gall to show up at a store just before closing time expecting somebody to mix three gallons of paint. What I wanted confirmed was, "But you were at Edie's on Wednesday night?"

"Around ten thirty." She clutched her throat. "If I'd been a couple of hours later, you might have found me lying on the bed beside her."

Myrtle cruised by just then to refill our coffee cups and asked Olive what she'd like to order. Olive looked at her watch. "Heavens, I didn't mean to stay. I need to get on over to Adney's. I just wanted to run in and say hello. Good-bye, everybody." She gave us all a bright smile, picked up her poinsettia, and hurried out with a clatter of heels.

"My monster is eating a woman," Cricket announced to the world in general. "He changed his mind. He likes womens with red hair."

⊰ 19 ⊱

Monday noon we went home to dinner and found Clarinda having a conniption. "I got a call from Daisy, and that sheriff was down at her place this morning axin' more questions about Henry. She said the way he acted, he'll arrest Henry any minute. We gotta do something!"

"He can't arrest Henry without evidence," I pointed out, "and he said the crime lab won't be done until at least the end of this week."

Joe Riddley looked steadily at me without changing the speed of his chewing.

"*You* might do something," I added, "but I made a promise to my husband. Why don't you take the afternoon off and go on down to Daisy's?"

When I got back to work, I pulled up a file of past-due accounts. Dealing with deadbeats suited my mood. One invoice, though, caught my attention: a bill for a big delivery of herbicide out to Josiah's grove the morning he had his stroke. I hadn't liked to send it to Edie in October or November—I'd thought I'd give her time to adjust to her daddy's situation and get some of her harvest in. Who the dickens would pay it now? Josiah wasn't signing any checks.

I was mulling that over, and waiting to hear from Clarinda, when the phone rang around one thirty. Instead of Clarinda, it was Meriwether DuBose.

"Did you have that baby?" I asked, all excited.

"Not yet. Two more weeks, the doctor says. But listen, I called to ask if you could come over here right now. To the warehouse. We've got a small crisis. Please?"

Meriwether was thirty-four. In the past fourteen months she had started up a new catalogue company, restored an old house, found love, been married, and gotten pregnant. Not to mention dealing with her autocratic old grandmother, Augusta Wainwright, and helping Augusta move out of the house where she'd lived all her life and settle somewhere else. Just dealing with Augusta would send most of us to the funny farm. But at no time in the past had I known Meriwether to sound so frazzled.

"What's the problem?" I flapped one hand at a deputy who had come in, motioning for her to set the warrant she'd brought down on my desk so I could read it while Meriwether answered. Multitasking is simply a fancy new name for what women have always done.

I perused the warrant, signed it, and handed it back while Meriwether explained, "Valerie Allen. She's terrified, and I can't calm her down. Can't you hear her?"

"I thought you had a yowling cat somewhere." I waved good-bye to the deputy as she left.

"No, a hysterical woman. And she's asking for you. Please, Mac? Can you come?"

Of course I agreed.

This was the second pretty day since Saturday's downpour, with a good wind. The nuts ought to be ready for the harvesters soon, but what if Henry wasn't there to oversee them?

I hadn't been inside the old brick warehouse down near the railroad tracks since a memorable afternoon when I'd been locked in there by a desperate murderer. In spite of knowing Meriwether was inside now with a raft of employees, my heart thudded as I pulled to a stop in her new paved lot and headed to the door.

I calmed down as soon as I stepped inside. The place looked real different full of tall shelves loaded with merchandise and with people moving up and down long aisles, pulling items off the shelves and putting them onto carts. An electric forklift purred its way down one aisle, and Tyrone Noland gave me a wave before deftly maneuvering a large box off the very top shelf. I gave him a thumbs-up, then turned to admire women filling boxes with Styrofoam peanuts from soft blue bins hanging from the ceiling.

I was sorry when Meriwether hurried toward me. "Oh, Mac, I'm so glad you've come."

"Place looks great." I'd rather look around than deal with a crisis any day.

She must have read my mind. "I'll show you around later." She led the way to her office, where Valerie sat in a chair by the desk.

Valerie and Meriwether might look a lot alike in certain lights. Both were blond, long, and slender. Both had large blue eyes that caught your attention. But Meriwether was beautiful, even nine months pregnant, and today Valerie looked a mess. Her nose and lips were red and swollen, her cheeks puffy from tears. She huddled in the chair, moaning, "I didn't do it. I didn't!"

"What's going on?" I asked briskly at the door, although any fool could see what was going on. Valerie was terrified. Fear hunched her shoulders and twisted her long legs around each other. Fear stood stark in her face as she looked back at me. "They think I killed Edie, but I didn't. I wouldn't do that! She was my friend!" She headed off into hysterics again.

"Get me some water," I told Meriwether. She went past me and fetched a cup from the water fountain. I crossed the office and emptied it over Valerie's head.

She spluttered and gasped. "What'd you do that for?" She wiped water from her forehead and looked in dismay at the widening stain on her jeans.

"To hush you up. I can't talk to you unless you calm down. I'm not sure I ought to be talking to you anyway."

"It's okay. I told them to call you."

I nearly jumped out of my skin. I hadn't seen Sheriff Gibbons sitting in a chair behind the door. Even if he hadn't been out of sight when I entered, I might not have noticed him. The sheriff is over six feet tall, but he has a way of blending into walls.

"Hello, Sheriff," I greeted him.

"Afternoon, Judge." He sat there in uniform, hat decorously on his lap, and gave me the formal nod of a colleague. Nobody would have suspected, listening to us, that he'd been best man in my wedding and would have become the guardian of our sons if Joe Riddley and I had died before they grew up.

"What's going on?" I figured he might give me an answer I could understand.

He nodded toward Valerie. "I'm trying to get some information from Miss Allen here. Her car was seen pulling out of Whelans' drive around seven last Thursday morning, not long before Mrs. Burkett was found."

The air left my body. Valerie? My mind went so blank, I couldn't think of a thing to say.

"I didn't kill her," Valerie cried, turned sideways in the big chair and scrunched up into a smaller ball than I'd known a six-foot person could make. "I didn't. I didn't know she was dead. She was dead the whole time, and I didn't know it." She started whimpering.

"Are you accusing her of the murder?" My voice wasn't steady, and I was wildly wondering whether I was there as a magistrate or as Valerie's friend.

"No. I'm gathering information, and thought you might be able to—uh—" He gestured toward the mess that was Valerie. "She asked for you."

I went over and shook Valerie by one damp shoulder. She must have cried a river and a creek. "Just answer his questions. He won't hurt you. I've known him all my life." Thank goodness it wasn't Police Chief Muggins. Charlie Muggins scares even me at times.

She sniffed and nodded. "Okay. I'll tell him. But you'll stay with me, won't you?"

"Of course, if you want me to."

Sheriff Gibbons pushed a chair my way. "I informed her she could call a lawyer—"

"A judge is better than a lawyer," Valerie interrupted.

"Honey, once I've heard your testimony, I can't have anything to do with the case." A magistrate doesn't try murder cases, anyway. All we do is hold a probable-cause hearing. If there is enough evidence for arrest, we send the accused to jail without bond and mail a letter to the superior court asking for a judge to be sent to hear the case. I had no more standing than Meriwether in that room. Less, in fact. She owned the building.

"That's okay." Valerie sniffed. "I still want you here."

"Don't you also want a lawyer?"

She shook her head. "I don't need a lawyer. I didn't *do* anything."

Buster and I exchanged a look. He nodded at me, and I guess he wanted me to ask her some questions. I tried to figure out the right ones to ask. "Why were you down at Edie's Thursday? I heard her say you moved out Tuesday morning."

Valerie gave me a miserable little nod and sniffed again. "Genna stayed over Monday night, and she—" Her voice trembled again, and she came to a full stop.

"She said some things that made you feel like you didn't want to live there," I suggested.

"Oh, I still wanted to live there, but Genna didn't want me to. She said I was trying to make Edie do things she didn't want to, and that Frank was staying overnight, and that I was . . . was . . . a tacky tramp." Valerie swiped tears away with one arm, but those were angry tears, not brokenhearted ones.

I reached out and patted her shoulder. "We both know that's not so. But if you moved out Tuesday, why were you back there Wednesday night?"

"I wasn't." The words were muffled. "Wednesday night Frank and I had a gig over near Louisville." She didn't mean the site of the Kentucky Derby, but Louisville, Georgia, with the "s" pronounced—seat of Jefferson County and not far down the road.

"But somebody saw you coming out of Edie's drive Thursday morning." I didn't bother to make that a question.

She nodded. "I know. I went over real early, before it got light, because I wanted, I—I—" Once she got started, she said it all in a rush. "I wanted to make the bears' Christmas outfits. As a surprise for Edie. I saw the Mama Bear you bought her. She brought it home Tuesday while I was taking out the last of my stuff, and she said, 'But heaven only knows when I'll get time to make it a Christmas dress.'" I could hear Edie saying it. "I'd been wondering what to give her for Christmas, and I'd already bought some material. You saw the bag, remember?"

I nodded.

"So Wednesday night, on the way back from Louisville, it came to me. I could make their outfits and surprise Edie. I couldn't make anything fancy, of course," she said earnestly, "but I could make Papa Bear pants and a little jacket like his Thanksgiving one, because Edie showed me how to make those. And I could make Mama Bear a jacket and a gathered skirt, sort of like my apron." Her voice trailed off on the last word. She was probably seeing, as I was, the charred ruins of her first-ever garment.

I touched her hair gently. "That was ambitious and kind. I'm proud of you."

She gave me a watery smile. Then she took a deep breath and shoved her hair back again—it had begun to creep over her shoulders. "I figured I could go in every morning for a couple of hours before class—my first one's not until eight—and she'd never suspect. The sewing machine's downstairs in what used to be her daddy's bedroom, so she couldn't hear it up where she sleeps. Slept." She stumbled over that fence, got up, and galloped on. "I figured if I left before seven, she wouldn't see me. So I went in Thursday morning and I got everything cut out and pinned, then I stuffed it all under the pillow on the bed. Genna always sleeps upstairs, so nobody ever uses that bed. I put the bears back exactly how she'd left them on the living room couch, and I even carried out all my threads and scraps in a plastic bag, in case she looked in the room. It was going to be a surprise." Her voice was bleak.

I felt bleak, too, and Meriwether was blowing her nose. Edie should have lived to see those bears dressed in Valerie's valiant efforts.

I turned to Sheriff Gibbons. "Do you have any more questions?"

He nodded. "Were you ever in Edith Burkett's room at the top of the house?" I suspected he'd found a fingerprint or two, and held my breath as Valerie started to shake her head.

She stopped, and nodded. "I took laundry up for her sometimes, and left it on her bed." She made a fist and bit her thumb, then admitted, "And two or three times I took a bath in her bathtub, if she was away for the night. She has a big old tub up there, and the tub on the second floor is short, so I'd go up and take a long bubble bath. I cleaned up real good, though." She needn't sound so ashamed. We weren't going to be telling Edie anytime soon.

"Did Frank ever spend the night?" I asked. We might as well deal with that while we were at it.

She hesitated again, looking at her lap. "Once." Her voice was low. Then she looked up quickly, defiant and indignant. "It's not what it sounds like, though. Not what Genna and Olive said. We'd ridden his motorcycle to practice, and on the way home it started to pour down rain." She lifted her chin. "We both got soaked, and I didn't want him to drive home in all that. Edie had already gone to bed, so I told him he could sleep in her daddy's bed if he'd leave first thing in the morning. He was gone before I got up, and I skipped classes that morning and washed the sheets while Edie was at work. But I never told her." Her voice was ashamed and forlorn.

"Did either of you ever drive Edie's car?" I persisted.

She nodded again, like a compliant child. "I did. She had

parked in the middle of the carport, and Frank needed to get his bike out of the rain, so I backed her car out and pulled over to one side. The next morning I moved it back to where she'd left it. But I had to move her seat. I couldn't get in with it where she'd left it. I was in such a hurry, I forgot to move the seat back or lock the back door when I came in after moving the car."

"When she asked about it, you lied to her," I pointed out.

She looked at her lap again. "I know. I didn't think she'd like it that I'd let Frank sleep in her daddy's bed. But I couldn't send him back out in the rain, and I couldn't tell her about the car without saying why I'd moved it."

Somebody sharper could have come up with all sorts of stories about why she'd driven the car, but I was coming to appreciate the limitations of Valerie's intellect.

She reached out and clutched my arm. "Did she die because I lied to her? Was that to punish me?"

"Heavens, no! God doesn't kill somebody to punish somebody else."

She didn't look real convinced. She might prefer a judge to a lawyer when she was in trouble, but when it came to interpreting God, I suspected she'd prefer a preacher.

I still had one question. "Does Frank have a key to Edie's house?"

She nodded without hesitation. "He was working on some things for her, so she gave him one so he could get in when she wasn't there."

"Did he give it back to her when you moved out?"

She looked baffled. "Edie didn't ask . . ." Her voice dwindled off. Even Valerie was smart enough to figure out the position that put them both in.

The sheriff had a question. "Did you go upstairs at any time yesterday when you were in the house?"

"Oh, no! I tiptoed into the downstairs bedroom and closed the door. When it was time to leave, I listened to make sure she wasn't up—"

That was as far as she got before she broke down again. I

couldn't blame her. I'd seen a lot more death in my lifetime than she had, but I couldn't imagine knowing I'd spent two hours in the house with Edie lying dead upstairs. The very thought made tears sting my eyes again.

Sheriff Gibbons has a tender heart, and I think he was having some of the same thoughts. He picked up his hat and stood. "I guess that covers it for now. Please don't leave town in the next few days, Miss Allen."

She looked up at him, startled. "But we have wedding gigs this weekend in Dublin and Augusta. They're counting on us."

Meriwether spoke quickly. "Why don't you let Valerie make you a list of places they're booked to sing these next two weeks? They just go out to perform and come right back each evening, right?" The last was for Valerie.

"Oh, yeah." Valerie's hair swung as she nodded. "We don't stay overnight or anything. Frank's mama would have a fit."

I told myself again that she was one woman I'd like to meet.

Meriwether handed Valerie a pen and a sheet of paper, and she started to write. After four lines, she shook her head. "That's as far as I can remember. Frank will know the rest."

"Frank will know the rest of what?"

We all turned, startled. Frank Sparks stood in the door, feet apart as if braced for a fight. Once again he was dressed all in black, from his boots and gloves to his leather jacket. A silver helmet dangled from one hand. "I heard you were over here, Sheriff, and thought I'd better mosey down. I don't know what you've told him, Valerie, but—"

Valerie started explaining. Frank listened in exasperation for only a couple of seconds, then commanded, "Hush! Don't you say another word without a lawyer."

"I don't need a lawyer," Valerie protested. "The judge is right here, and I haven't done anything except go down to Edie's the morning she was killed, to—"

He caught her and clapped one hand over her mouth. "Hush!"

The sheriff turned to him. "Where were you the night Ms. Burkett was killed?"

"Ask my lawyer." He tugged Valerie's hand. "Come on. We're out of here."

On their way to the door, Valerie's foot caught on the leg of a chair and she went sprawling. He helped her up and led her out. In a minute or two his Harley roared away.

Meriwether chuckled. "That child can't walk across a room without running into something or tripping over something else. She stays black and blue."

"You don't think he hits her?" I asked.

"Heavens, no. He adores her. She adores him, too. She just hasn't figured that out yet. She thinks she ought to be loyal to some sailor who got a crush on her right before he shipped out, and then proposed by mail. I'm working on helping her see she isn't bound by that. And while most women's bruises may be caused by beatings, Valerie's are all her own."

Mama always said nobody really knows what goes on inside a love affair except the two people involved, and most of the time even they aren't real sure.

We all jumped when Meriwether's security alarm started to clang. Buster rose to his feet, but she waved him back. "It does this all the time. There's a short or something." She hurried out.

"Don't turn it off permanently," I called after her. "It could be somebody wanting you to do exactly that." I didn't know if she'd heard me or not.

The sheriff walked me to my car. He was holding the door when his cell phone rang. "Yeah?" He listened only a second, then held the phone away from his ear.

In spite of the clanging alarm, I could hear a tinny voice coming through the phone. Somebody had sure lit Shep Faxon's cauldron.

"Sheriff, I got Genna Harrison in my office pitchin' a fit,

and I can't do a thing with her. The way she's carrying on, I'm scared she's gonna hurt somebody. Get over here and calm her down, you hear me? She came over here wantin' to know why Edie hadn't left her all that money they got from selling her daddy's pharmacy and their big house, and she won't believe me that Edie didn't say a thing about any money or investments. Genna claims I've stolen her inheritance, and she's scaring the living daylights out of us. My secretary is in with her now, while I stepped into the bathroom to call you on my cell phone. Come quick."

Sheriff Gibbons laughed. "Surely you can handle a little lady, Shep. An old hand like you?"

"It's not the little lady I'm scared of, Sheriff. It's that gun she's waving all over the place."

❧ 20 ❧

I arrived back at the office in time to take a call from Clarinda. "Where you been? I been callin' and callin' you."

"I had to go out a minute. What did you want?"

"I wanted you. Daisy's down here pitching a fit. It wasn't bad enough they asked her to clean up Miss Edie's room this morning, with all that blood in it. Then the sheriff's men came back down here nosing around, acting like it's only a matter of time until Henry's in jail. And now Henry's run off like a wild man. Daisy' plumb frantic with worry."

"Where'd Henry go?"

"How do I know? Daisy showed him some paper from his grandmama's Bible, and next thing we know, he's grabbed it and hightailed it out of here. That's when Daisy went crazy. She says that paper kills people. Can you come down here? I don't know how to handle her."

Handling frantic mothers is not on my résumé, but keeping Clarinda happy means I frequently develop new skills. "I'm coming," I said, trying not to think about all the work piling up on my desk. "If Henry comes home—"

"We'll sit on him 'til you get here if we have to," she promised.

When I drove out Oglethorpe Street toward Whelan Grove Road, the new superstore had so many cars in its parking lot, I wondered who was back running the town.

The Joyners lived in a brick ranch house beyond the

grove, across the road and down a bit from Josiah's, built on a two-acre lot Josiah's daddy had given Pete's mother, Mary. The little white house he'd built for her was now a toolshed and garage to one side.

Pete loved plants and specialized in daylilies, so his yard was a thing of beauty in summer. Today it all looked cold and dead, just like Pete. I decided to offer Daisy a magnolia and a holly to plant in the yard, if she'd have them. They'd make the place more colorful in winter. I mentally added a few camellias to the truck. Camellias are evergreen, they bloom all winter, and their blossoms are prettier to me than rubies, garnets, and amethysts.

Clarinda met me. "He's still not home." The front door opened directly into the living room, which was paneled in dark walnut and decorated in green and cream with touches of red. I wished it didn't remind me so much of a funeral parlor.

Daisy sat uneasily in a green brocade armchair, twisting a tissue in her hands until it was worn to shreds. Nothing about her was still. Her gaze darted from me to her lap, roamed around the room, then made another round-trip. Her knees quivered in their brown corduroy pants. Her feet tapped the creamy carpet. Her lips trembled.

"Have you talked to the sheriff? Did he tell you why his men are so dadgum sure they can arrest Henry?" Clarinda demanded, lowering herself with an "oof!" onto one end of the couch as I sat down on the other, nearest Daisy.

I hesitated, but it wouldn't be a secret as soon as the crime lab sent back a report, and those deputies had no business scaring Daisy with tones of voice and facial expressions. I'd watched them do it to other suspects' families, and it made me mad.

"They found a pair of his coveralls down behind some bushes near the equipment barn. They've sent them off to be tested to see if somebody else could have worn them."

"O' course somebody else wore 'em if they were worn to kill Miss Edie in!" Clarinda's loyalty to her family runs strong and deep. "Henry never killed anybody, and if he did, he's too smart to leave his own coveralls under a bush for any half-wit deputy to find."

"He went missing a pair not long ago," Daisy offered eagerly. "I don't mind what day it was, but he'd put them on fresh the day before, and he usually wears them two days if he don't get them real dirty, to save me having so much wash. But he showed up here the next morning saying he thought he'd left them on a hook in his shed, but he must not have, because they wasn't there. I told him, 'I can't have you losing clothes like you used to in grade school.' That boy was so careless with clothes back then, the principal said he was gonna change the sign on the LOST AND FOUND box and just call it HENRY'S BOX. And in fourth grade—" She seemed eager to escape into Henry's childhood, but it was Henry's present I was worried about.

"You need to think back to what day that was," I told her. "Remember anything you did that day to fix it in your mind, and write it down so you'll remember."

"In case you have to testify in court." Clarinda has worked for judges too long.

Daisy gasped and covered her face with her hands. "I can't. I just can't!"

"It hasn't come to that yet," I reminded her. "Tell me what happened today."

While we waited for her to collect her thoughts, I wondered if she'd tell me much. It wasn't as if we were friends. Pete used to come in and out of the store a lot, but his wife seldom left home. I'd heard she had whatever that disease is that makes people afraid to go into crowds. The three of us weren't much of a crowd, but as she looked quickly at me, Clarinda, and back at her lap, I felt sure she thought her house had one too many people in it.

"Clarinda said Henry stormed out of here this afternoon." I prompted her when the silence grew long.

She nodded. "It's that paper. That wicked paper." Her

frightened whisper was worthy of a horror film. I shivered, although the house was too warm and stuffy.

For a minute or two, the only sound in the room was the soft hum of the refrigerator in the kitchen. Daisy didn't seem to hear it. I don't know when I'd seen a woman look so wrung out. "Tell me about Henry," I prodded.

Before Daisy could answer, Clarinda jumped in. "He came home midafternoon for a little break. Daisy and I were sitting here having a glass of tea, so I fixed him some. He asked what we'd been doing all day, and Daisy told him two of the sheriff's men had asked her to clean up Miss Edie's room. That made him mad to start with."

"It was awful," Daisy put in. "Plumb awful." She shuddered at the memory.

"Then Daisy said the same men had come down here asking again about the night Miss Edie died, and she mentioned to Henry that she'd had to tell them about taking her medicine for a migraine and going to bed early, so she couldn't exactly swear he was here that night."

"But I'm pretty sure he was," Daisy added anxiously.

Clarinda nodded, and continued. "Henry started fussing at her, saying he had nothing to do with that murder and she knows it, but she's the only alibi he's got. Then Daisy says she knows what's killed everybody, it's that paper from his grandmama's Bible. She says everybody who touches that paper goes crazy and dies. He asks, 'What paper?' and she fetches it to him. Next thing we know, he's running out of here like a wild man—"

I'd heard that bit, so I waved her to stop. "Do you know what made him so mad?"

Daisy lifted her head. "It was that paper. That wicked paper!"

"What is it?" I asked.

She clutched the arms of her chair like it might lift off with her any minute. "I don't know, but I wish I'd burnt it up. Why didn't I when I had a chance? I found it in Pete's mama's Bible one Friday when I was dusting. I pulled out the

Bible and that paper fell out. I saw Pete's name on it, so I showed it to him when he got home from work. He collapsed on that couch right where you are now, like a strong wind had blown him over. Then he got up and started pacing. He paced up and down all night long, muttering things I couldn't hear. When I got up to get breakfast, he was sitting at the table with his head in his hands. All of a sudden he jumped up and said, 'I've got to talk to Josiah. I'll be back in a little while.'

"I told him, 'It's Saturday. You don't work Saturdays until harvest time, and we were goin' to town.' He said, 'I'm fixin' to get me an explanation. I'll be back in a bit, and we'll go to town.'"

She slumped in her chair. "The next time I saw him, he was dead, and Mr. Josiah might as well have been. The paper was still in Pete's pocket, but it was crumpled up, like he'd taken it out and put it back in a hurry, and it had a little corner missing. It killed him, Judge. I know that as sure as I'm sittin' here. And when Henry saw it this *after*noon"—she emphasized the first half of the word, as country people are wont to do—"it was like Pete all over again. He started talking wild, said he wanted an explanation, and tore out of here like the devil himself was on his tail."

"But you don't know what was on the paper?"

"No'm." Lacking another tissue to shred, she twisted the corduroy over her thin knees and did not meet my eyes.

"Daisy, can you read?" I asked as gently as I knew how.

She hesitated, then shook her head, her head still down. "It shames me," she mumbled, "and I was so afraid Miss Edie would find out, her carin' so much about reading and such. I never learned much past my name."

"Why not?" I knew the story I would hear. I've heard it so many times in one form or another from her generation. Anyone who doesn't believe we have nonreading adults in this country needs to think again. And these are not dumb people. The rest of us ought to try for a week to cook a new prepackaged food, operate anything from a radio to a microwave, or take new medicine on schedule without being able to read. It takes a good bit of intelligence and native wisdom to survive, much less survive without being found out.

Daisy's voice dropped to a whisper, and I had to strain to hear. "Mama died when I was in first grade, and I went to live with an auntie. She had littler children, and she needed me to mind them so she could work and feed us all. When I got bigger, I kept meaning to go back, but I was working and needed the money. Then I married Pete. He tried to teach me some, but he wasn't a real patient man, and the more he tried to teach me, the more nervous I'd get. I thought about axin' Miss Edie, but I was too ashamed." She paused, and the room was silent for a long minute. Then she lifted her head. "The only two words I knew on that paper were 'Peter Joyner.' That's why I showed it to Pete." She jumped up and began wringing her hands. "It killed him, Judge, and it killed Miss Edie. Now it will kill my Henry, too!" She flung herself around the room, muttering and rubbing her hands like Lady Macbeth.

As she circled close to me, I realized what she had just said. "Did you show the paper to Edie?" I asked gently.

She veered over toward the window and stood there clutching the drape, as silent as if she had not heard.

"Did you?" Clarinda wasn't gentle at all. "Did you bother Miss Edie with that?"

I raised one hand in protest, but Clarinda's roughness made Daisy protest, with misery in every line of her body. "I didn't mean to harm her. I'd never have harmed Miss Edie. You all know that."

"But you showed it to her?" I pressed her.

I could barely see her nod. "Yessum. I stuck it back in Mary's Bible after I took it from Pete, and I forgot all about it. But I picked up that Bible last Sunday a week, because I needed comfort. Sometimes just *holdin'* the Good Book brings comfort, you know?" She covered her face before I could nod. "Ain't nothin' gonna comfort me if that paper takes Henry, like it did my Pete and Miss Edie." She fell into a nearby chair, flopped her head against its back, and filled the room with her wails.

I walked over to the window and looked out, partly to reassure myself that a sunny, sane world still existed. When she stopped for breath, I prodded her. "So you found it again Sunday afternoon."

She jumped up and started circling the room again. She followed a worn dip in the carpet, which I figured was her regular route when agitated. "The Bible opened right to it, like a sign or something. Sign of evil is what it was! All these years since Mary died, I left that Bible sitting right there on that shelf. Why I had to pull it out this fall, I do not know. It has brought me nothing but trouble. When I saw the paper that killed Pete, seemed like I just had to know what it was. So I carried it up to the grove, looking for Henry. He works Sunday afternoons during harvest. When I got to the house, Miss Edie was gettin' out of her car, comin' back from church, so I told her I'd found a paper with Pete's name on it in Mary's Bible. I didn't tell her Pete had it first. I said my migraine was so bad, I couldn't see to read it, so could she read it and tell me what it said. She—" Daisy turned her back to us and stopped. Her voice faltered.

"Go on," Clarinda ordered.

Daisy took a deep breath, put her palms together, and lifted them in front of her mouth. I had to listen carefully to hear her. "She looked at it a minute, then she got real pale. Maybe there's poison in that paper, I don't know. I never come over queer holding it, but everybody else sure has. I was afraid she would faint, she was so white. I helped her real quick into the house and got her some water. She sat there just looking at the paper for a long, long time. Finally I reached to take it back, figuring I'd put it back in the Bible where it couldn't do more harm. 'I'm sorry to bother you with this,' I told her. 'I was coming looking for Henry.' She pulled the paper away from me and axt, 'Henry hasn't seen this?' I said, 'No'm, I haven't showed it to him yet,' and she said, 'Don't bother him with it right now. Let me keep it a few days. I'll see what I can do. And I'll bring it back. I promise.' She worried me, her voice was so faint.

"'Is it bad?' I asked. And she said, 'Very bad. Shameful.' She rubbed her head like it was aching, then she said, 'I need to think. You go on home now. I'll bring you back your paper in a day or two.' She did, too. She come down here Tuesday around dinnertime and told me she'd taken care of things, that I should put the paper back in the Bible and not say anything about it to Henry until she could talk to him." Daisy stopped pacing and lifted her hands to the ceiling. "May God forgive me, that's the last time I ever saw her. That paper I give her killed her just like it did my Pete. If it takes Henry—You gotta find him, Miss Mac. You just gotta. I can't lose Henry along with everybody else!"

⊰ 21 ⊱

"I need to think, too," I told Daisy. "I'll call you later." I turned to Clarinda. "You'll be staying down here?"

She pursed her lips, disgusted I hadn't come up with a magic answer to Daisy's dilemma right away. "I'm not goin' anywhere until we sort this out. But you think fast, and find out what's going on before they arrest Henry. We don't want any more trouble around this place. Besides, I got to cook all day tomorrow for my sorority luncheon Wednesday."

"That's right." I reached for my pocketbook. "Keep your priorities straight."

I did want to know what was going on, though. Whelan Grove had had enough tragedies. I didn't want Henry to be another.

"There has to be something we've all missed," I muttered as I drove back to the store in Hopemore's afternoon rush minute. It was more prayer than complaint. "But what?"

The amazing thing about prayer is that sometimes when we think we're simply asking for what we want, we're actually being led to ask so we'll recognize an answer when it comes. That afternoon, the words were hardly out of my mouth when a siren wailed behind me. As I swung off the highway to let a paramedic van pass on its frantic way to the emergency room, I thought about the day Josiah and Pete were rushed to the hospital. Pete was already dead and Josiah unable to speak. So who called 911?

Before I could mull that over, as if my life weren't complicated enough, my cell phone rang. "Judge?" the sheriff asked. "Are you near your office? I need a warrant for arrest."

"Shep actually charged her? Let me come down there. It's on my way back."

I arrived to find a very shamefaced Genna slumped sullenly before the magistrate's bench. Her clothes were wrinkled, her hair disheveled, her face streaked with mascara. As soon as she saw me, she immediately started talking. "It was all a mistake, Mac. I wouldn't have hurt anybody. I just wanted him to tell me about Edie's money, and he wouldn't."

Shep Faxon stood angrily to one side.

I held up one hand. "Wait a minute, Genna. Shep, you sure you want the sheriff to charge Genna here with aggravated assault?"

"I sho' do, Judge. The way she was wavin' that gun around, she coulda killt somebody!" I kept my dignity, but something in me wanted to stand and cheer for anybody who could so thoroughly ruffle his feathers.

I signed the paper the sheriff handed me, then before I set bond, I ascertained several things. Adney was working a circuit down toward Jacksonville for the next two days, and Genna had decided to go ask some questions about Edie's will before he got home. She had a permit to carry the gun because she was nervous when Adney was away. She had never used it before. The sheriff now had the gun in his possession. Genna was not likely to pose a threat to the community if I released her until her court date. And she didn't have enough money in her checking account to post bond.

I saw what Cindy meant about Genna being useless without Adney. She couldn't think of a single way to get out of jail until she called him on her cell phone. I was surprised she'd had the gumption to go see Shep without him. Adney said he'd call Olive. She came waltzing into the detention center half an hour later so indignant, you'd have thought we'd all been pistol-whipping Genna for hours. She thumped down the deed to some land Adney owned like we were planning to use it for nefarious and probably illegal purposes, and swept Genna off saying, as they went out the door, "Let's go get you freshened up, and we'll have dinner at the country club. You look like you could use a drink." From the glares they both shot back at me as they headed for Olive's car, I wouldn't be selling plants to either of them anytime soon.

The sheriff grinned at Shep and me. "All in a day's work, right?"

Shep Faxon wiped his forehead, which had beaded with sweat during the process. "Not in my day's work. I don't mind tellin' you, when that girlie jerked out that pistol and started wavin' it around, I thought my time had come. I didn't think she'd shoot me on purpose, mind—"

"She doesn't know you well enough," I retorted. "You can leave that to your friends."

I left them to whatever it is men talk about when they huddle together in hallways, and moseyed down to the 911 operator's desk.

Hope County was later than some in getting a 911 system because we're underpopulated, as Georgia counties go. Opponents pointed out that we don't have constant emergencies like crowded counties, which keep whole banks of operators busy twenty-four hours a day. They objected to paying for twenty-four-hour service when some days we don't get a single emergency call and some of the calls that do come in— about minor fender benders or women wanting a ride to the hospital when they're in labor and their husbands are at work with the truck—aren't "real" emergencies.

Proponents argued that those are real emergencies when they are happening to you, and in addition, we get a number of domestic violence calls and have a lot of fires in winter, because our weather is mild enough that some houses still aren't well heated and folks rely too much on space heaters, then leave them unattended. They also argued that because of television, folks in Hope County knew that other people could dial 911 in any emergency and get help without having to look up and dial a whole number for the hospital, the sheriff, or the fire department.

I hate to admit it, but the argument that swayed the vote was that we didn't want newcomers thinking they'd moved to a hick town.

The county commission compromised by installing a 911 line at one of the desks in the sheriff's office and making sure that whoever is on that desk gives those calls priority. Otherwise, he or she is free to work on other tasks.

As I had hoped, I found the desk staffed that afternoon by Mary Ball, whom I had known since she had long brown pigtails and a lisp. She used to skip into the store on her way home from school and ask for a "lemon thucker"—the only child I ever knew to prefer lemon ones.

"Hey, Mary," I greeted her. "This isn't an emergency, but if you aren't busy and can give me some information, I'd be grateful."

"Sure, Judge. What do you need?" Her voice throbbed with curiosity. "Are you detecting?"

Mary reads too many mystery novels. Sure, I've occasionally been in the local paper for helping the police identify a killer—although our police chief, Charlie Muggins, generally takes the credit and makes it sound like I got in his way. However, Mary is aware of Charlie's many deficiencies, so she generally gives me *more* credit than I deserve. I didn't want her going around the detention center bragging that she'd been helping Judge Yarbrough on a case.

"Shut your mouth, and don't you dare let the sheriff or Joe Riddley hear you asking that," I told her. "I'm just curious who placed the 911 call from Whelans' place."

She looked at me uncertainly. "You did," she finally said. Bless her heart, she probably thought I was getting prematurely senile.

"Not that call. The earlier one—back in September when Pete Joyner had a heart attack and Josiah Whelan had his stroke. Who called the paramedics?"

"I didn't take that call. Do you know exactly when it was?"

"Let me see." I tried to remember the invoice I'd been looking at earlier. "It was the third Saturday in September, because we delivered some herbicides down there that morning."

With that information, she found it almost at once, but her forehead creased in a puzzled frown. "It says here the caller was Smitty Smith, but that can't be right. Wasn't he in juvey?"

"No, he'd gotten out the day before." Joe Riddley had come home Friday night and informed me that as of the next morning, Smitty would be working for us after school and on weekends. I'd told him, "You can hire who you like, but you better keep Smitty out of my road." Smitty had never been high on my Favorite People list, and he'd gone down considerably one afternoon when he'd taken potshots at me and pretended he was shooting at squirrels.

When Smitty showed up the next morning, Joe Riddley assigned him to help Paul, our deliveryman, load and unload the truck. Paul's hard of hearing, so Joe Riddley said he wouldn't be bothered by Smitty's foul language. I'd forgotten that Smitty's first day was the same day Paul made that big delivery of herbicide to Whelan Grove.

Trust Smitty to have a cell phone, probably paid for with some of his ill-gotten gains before he was arrested. But thank heavens he did. It might have saved Josiah's life. Pete was dead before the paramedics got there.

I'd avoided Smitty ever since, so how the Sam Hill was I going to invite him into my office for a chat without raising eyebrows all over the store—not to mention word getting back to Joe Riddley? I didn't plan to do any detecting, mind, or put myself in any danger—although talking to Smitty privately would require a bit of caution. I just wanted to satisfy my natural curiosity about what went on that day and ease Daisy's mind.

Call it luck or call it providence, Smitty was standing

down at the back corner of our parking lot having a smoke
when I pulled in. I have strong feelings about kids smoking,
and I don't mind airing them, but right then I was willing to
overlook Smitty's health to talk about Pete Joyner's final
morning.

I moseyed back that way. Smitty dropped the cigarette
like it had burnt him and gave me a smarmy smile while he
surreptitiously ground it out with one toe. "Afternoon, Judge.
You want something? I'm on break."

It was chilly to be standing in a parking lot near dusk, but
I didn't mention that. I was busy figuring out that as smart as
Smitty was, there wasn't any point trying to work around to
what I wanted. I might as well be honest. Maybe it would in-
spire him.

"I understand you made the 911 call the morning Josiah
Whelan had his stroke. Did you see or hear what went on
down there before that?"

He tilted his chin and managed to convey the impression
that he was lounging against something, though he was five
feet from the nearest wall. "I might have. "

"So what happened?"

He gave me a considering look, like he was calculating
what it might be worth to me. Something in my eye made
him shift in his tracks and admit, "I don't know exactly. The
old man is watching us unload when the ni—" He caught my
eye and said quickly, "The black dude comes down the drive
in a truck. He calls out the window to old man Whelan, 'I
need to talk to you. It's real important.' So old man Whelan—"

"Mr. Whelan," I corrected him.

"*Mr.* Whelan." The way he emphasized it, it was more in-
sulting than the other had been. "He heads over that way, and
the black dude climbs out of his truck and they go over next
to a funny little shed with a chimney. We were unloading
stuff, so we didn't pay them much attention. I did see them
both start waving their arms, but didn't think much about it.
Then I needed to—uh—" His eyes slid away from mine.

I suspected the sentence should end "have a smoke," but I didn't interrupt, and ignored the blank in his sentence as he went on.

"—so I went around behind the shed. I didn't mean to listen, but they were talking loud and couldn't see me." Like any good storyteller, Smitty stopped until I prompted him.

"So what did you hear?"

"Well, they were in the middle of something by then. First the old—Mr. Whelan goes, 'You got no call to come around here saying stuff like that. Git, now! Git on home!' Then the black dude goes, 'I got this paper to prove it. I'm not tellin' you for me, but for Henry. You gotta do the right thing by him. You know what you done.'

"'I ain't done nothing,' Mr. Whelan yells. 'I don't know what you got in your hand, but what you're sayin' is a pack of lies and you damn well know it. You've worked shoulder to shoulder with me well nigh on fifty years. You know what kind of man I am.'

"'I know what you done, too,'" the black man goes. 'It says so, right here. I don't want nothin' for me, but you owe Henry. I've done called him to get down here tomorrow, and I'm gonna tell him what's what. He deserves to know.'

"Mr. Whelan goes, 'I'll see you in hell, first! Lemme see that!' I hear paper tearing, and the black dude goes, 'Don't you tear that! It was in my mama's Bible. It's all there, in black and white.' Then he gives a sob, like, and says, 'Ain't that funny? Right there, in black and white.'"

Smitty was not only rolling the story off like lines in a play, but his face and his body were changing as he spoke. I could almost see Josiah and Pete standing before me. "You ought to try out for that play they're doing over at the Du-Bose Center," I told him. But I didn't doubt his word. I'd heard him recite whole conversations before, and he was a reliable witness. Not reliable in a lot of other ways, maybe, but a reliable repeater of what he had heard.

He got distracted by what I'd said. "You think I could get a part?"

"They'd be lucky to have you. But what happened then?"

Smitty shook his head. "It got scary. Mr. Whelan starts yelling so loud, I look around the corner. He's jumping up and down and waving his fists, and screaming, 'Git on home, you hear me? Git on! Git on!' He kept screamin' and screamin',' then I heard this funny sound, like chokin' or sump'n, and he fell down on the ground and started jerking, makin' real funny noises. The black dude fell down on his knees beside him, yellin', 'Don't you die on me! I didn't mean you to die!' And he took the old man under his arms and started dragging him down the road. The old man was yelling so, I thought sure Paul would come help, but he didn't. I didn't know *what* to do."

"Paul's almost deaf," I reminded him.

"I hadn't been around him long enough to know that. I figured he didn't want to get involved. I was about to go back in, too, and leave them to it when all of a sudden the black dude grabs his chest and pitches down on top of the old one, like somebody in the movies. That's when I whipped out my phone and called 911."

"Good work," I told him. "You probably saved Josiah's life."

I don't know which of us was more surprised by that praise.

⇥ 22 ⇤

It didn't take a Sherlock Holmes to guess that paper was Pete Joyner's birth certificate, naming Josiah as his daddy. It made me sick. How could Josiah work beside Pete all those years and never let on who he was? Now Henry must be heading to the one person he figured could give him some answers, and he probably didn't know how bad Josiah's condition was. I hated to think of him storming in on poor Josiah without anybody else around.

I tried to reach Joe Riddley, but they said down at the nursery he'd gone to run an errand, so I left him a note on his desk and a message at the nursery: *Gone to see Josiah. Back around seven or so. Go on home and make a sandwich.* He and Bo wouldn't miss me much. There was an old World War II movie on television, and Joe Riddley's life isn't complete without one of those every week or two.

I drove as fast as I dared and faster than the law allows, glad to be going against traffic. Augusta, like other cities in America, is gobbling up charming little towns and the farm-land around them as hoards of people flock out of the city to "get away from it all." They leave at dawn, reach home at dusk, drive an hour each way every day, and spend their weekends paying homage to the house god. Oddly, they don't seem to realize that their subdivisions—and others sprouting up around them—will change those towns and farming communities into places exactly like the ones they left. I dread the day when I hear somebody refer to my home-town as a "bedroom community."

I knew why I was fuming at development, though. To keep from thinking about the way Josiah used to play with Pete and me when we were little, teasing us to make us gig-gle, lifting us to branches so we could climb a tree, standing below in case we fell, swinging Pete up over his head while Pete shrieked with laughter.

I also remembered Pete, when he was about twelve, pulling Edie as a chubby toddler around and around the driveway circle in a little red wagon. Starting when he was a teenager, Pete spent a lot of time working beside Josiah in the grove. Josiah used to brag that Pete knew the business better than he did.

How could he? I wanted to scream. *How could he go his whole life denying his own son?*

I thought I would smother from anger and grief.

I wondered why I hadn't suspected, all those afternoons I'd sat under the trees with Sally while Josiah teased me and Mary brought me buttermilk. I couldn't remember Josiah paying her any special attention, but I was only a child. Had anybody else noticed? Maybe not. Like Mama used to say, "The hardest things to notice are those you've looked at all your life."

Then I remembered Clarinda saying, "The Joyners have worked for Whelans since Elijah took off in the heavenly chariot. Some folks say—but never mind that." Obviously, in her community, some people knew.

Those thoughts occupied me until I reached Golden Years. The winter sun was going down by then, slanting broad rays across the parking lot. Since I didn't know Henry's car, I didn't waste time looking for it, but clutched my coat around me against the wind and ran to the front door. I scribbled my signature on the visitors' register and dashed toward Josiah's room.

I'd known the way, and Henry must have had to look for the place, because although he'd been gone from home quite a while, he was just entering Josiah's door as I came down the hall. I almost didn't recognize him in jeans and a red T-shirt.

I got to the doorway in time to see him step toward the bed, and to watch his shoulders sag as he caught sight of the wrecked man in the bed.

"Hello, Henry," I said from behind him.

He whirled around. "Miss Mac! What you doin' here?"

"Same thing you are, I reckon. Looking for some answers. Is Josiah awake?"

He nodded. "I guess you could say that." His voice was bitter.

I pushed past him to the side of the bed. The smell of urine and age nearly overpowered me, and I could scarcely see with the blinds closed. On the pillow, though, Josiah's eyes shone in the dimness. He made a series of garbled noises and raised his good hand.

"Hello, " I said cheerfully. "I've come to see you, along with somebody else. I'm going to open the blinds, okay?"

I interpreted a series of grunts as permission. The light was not kind to Josiah's face, but he seemed to welcome it on his skin. His sunken condition still shocked me, but not as much as it did Henry. From his expression, I suspected he wished he could turn and run.

I pulled the visitor's chair close to the bed. Might as well be comfortable. This could take a while. "Here's Henry Joyner, come to see you." I motioned Henry to come closer.

"Hey! Hey! Hey!" Josiah bobbed his head with excite-ment. His good hand rose a few inches from the coverlet and tears dribbled down his cheeks and onto his pillow. Is any-thing sadder than not being able to wipe away your own tears?

I reached for a tissue and dabbed his cheeks. "Is that bet-ter? Joe Riddley couldn't come, but I wanted to stop in and say hello."

His hand reached for mine, so dry it whispered against my palm.

"Henry wanted to see you, too, and tell you how the harvest is going." I nodded at Henry.

Henry still hadn't moved.

I pointed for him to go around to the other side of the bed. He did. As he stood looking down, I watched his tense anger dissolve into pity for the man he'd loved all his life.

He bent down and his voice was husky. "Hey, Mister Josiah. We're doin' our best to get the crop in, in spite of all this rain we've been having. You're going to have a good yield this year, particularly from the Schleys."

"Unh. Unh. Unh." Josiah nodded his head and tried to smile.

"And those new Sumners are going to make good this year, too. I'm not sure about the Desirables, though. Their limbs break pretty easy."

"Unh, unh, unh!" Josiah took his good hand from mine and made chopping right-angled motions.

I had no idea what he was doing, but Henry nodded. "Daddy told me you have to bend the branches at right angles to the trunk. I saw where you'd done that on some of them, and they're holding up so far, but we'll have to see how well they produce before we put in any more."

Josiah nodded and reached his good hand across his shrunken body to grasp Henry's. "Pee? Pee?" he asked.

I looked around for a urinal, but Henry seemed to have less problem than I did understanding what the old man wanted. "Daddy's not with us anymore, I'm afraid. He passed in September, right after you got sick. Heart attack."

"Pee? Pee!" Josiah's eyes filled with tears again, and I did tissue duty for a second time. "Eee. Eee." Streams coursed down his cheeks.

Even I could understand that. "Yes, Edie's gone, too," I agreed, wiping his face again and again. "We all miss her very much."

He turned his gaze to Henry, and another stream of garbled words came from his mouth. When he saw we didn't understand, he got frustrated and started slapping his good hand on his own chest and then at Henry. "Gwo. Gwo. Gwo! Uuuu. Uuuu. Gwo!"

It sounded like a vowel exercise to me, and I could tell Henry was baffled, too.

"Don't get overexcited," I told him, pinning his agitated hand with my own. "Henry's got some questions to ask you. Will you try to answer?"

Josiah didn't nod, and I wasn't sure he understood.

Henry reached for his shirt pocket. "Mama found something last Sunday a week, in Grandmama's Bible. Mary, Daddy's mama. Do you remember her?"

"May." Josiah nodded.

I began to wish I hadn't come. Henry was handling this fine. He looked over at me, and the way his nostrils flared, I suspected he wished I weren't there, too. But Josiah had reached for my hand again, and was clutching it so tight he nearly cut off my circulation.

Henry pulled out a crumpled piece of paper. When Josiah saw what it was, he pushed his head deeper into the pillow. Anybody could tell that he recognized it. His eyes turned anxiously to meet mine. "Eh," he said. "Ehmay."

I tried to keep my disgust from showing. "Listen to Henry," I told him.

As Henry held the paper toward him, though, I could see that it was not, as I had expected, a birth certificate. It seemed to be a letter.

Henry waved the paper over the bed so it rattled—or was that his hand trembling? Josiah squeezed his eyes shut and pursed his mouth, refusing to look at it.

"This is a letter from your daddy, Mister Josiah, acknowledging that my daddy—'Peter Joyner, son of Mary Joyner,' it says right here"—Henry pointed with a long brown finger—"was his grandson."

Josiah squeezed his eyes tighter, as if that could make us go away.

Henry's voice trembled and broke as he asked, "Are you my granddaddy? Are you? Why didn't you ever tell us?"

Josiah's eyes flew open. "Oh!" He lifted his fist and brought it down in fury on the coverlet. "Oh! Oh! Eh! Eh!" When we didn't understand him, his shouts rose louder and louder.

A nurse rushed into the room. She was almost broader than she was tall, and she pushed me aside like a minnow. "It's okay, Mister J." She bent over her thrashing patient. "It's okay. I'm here. You're going to be all right." She looked from Henry to me with a glare. "You all need to leave. You're upsetting my patient."

"Not half as much as he's upsetting us," I snapped. "We're trying to get some information out of him, and he's refusing to answer. He was perfectly fine, until—"

"I'm sorry, but whatever it is you need to know, you'll have to find out some other way. We can't have him excited. It's not good for him."

I might have argued further, but a voice growled in the doorway. "Little Bit, why are you plaguing the living daylights out of Josiah?"

❧ 23 ❧

Joe Riddley crossed the room and put his hand on Josiah's shoulder. "Calm down, old buddy. I'm gonna take Mac out and let you get some rest. We'll be back another time, okay?"

Josiah looked up at him, pleading with his eyes for somebody to understand. "Eh. May. Pee. Hey! Eh. May. Pee. Hey!" Maybe it was a weird way of counting.

Joe Riddley tightened his hand on Josiah's shoulder, then turned and led the way from the room. "Come on, MacLaren. Henry." We followed him out.

I looked back at the bed as I left. The nurse was just straightening up from smoothing his covers. "Could we talk to you a minute?" I asked her.

She nodded, and bent to tell him, "I'm going to walk them out the door, then I'll be right back. Okay?"

He turned his head away, dismissing us.

The nurse closed the door behind her. Henry was already striding around the corner toward the front door. I figured I'd better start right in before Joe Riddley could start in on *me*.

"Can you tell what he's saying when he yells like that?"

The nurse, identified on her name badge as JANE GROGG, shook her head. "Not always. 'Oh' means 'no'—I know that because he says it a lot." She smiled, showing a gold tooth. "And 'Eee' was what he called his daughter, Miss Edie. He misses her so much. We all do, too. I swan, I never imagined when she came last Tuesday morning that I'd never see her

again. And toward the end, Mr. J. got so mad at the lawyer
that we had our work cut out calming him down and didn't
even get to tell her good-bye. Who'd have thought she'd go
before him? It just goes to show, don't it? Well, I better get
back to my patient. You all come back soon, and don't feel
bad about what happened in there. Folks who have strokes
are prone to get real emotional."

Folks who've just had a shameful secret uncovered are
prone to get emotional, too, but I didn't point that out.

As I trotted behind Joe Riddley to the parking lot, I expected a lecture on running off and getting involved in mysteries. Instead, he went striding toward Henry, who was
standing beside a sporty yellow convertible parked under a
halogen light, rhythmically pounding one fist on its hood.

"Son?" I heard Joe Riddley ask in a mild voice. "You
want to talk about what's wrong?"

I panted up behind him, shivering. It was really cold now
that the sun was down.

Henry turned, his face twisted with rage and grief. "Don't
call me son! I'm not your son. I'm his grandson! How could
he—how could he—how could they—?" That's as far as he
got.

"Mind telling me what that's all about?" Joe Riddley inquired.

Henry fumbled in his pocket, pulled out the crumpled
paper, and handed it over.

Joe Riddley read it silently, then handed it back. "It wasn't
Josiah." I don't know who was more surprised, Henry or me.
Joe Riddley spoke like he knew what he was talking about.

"Of course it was *Josiah*." The word was ugly in Henry's
mouth. "All those years—all those years!" He pulled back
one leg and kicked the tire so hard the car shuddered.

"It wasn't Josiah," Joe Riddley repeated. "Josiah was
overseas in the army back then."

"How do you know so much?" I demanded from behind
him.

He answered me without turning away from Henry. "Because Josiah always called me his little buddy, and after he went in the army, he sent me postcards a few times a year. He sent me a card from Germany for my sixth birthday, along with a little American flag, saying he sure had missed America the year he'd been gone and he hoped I'd grow up to be proud of my country. I gave that flag to Mary as a present for the baby when Pete was born seven months later. It was the best thing I had to give."

"But I remember him tossing Pete into the air," I protested. "I remember that real clear."

"Then Pete must have been at least two, because Josiah didn't come home from Germany until he was eight." That made sense. Surely Josiah wouldn't have thrown an infant up in the air.

"But why would his daddy write that letter, then?"

"It must have been Edward, Josiah's brother." Joe Riddley spoke slowly, working it out as he went along. "Ed was in a car wreck and died, and now that I think about it, that was the winter before Pete was born. But Ed lived a couple of days in the hospital. Maybe he told his daddy what he had done. I know it was that winter, because his was the first funeral I ever attended. Daddy told Mama that a boy of six was plenty old enough to go to a funeral, and I ought to go to at least one before somebody in the family died, so I'd know how to behave when I needed to."

"That must be what Josiah was trying to say." I was trying to put it all together. "'Eh, May, Pee, Hey' must mean Edward, Mary, Pete, Henry. It wasn't Josiah, Henry! It wasn't!" I felt like a huge rock had been lifted from my back.

Henry glared from one of us to the other, his eyes bloodshot from too much anger and unshed tears. "Is that supposed to make me feel all better?"

"No." Joe Riddley sounded as sad as I felt. "I'm not sure Edward would have done the right thing by Mary if he'd lived. I got whipped once for repeating in public something my mother said to Daddy about Edward Whelan being more interested in Edward than in anybody else. I don't even know what the right thing would have been around here back then. But I do know that before the baby was born, Mr. Whelan built Mary her little house and deeded her two acres of land. That must have been when he gave her the letter, too."

Henry cried out, his mouth twisted with rage, "Two acres! Is that what my daddy was worth?"

"You know better than that," Joe Riddley said sternly. "The Whelans loved your daddy. Not like they should have, maybe. Old attitudes die hard. But they did make sure he and Mary always had food to eat, a roof over their heads, and good jobs on the homeplace. Respect, too. And Josiah's done you no harm. He loved you, coming up. I'm not sure he knew until just now what Edward did."

"Pete told him," I said quietly. "It was reading that letter that gave Josiah his stroke. And trying to save Josiah's life killed Pete."

"How do you know so much?" Joe Riddley threw my question back at me.

"Smitty overheard them." I repeated what Smitty had said. Then I turned to Henry. "Josiah is a sick old man."

Henry blew through his nostrils and turned so his face was shaded from the light. "Nobody told me how bad he is. But I can't stay around here, knowing all this. I ought to get in this car right now, ride off, and never come back." He was talking more to himself than to us. "I haven't left a thing in Georgia I can't find somewhere else."

"Your mama's here," I reminded him.

"I can send for her when I get settled somewhere. She was brought up down near Valdosta, anyway. She never saw Hopemore until she married daddy."

"The sheriff won't let you leave yet. He thinks you killed Edie. I suggested Saturday you ought to hire a lawyer. Now I'm warning you." It had occurred to me that this gave Henry what Buster hadn't had before: a good motive for murder.

Joe Riddley put his hand on my shoulder and squeezed, but somehow he didn't feel mad. It was more the "I'm right here with you, Little Bit" kind of squeeze.

Henry rared back like a startled horse. "He's got no evidence against me. Sure, somebody stole my machete out of the shed—"

"He's found more than that."

"What?"

"A pair of your coveralls showed up under a bush."

"I told him a pair went missing."

"He's sent them to forensics. They had blood on them."

"*What?*"

I nodded. "He ought to get a report back sometime in the next few days. Let's hope there's evidence somebody besides you wore them."

"There better be, because I did not kill Edie." He waved the paper at me. "But when you tell him about this, he'll think I had a motive, won't he? And executing me would solve a lot of problems around here."

He jerked his door open and jumped into the car. We barely had time to get out of the way before he backed up and roared off.

Joe Riddley must have seen how worn out I was, because he suggested we stop at a good steak place on our way home. It was a bit out of our way, the place where people took their honeys, so I hoped maybe he wasn't too mad.

When we got there, I let him go on in and stayed in my car long enough to call Clarinda. She said Daisy was a little calmer, and I explained what had just happened. "Some folks been suspecting something like that a long time," she told me. "Both Pete and Henry got the Whelan eyes." She grunted a couple of times, then said, "Edward," like she was thinking that over. "That figures. He always was the wild one. I couldn't figure Josiah for—well, you know. You think Henry's on his way back to Daisy's?"

I sighed out my distress. "Your guess is as good as mine. Meanwhile, I'd better go join Joe Riddley. We've stopped by Candlelight Inn. We came in different cars, and he's already inside. If I don't get in there pretty soon, he'll order my steak well done to spite me."

Clarinda cackled. "Everybody in there who doesn't know you two will think you're married folks having an affair on the side, coming separately and all. Go add spice to their dinners. Snuggle up to him real good."

I went in, came up behind him, and gave him a hug around the neck. "You'd be a nice person to have an affair with," I whispered in his ear.

The speed with which he disentangled himself and the sour look he gave me dispelled anybody's false impression. "You don't need to try and sweeten me up." He reached for a roll and the butter. "You know good and well that following Henry to Josiah's comes under the heading of meddling in things that don't concern you, which you had flat-out promised me you wouldn't do again."

I waited while the waitress set salads in front of us, then asked her, "Did he tell you I wanted my steak well done?"

"Oh, no, ma'am, he told us you like it medium."

I was about to give him a smile of thanks when I saw that he'd had them put ranch dressing on my salad instead of bleu cheese.

"Wouldn't want to waste an expensive piece of meat." He picked up a big chunk of bleu cheese from his own salad and smacked his lips before eating it whole.

I tried to scrape dressing off my lettuce, but it might as well have been welded on. "You have to agree it was good you were able to clear up that misunderstanding," I pointed out. "If I hadn't gone, you wouldn't have followed me, and Henry would still be thinking Josiah was Pete's daddy and hadn't admitted it all those years. Remember how we were talking in Sunday school a week or so ago about the way God brings good out of things that don't seem good at the time? Maybe—"

"Don't you go blamin' God for your meddling in Josiah's business," Joe Riddley warned. "I can't get out of this booth fast enough if lightning strikes."

"You really think Josiah didn't know Pete was Edward's son? Now that I know to look for it, Pete had a lot of mannerisms that were like Josiah's daddy. And the Whelan eyes."

Joe Riddley swabbed up the last of his dressing with a piece of lettuce. "Folks can generally miss something right under their noses if they choose not to see it. Like you not seeing how dangerous it is for you to get mixed up in this stuff. One of these days your guardian angel is gonna throw up her hands and go home, and I'm gonna be looking for a replacement wife."

"You wouldn't dare!"

He set down his fork after finishing the salad and gave me a solemn look. "The day after your funeral. I swear it, if you don't straighten up and fly right. Now start eating. You know I don't like driving these roads after dark."

I bent toward my salad plate and started picking out bits that hadn't been slathered with dressing. He motioned to the waitress. "Could we have another salad with bleu cheese dressing, please? I got her order mixed up."

After she removed the plate, he covered my hand with his. "You know I love and appreciate you, honey. I even appreciate the fact that once you get your teeth into something worthwhile, you don't let it go until it's finished. Lulu takes after you that way. But I don't want to lose you. Recent months have taught me to be glad for every day we've got together, and I want a lot of them."

My throat was all choked up, but I managed to gulp out, "Me, too."

"So I want to make you a deal. Don't you go places without me. Let me know ahead of time, and I'll come along. Can you agree to that?"

"I'd be proud to have you."

Neither of us imagined then how hard that bargain was going to be to keep.

When we got home, I took off my clothes and put on a robe, planning to put my feet up a while before bed. I'd barely gotten settled good on the sofa, Lulu's head in my lap, when the phone rang. "Can you get that?" I asked Joe Riddley. His recliner was beside the phone.

"It's probably somebody wanting you down at the jail." But he muted the television and growled, "Yes?" into the receiver. In an instant, he turned into Mr. Sweetness and Light. "Why, sure, she's right here." He held it in my direction.

As I padded barefoot across the room, I muttered, "If I have to go back out tonight, I may shoot somebody. I don't remember you having to go out that much at night."

"That's because you always turned over and went back to sleep."

I snatched the phone and said, in a voice a tad less than charming, "Judge Yarbrough."

"Mac?" Meriwether's voice was more amused than worried.

"Oh, honey, I was afraid you were a pesky deputy wanting me down at the jail. Has the baby come?"

"Stop asking me that." Now she sounded more like a normal pregnant lady, crabby as all get-out. "The baby hasn't come, I am sleeping terribly, and I feel big as an eighteen-wheeler. But what I wanted to tell you is that we solved the mystery of the ringing alarm. For two weeks, our security alarm has gone off at all hours. Nobody could figure out who was tripping it."

"Well, tell me. Who'd be dumb enough to break in in the middle of a workday?"

She laughed. "Three baby kittens. Apparently they've been moving around at night, which triggered the motion sensors. They were living in a big wicker basket, and this afternoon Tyrone startled them when he was putting up merchandise. When he tried to grab them, the black one took off straight up the shelves and leaped for another shelf, but she caught on the security wire to the back fire door—which we keep armed—and yanked it out. She fell and tumbled right into Tyrone's arms. When I got there, I don't know who was happier, that kitten or Tyrone."

"I guess you're pretty happy, too, to know nobody's breaking in."

She laughed again. "I am. And the kittens are darling. We can't keep them in the warehouse, obviously, but Tyrone wants the one he caught. Says he's gonna name her Holly. I'm trying to find homes for two gray males. Do you reckon Ridd and Martha might take them? They could keep the mice down in their new barn."

"We've already named them Mac and J.R.," I heard her husband call in the background.

"I'll ask Martha about the kittens," I told her, "but you tell Jed for me that Ridd's got two new pigs, and I've named them Jed and DuBose."

When I hung up, I headed to the kitchen for a bowl of ice cream with hot fudge sauce. "One of these days I'm gonna diet," I promised Lulu, who was hovering at my feet hoping she'd get a scoop of ice cream, too, "but I can't as long as ice cream and hot fudge keep appearing in the refrigerator. You and I both know *I* don't buy them."

"You fixing ice cream?" called the culprit from the next room.

I fixed us each a bowl and gave Lulu a couple of spoonfuls, then let her out into the backyard. As I carried ours to the living room, I said, "If you'll turn that thing off a minute, I'll tell you what Meriwether said."

The day would have ended on a cheerful note if the telephone hadn't rung again.

❧ 24 ❧

"Oh, Mac, I'm so sorry to bother you this late." It was Genna, breathless and flustered. "I meant to call you this afternoon, but things got hectic and I completely forgot."

She scarcely gave my ears time to absorb one sentence before she was off and running with another. I was still getting my head around "hectic" as a description for her afternoon when she was halfway around another track. ". . . called and asked what I want Edie buried in. I can't decide something like that! I mean, I wouldn't have any idea what she'd like to wear. It won't be an open casket, of course . . ."

My memory darted to Edie as I'd last seen her and I shuddered. No, it wouldn't be an open casket.

I felt so dizzy, I pulled up a straight chair behind me and sat down. Genna was still rattling along.

". . . don't think I can stand to see the room yet. But they want them by ten tomorrow morning, and I understand you found her, so you've already been up there, so I wondered if maybe . . . I mean, I know it's a lot to ask, but Cindy said she thought you might be willing to. If you don't want to, just say so, but if you would, I would be eternally grateful. Adney would, too. I thought about asking Alex, but I don't know her all that well, and Olive—she and Edie didn't dress anything alike—"

"You want me to pick a dress for Edie to be buried in?" I'd finally pieced that much together.

"Oh, would you?" She acted like I'd offered, not merely asked for clarification. "That is wonderful! I am so grateful. If ever there is anything I can do for you, please let me know. This has all been so hard on Adney and me. We could not have gotten through it without you and your sweet family, and I want you to know that. We both appreciate you."

That woman at the jail a few hours ago must have been Genna's evil twin. Before I could say another word, Genna cooed, "The sheriff said they're finished with the house, so I'll meet you over there at eight tomorrow morning to let you in. Remember, the funeral home needs the outfit before ten. Thank you so much."

I stood there holding a buzzing phone, wondering how different my life might have been if I'd mastered the fine art of manipulation.

On my way back to the sofa and my melting ice cream, I grumbled, "Genna's conned me into picking out a dress for Edie to be buried in. You coming with me in the morning?"

"I told you, I'm going wherever you're going."

Which is why Genna met us both down at Edie's the next morning. She unlocked the door, then turned to leave. "I've got an aerobics class, but if you'll turn that little doohickey in the doorknob when you leave, I'll come back later to lock the dead bolt." Her fear of crime in the neighborhood seemed to have evaporated now that Edie had nothing left to steal.

Seeing Edie's blue Saab in the carport had made me think, for one quick second, that the past week had been a bad dream and she'd be inside wondering why we were barging in without ringing the bell. I left my pocketbook with Joe Riddley, who elected to read the paper at the kitchen table. Just as I reached the stairs, I realized I hadn't brought anything to carry the clothes in, so I went back to her pantry to hunt for a plastic bag. Like us, she kept a big bag of bags hanging on a pantry nail. As I grabbed one, I saw, behind the bag, a ring holding several keys. I wondered if the sheriff's men had noticed it. I'd tell him later.

I climbed to Edie's room with a heavy heart. It felt odd to

wander around in her house without her permission. Before I climbed the last disheartening steps, I smelled the blood.

I'd smelled blood all my life, of course, growing up on a farm. On frosty autumn mornings Daddy used to butcher hogs down behind our house. Their blood on the breeze made my brother hop around in excitement, anticipating fresh livermush and bacon. This frosty morning, though, the scent of blood buckled my knees. I had to lean against the narrow stairwell wall for an instant to regain enough strength to keep climbing.

Even Isaac had been shaken by the room as he first saw it. "I'd never seen so much blood in one place," he'd told me, his ebony face grave. Then he'd hurried to add, "But it's gone now. The bedding and rug were bagged and taken away for evidence, and Pete's wife, Daisy, has scrubbed everything, even the ceiling. You won't see anything except an empty room."

He'd forgotten how the smell of blood lingers, clinging to the very air, as if loath to let go of its hold on life.

I covered my mouth and nose with one hand and hoped the scent of almond lotion would see me through the ordeal.

I thought about calling to Joe Riddley in the kitchen below. But what would I say? That I was too sick at my stomach to enter a perfectly empty room to perform one last service for our friend? I certainly couldn't ask him to pick out her burial clothes. We'd be holding a funeral where the guest of honor's dress didn't match her shoes—if the shoes matched each other. No, I owed it to her to see her decently buried. "I think I can, I think I can," I chanted from one of Cricket's favorite storybooks as I forced myself up the final five steps, wondering why any woman past fifty chose to sleep on the third floor.

Then I reached the threshold, stopped, and gasped.

What I saw was not a room of death, but an incredible view. Josiah had given his daughter a magnificent gift. The room rode the treetops like a ship on a green sea, and on a clear day you could probably see Augusta.

No wonder Edie had come back to this room when her husband died. It should have been her sanctuary, not the scene of her murder.

Then my eyes refocused on a few dark spots on the windows that Daisy had missed, and my breakfast gave fair warning it was coming back. I barely had time to dash into the dainty bathroom Josiah had installed in half of the back wall, next to the big walk-in closet.

Afterwards, I soaked a washrag and wiped my mouth. "You weren't supposed to *die*," I muttered angrily. "That wasn't what we were worried about at all."

Only my fury that this had happened to her—and at Genna's halfhearted grief—sent me back into Edie's room.

I stood looking around me, wondering if I might recognize any clues the sheriff's people had missed. All I saw was a stripped bed, one teddy bear leaning against the wall under the bank of front windows, a jewelry box sitting crookedly on Edie's dresser, and a collection of Hummel figurines on her chest of drawers. The carpet had been lifted, all the bedding and at least one chair removed. Light squares on the wallpaper showed where pictures had hung. Only the wall with the door to the stairs remained untouched. There, a bulletin board over Edie's computer displayed several articles describing her winning bridge tournaments, and she kept her trophies in an old oak china cabinet in the corner that had probably held picture book dolls when she was younger.

Averting my eyes from the spots Daisy had missed on the windows, I raised several to let in fresh, cold air before I headed to the closet. I had only performed this service twice before, for my mother and Joe Riddley's. Now, as then, I found myself teetering between practicality and respect for the dead. Should I choose a good outfit that somebody else could still get use out of, or pick something old and have people—in this case the funeral home staff—think we didn't have proper respect?

Put me in any old thing, Mac, and give the good stuff to people who need it. I could hear Edie saying it. Lately she'd been lobbying for the Magnolia Women's Club to start a closet of gently used professional clothes for women going back to work. Maybe we could start it in her memory and begin it with her own clothes.

I was reaching for a navy suit she'd had for years when I heard somebody clumping up the stairs. So help me, my heart nearly stopped. I could tell it wasn't Joe Riddley. "He had to let them come up," I reminded myself.

Olive poked her head around the door. "Hey! I thought I'd find you up here."

She paused as I had, but it wasn't because she was sickened by the smell or entranced by the view. "Why on earth would Edie want to sleep all the way up here? Those stairs are a killer."

Her eyes roved restlessly from the bare bed and floor to the lone teddy bear near the windows. "I guess that poor little fellow was too far away to get messed up." She came to the closet like a slim dark shadow. "I didn't know Genna was fixing to ask you to do this. You don't need to bother. I can handle it."

Until that minute, I'd have gladly handed the job over to the first volunteer. Now I was bound and determined Olive wouldn't get it. I held the navy suit close to my chest. "Genna asked me to do it, and I've already chosen this." I pulled out a tailored white blouse with a ruffle at the neck. It was businesslike and feminine, just like Edie. I bent and grabbed her navy pumps, remembering Edie wearing that same outfit to Wick's funeral just last spring. A lump rose in my throat and threatened to choke me.

Olive wrinkled her nose. "Those old things? Why don't you—?" She reached past me to pull out one of Edie's really nice dresses, a swirl of pink, green, and magenta silk from the days when she and Wick flew to New York for plays. Olive held it up against her sallow face and sashayed over to the full-length mirror on the bathroom door. She preened a little at the picture she made. "Edie had good taste, when she chose to exercise it."

That was a bit much from somebody who thought black and gray were the only colors on the color wheel.

Contrary to what Olive later claimed, I did not snatch that dress from her. I did take it firmly and hang it back in the closet. "Edie wouldn't want us wasting a good dress to bury her in. I'll talk to Genna about what to do with the rest of these clothes."

"She'll probably put them in a garage sale with the rest of the stuff in the house." Olive moved restlessly around the room and stopped to rummage in Edie's jewelry box with an appraising eye. Only Mama's good training and my respect for the office of judge kept me from stomping over there to give her a good smack. She picked up a small figurine from the dresser and examined its bottom. "Pity she chipped this. It may be prewar Dresden. But look at all the Hummels on her chest." She headed in that direction and began to lift them to examine their bottoms. "These are old enough to be worth a little." She started setting them on a nearby table.

"They were Edie's mother's," I said, less than charitably. "Genna may get them and the rest of the stuff in the house"—I emphasized the words she had used—"but she'll have to wait until Josiah dies. They're still his—along with the house and the grove. And Genna may not get them when he's gone."

I had her attention now. "What do you mean?"

I wished I hadn't let my temper run away with my tongue. "Oh, just that there may be other relatives, that's all. Edie didn't have any money, either—you need to tell that to Genna. Her daddy lost every cent he had, and was deep in debt when he died. Edie paid every cent she got to his debtors."

She stared. "How do you know?"

"Never mind how I know. It's the truth." I gathered up the suit and blouse and headed for the chest. "Now, if you'll excuse me, I need to find some underwear." Mama always said, "Honey, don't you neglect to put underwear on me for my funeral. If they ever have to dig me up, I don't want them thinking I wasn't respectable."

I thought Edie would want to be respectable, too.

In the mirror, I saw Olive watching me as I opened dresser drawers. I looked away. When I looked back in a few seconds, I watched her put her hand on the top of the chest and lift it up. There was a tray above the top drawer that I hadn't suspected was there. I took out some panties. "Now let me find a slip," I murmured, rummaging around while a slip lay there in plain view.

Out of the corner of my eye, I watched Olive in the mirror.

She took out a white case, opened it, and slid a strand of pearls into her pocket. A gold necklace followed, then I saw her lift a letter and examine it with a gloating smile.

"Well," she said carelessly, turning away and sliding the letter into her pocket with the jewelry, "I guess I'll be going if you don't need any help."

She ambled back toward the door and started slowly down the steps. I heard her pick up her pace after two or three steps.

I followed. "I'm all finished," I explained as she turned to give me a surprised look at the bottom of the stairs.

"You don't have panty hose." She was moving toward the main staircase.

"She won't need panty hose. Do you reckon Genna wants me to take this stuff straight to the funeral home?" I was crossing the upstairs hall right behind her.

"You might as well."

She doubled her speed going down the main stairs and was almost running by the time she headed toward the kitchen. I waited until she was at the door, then called, "Stop her!" Joe Riddley could hold her better than I could.

Wouldn't you know, that man wasn't there? I arrived at the kitchen to find his newspaper lying folded on the table beside my pocketbook. The screened door of the porch slammed behind Olive.

"Stop, thief!" I dumped Edie's clothes in an unceremonious heap beside my pocketbook and hared after her.

When I reached the back steps, Olive was heading to her car. "Stop, thief!" I yelled again.

She fumbled frantically for her keys, then threw the purse hard at me. Long legs churning, she ran across the drive and down into the grove.

There was no way I could catch her on foot. We'd come in Joe Riddley's car, and I didn't have its keys. But a green tractor stood outside the equipment shed by the gas pumps.

I used to love to drive my daddy's tractor as a girl. I'd even driven Ridd's tractors off and on in recent years, for the fun of it.

I swung myself up into the cab and saw the keys in the ignition. With a prayer of thanks, I started the engine. Somebody had just filled the tank with gas, and it moved like a charm. I headed through the grove after Olive as fast as that thing could chug.

If she hadn't paused to catch her breath, I might not have caught up with her, but there she suddenly was, three trees ahead of me, clinging to the trunk, gasping. When she saw it was me on the tractor, she took a deep breath and darted around the tree and down the next row.

I followed.

She ran around another tree and headed back the way she had come.

I followed. The tractor wasn't as lithe as Olive, of course, but I could keep her in view.

Pecans crunched under my tires and flew every which way. The medians were mowed, but Henry's crew hadn't harvested this area yet. Down one row at the far end of the grove, I saw the shaker making its funny progress in our direction. I hoped Josiah and Henry would forgive me for the nuts I was destroying in the process of trying to save Edie's pearls.

I also wondered what the men operating the shaker must

think of the crazy tractor dashing between trees and up and down rows.

Olive and I both knew she couldn't hide from me, no matter how many trees she darted around or how many rows she tried. The only thing bothering me was what I'd do with her when I caught her. Where the dickens was Joe Riddley? Some bodyguard he had turned out to be. What if Olive had come upstairs to murder me, instead of to steal what little Edie had left?

I wondered how she had known about that secret tray in the chest. Genna must have told her. The bedroom furniture had been Wick's wedding gift to Edie, and I'm sure he showed off that nifty feature to both his wife and his daughter.

Which brought up a disturbing likelihood: that Olive had killed Edie for the snuffboxes, jewelry, and silver, with jealousy fueling her fire, and this morning had come back for things she'd missed the first time. I'd bet my final dollar Genna hadn't told her about that tray until after Edie died. I'd have to tell Sheriff Gibbons about it, and about the keys in the pantry. His men hadn't been as thorough as he expected them to be.

In that second while I wasn't paying close attention, Olive pivoted and made a daring lunge past me, heading back down the grove away from the house. I had to stop and turn. By then she had vanished.

Five trees ahead of me, the shaker and a huge tree were dancing their jig to the accompaniment of a storm of nuts. It takes a shaker two minutes to shake a tree and move to the next one. As they finished the fifth tree and came toward the fourth, I caught an agitated flash of black among the leaves of the third.

"Stop!" I shouted. They couldn't hear me above the roar of my machine and theirs. "Stop!"

I revved that engine and rolled down the row as fast I could go, straight for the shaker.

To this day I wonder what those men thought when they

saw a tractor barreling straight for them, driven by a small woman with a beauty parlor hairdo. None of them spoke enough English to tell me. But at least they stopped. They watched warily as I hiked up my skirt and climbed down.

I also wonder whether I'd have done better to have let them shake Olive out of that tree. Instead, I cocked my head and called up to her, "You might as well come on down. I know you're there, and I saw you take the pearls and Edie's gold chain."

The men broke into frantic chatter and shook almost as much as their machine when Olive appeared among the branches. For once she looked like a real French waif. Her cheeks and hands were smudged with dirt, and she had leaves in her wind-ruffled hair. As she sat on the bottom branch and accepted their help getting down, I saw a flash of white cotton through a rip in her slacks. So much for red bikini underpants.

Once on the ground, she glared. "Now I suppose you'll want to call the police?"

"Oh, no," I assured her. "We're outside the city limits. I'm going to call the sheriff."

My cell phone was in my pocketbook at the house, and I couldn't ask the men to hold Olive until I fetched it, so I cupped my hands and called, "Joe Riddley? Joe Riddley!" in the voice that used to bring our boys to dinner from our neighbor's cattle pond two fields away.

The men immediately cupped their hands and began to call, "Joe Reedley. Joe Reedley."

"*Mi esposo,*" I explained, drawing on my small store of Spanish. "*A la casa.*"

For all I knew, I was saying I liked my husband on top of a house, like pie à la mode, but one of them grinned and nodded. "*Sí.*" He started out for the house at a run. The others watched Olive so carefully she didn't dare run. They obviously thought we were the day's entertainment.

Joe Riddley arrived in the backyard the same time the worker did. I saw them jump into his Town Car and head down under the trees. Joe Riddley got out of one side and the Mexican worker climbed out of the other, pausing to stroke the silver finish with his hand. "What's this fellow saying about you bein' up a tree?" Joe Riddley demanded.

"It was Olive." I'm too polite to point, but I nodded in her direction. "Call the sheriff. She stole Edie's pearls. She may have killed her, too."

The men understood enough of what I said to take a few steps back in a circle of wonder.

The sheriff came himself. He listened to my story and put Olive in his cruiser. She never said a word except "I want to call my lawyer." She glared at me whenever she looked my way, but as she was climbing into the backseat of the sheriff's cruiser and thought I couldn't see her, she had a funny expression on her face. I would have sworn it was a smirk.

"Where the dickens did you get to when I needed you?" I demanded when Joe Riddley and I were alone.

He looked sheepish. "I'd been wanting to get a good look at Josiah's new sorting equipment. I thought I'd just nip out there and take a gander while you were upstairs."

I was about to tell him what I thought about his future as a bodyguard, but a reporter and photographer from the *Hopemore Statesman* showed up right then. After the reporter interviewed me, that pesky photographer insisted on taking a shot of me beside the tractor. My picture would appear on the second page the following Wednesday, under the headline "A Judge of Many Talents."

I'd always thought of driving as a skill, myself.

❧ 25 ❧

When Joe Riddley and I took Edie's burial clothes by the funeral home, the woman at the front desk wanted to discuss all of Edie's wonderful accomplishments and wonder how Hopemore was going to get along without her. Since I was wondering the same thing, that conversation took longer than Joe Riddley thought it needed to.

We barely made it to a business association luncheon that I'd have skipped if I hadn't been president of the group that year.

After lunch I returned a call from Alex. "The sheriff's office called me with some message about why Olive isn't coming in," she told me, "but they mentioned your name, so I thought I'd get the story from the horse's mouth."

"This is one weary horse. But here's what happened." I didn't tell her about the chase in the pecan grove—I figured both Olive and I deserved to hang on to a little dignity as long as we could—but I told her I'd seen Olive taking some things from Edie's room and turned her over to the sheriff. I finished up, "You don't reckon Olive could have killed Edie, do you? I mean, I know they were both librarians, so you might find it hard to believe—"

She snorted. "You don't know librarians like I do. But I am surprised Olive would steal the stuff with you right there. She's generally real meticulous in her work. I don't know if she killed Edie—and I hope not, because I don't need to lose another staff member right now—but I do think she put those keys in Edie's pocketbook. A woman came by today saying she'd lost her keys a couple of weeks ago, on a day when she, her daughter, and her grandson went to Augusta to shop. She'd thought she must have left them somewhere up there, but she said that last night she asked God to help her find them, and this morning, just as she was waking up, she pictured them, clear as anything, on the floor of our ladies' room. Can you believe she thinks God bothers with something as trivial as lost keys?"

Having been granted answers to a few trivial prayers myself, I murmured, "Well, there is a verse in James that says, 'You have not because you ask not.'"

"Maybe so." Alex sounded dubious. "But I'd be embarrassed to pray for anything so dumb. Anyway, after she woke up, she remembered that while her daughter returned books on their way to Augusta, she took her grandson to the bathroom and he got to playing in her purse. She wondered if he'd dropped her keys and she'd not noticed."

I knew Alex was thinking the same thing I was: Olive could have found them and put them in Edie's purse. But why?

I couldn't think of a single reason, but what I wanted to know right then was, "Did you ask that woman why somebody with a grandson—especially somebody who prays for help with lost keys—has a brass tag from a porno Web site on her key chain?"

Alex's laugh rumbled across the wire. "Not me, girlfriend. She's a library patron. But you want her number? Call and ask her yourself—and let me know." She sighed. "You can also come over here and work my front desk. I'm as shorthanded as a one-armed short-order cook."

I declined both offers, pleading that I was seriously behind in my work.

All that time Joe Riddley had sat at his desk reading spring seed catalogues like they were candidates for the *New York Times* best-seller lists. "Go on down to the Christmas tree lot," I told him crossly. "I can't work with you rustling those pages."

"I'm not leaving you here alone." He picked up another catalogue.

"I've got five employees protecting me, and a few customers to cheer me up if I get lonesome, and I promise not to leave the building without giving you a call."

"And waiting for me to answer?" I have been known a time or two to tell him I've called when I've just let the phone ring once and hung up.

"I'll wait for your permission. How's that? I expect to be right here working on the next payroll. While you're down there, why don't you find us a nice little tree?"

This would be our first Christmas in the new house, the first time in nearly forty years that we hadn't had a twelve-foot tree. "How about getting one I can reach the top of?"

He grabbed his cap. "One three-foot tree, coming up." I don't know who was more relieved when he left. I love the man dearly, but he makes a better husband than watchdog.

Before I could get much done, Buster stopped by. He dropped into my visitor's chair, turned his hat around between his hands, and muttered, "I thought you'd like to know how things turned out."

I nodded encouragingly and turned my chair around to face him.

"She didn't do it, Judge."

"She certainly did. I saw her take them with my own eyes."

"Oh, she had the two necklaces in her pocket, like you said. But she claimed she was picking them up for Ms. Genna Harrison, and Ms. Harrison confirmed it."

"What? Did Genna come down to bail her out?"

He grinned. "Tit for tat? No, I think Ms. Harrison got enough of our hospitality yesterday. On the way to the detention center, Ms. Harrison called her brother—"

"Could you just call them Olive and Genna, so I can keep it straight?"

He twitched his shoulders. The sheriff doesn't like calling women he doesn't know well by their first names. "Well, Olive called Adney Harrison, who was working in Savannah today. He got Shep Faxon to come down. Shep talked to Olive and called Genna, and Genna told me over the phone that it was all right for Olive to have the stuff—that Olive was bringing it to her."

"You believed that?" I thought of the crafty expression on Olive's face as she lifted the lid of the chest and the smirk as she climbed into his cruiser. "Why didn't Genna get the necklaces herself this morning before she left? Or why didn't Olive wait to come looking for them until after Joe Riddley and I left? Or why didn't she come upstairs and simply announce, 'Genna told me to come look for a couple of necklaces the robber may have overlooked'?"

"Your guess is as good as mine. But you know as well as I do that without a charge, I couldn't hold her. While we had her there, though, acting on what you said down at the grove, I did ask her to reconfirm her alibi for the night Ms. Burkett was murdered. She had told us she was at home asleep. She conferred with counsel and said she hadn't quite told the truth—she actually stayed in a motel in North Augusta that night. She said her brother doesn't like her staying in motels alone, so she hadn't wanted him to know. Her story is that she rented a truck late Wednesday afternoon and drove a couch to a store in North Augusta, but they close at six on Wednesdays. Since they would reopen at eight the next morning, she decided to sleep up there so she could go to the store first thing and get the truck back before she had to go to work."

"But she was in Hopemore. She said she bought paint—"

"I know. She drove back to Hopemore, drove down Ms. Burkett's drive like she said, and she went to buy paint. After that, she claims she wasn't sleepy, so she got the bright idea to drive back to North Augusta and go to the store early in the morning, to save a second day's truck rental. On her way back to Hopemore Thursday noon, she heard about the murder on the noon radio news."

I thought that over. Olive hadn't mentioned the drive back to North Augusta when she'd been cataloguing her woes over at Myrtle's. "She could have killed Edie and then driven to North Augusta. You aren't positive when Edie died, are you?"

"Nope, but we know it was after twelve thirty, because Adney Harrison called Ms. Burkett at twelve thirty that night. Said he was concerned because he knew his wife wasn't there and Valerie had moved out, so he called to be sure she was okay. He said Ms. Burkett was a night owl, so he expected her to be awake, but he woke her up. They talked about five minutes—that checks out with his phone record—and he says she thanked him for his concern and said she'd see him when he got back to town. The medical examiner thinks she died before two."

"So maybe Olive stuck around until after twelve thirty, killed her on her way out of town, and checked into the motel real late."

I could tell from the way Buster shifted in his chair that I wasn't going to like the answer. "She checked into the motel in North Augusta at twelve thirty-five."

"So maybe she checked in and drove right back? What's one more round-trip when she'd already done two?"

"The desk clerk probably wishes she had, but she didn't. She asked for a nonsmoking room on the side away from the expressway, telling him she has bad allergies and traffic noises bother her. Then she came stomping back ten minutes later, claiming that somebody had smoked in there sometime in the past, because she could hardly breathe. He found her another room, and she moved her stuff in. She called thirty minutes later to say she had gone to take a shower and the shower head was missing. He didn't have a replacement at that hour, so he offered her a third room, but the only one they had was on the expressway side. The clerk said by then Olive was getting pretty hot under the collar about dragging her stuff in and out of rooms and moving her truck, and said she doubted she'd get a wink of sleep. She demanded a discount on the room, but he wasn't authorized to give it to her. He did help her carry her things down to the new room at one forty—he remembers because he made a note of when he was away from the desk. He thought he was finally done with her for the night, but she called twice more. The first time she asked for a wake-up call at seven, and the second she complained about trucks shifting gears on the expressway ramp and asked if he had any earplugs. He took her down some cotton balls from a first-aid kit. He said it was two ten when he got back to the desk."

"Sounds like our Olive," I said glumly. "If it had been anybody else, I'd have thought she was setting herself up with an alibi for the time of the murder, but that woman is just naturally contrary."

Buster turned his hat around some more. "We got one more bit of news you aren't gonna like, either. The forensics report came back on the orange coveralls. Nobody else wore them but Henry."

"But you said the blood on them was smeared, not in spurts."

"I know, but you can't always reconstruct how things happened. Maybe he tried to wipe it off while it was wet."

"But why would Henry kill Edie? He's known her all her life, she gave him a job—".

A six-foot man can't disappear into a normal-size wing chair, but the sheriff was giving it a good old-fashioned try.

"There's more, isn't there?"

He nodded, clearly miserable. "I wish Clarinda wasn't connected to the Joyners."

"Clarinda's connections have nothing to do with this."

"I'm afraid they do. Shep was in my office when the forensics report arrived. I didn't tell him what was in it, of course, but he asked if it looked like Henry Joyner could have killed Edith Burkett. When I asked why he thought that, he started his good-ole-boy shuffle and dance, then said he reckoned it wasn't too much of a violation of client confidentiality to tell me what happened last week. He said Edie Burkett called him late Monday, real upset and wanting to see him right away. She went down to his office and showed him a letter from her granddaddy, claiming Pete Joyner was his grandson. She said she had taken it to Josiah and asked him if he was Pete's daddy, too. She claimed Josiah told her he thought Pete must have been Edward's son—although neither Shep nor I can figure out how she understood him, the shape Josiah's in."

He held up a hand to keep me from interrupting, just like he used to do on our way to elementary school. "Wait, let me finish. Shep said he was still trying to get his head around that when Edie started insisting that she and her daddy needed to revise their wills to do the right thing by Henry. Shep claims he tried to explain to her that what Henry didn't know wouldn't hurt him— Don't get all het up, Judge. You know I'm just quoting Shep. Shall we say he was trying to dissuade her from doing something he considered rash? Edie wouldn't budge. She said Pete died before justice was done, and with the precarious state of her daddy's health, she and Josiah both wanted Shep to draw up a new will for him right away, and to go with her to Golden Years on Tuesday morning so Josiah could sign it. She said she would come in later to revise her own will. Then she sat there telling Shep exactly what to put in Josiah's new will. Since she had Josiah's power of attorney, and Josiah would have it read to him the next day, Shep did what she asked. That will left everything to Edie for her lifetime, but after her death the pecan grove, house, and all its furnishings—the whole shebang—would go to Henry. Edie insisted that her daddy could understand what he was signing, even if he can't speak."

I know now that Josiah had tried to tell Henry, "The grove goes to you."

"I'd agree with—" I managed to cram that much in edgeways before the sheriff again held up a big hand and said, "I'm almost finished. Shep said that Tuesday the two of them took the new will to Josiah, Edie read it to him, and he signed it in front of two witnesses."

"Did Shep say what he said to upset Josiah afterwards?"

The sheriff shuffled his feet. "You don't want to know. Sometimes Shep makes me ashamed to know him." He stood. "But that gives us motive, means, and opportunity, Judge. I'm on my way to pick up Henry now. If you'd call Clarinda and ask her to go down and stay with Daisy, I'd appreciate it."

He left without giving me a chance to say another word.

What was there to say?

❧ 26 ❧

"You got Olive arrested?" Walker asked in disbelief. "Adney's sister?"

"She was robbing Edie's house."

"Poor Adney, with two crazy women on his hands right now."

"Genna isn't crazy," Cindy blazed. "She's just stressed out. Anybody would be."

"Olive was Edie's friend," Walker protested. "Why would she rob her after she was dead?"

We were sitting at their breakfast room table later that evening, sharing what Walker has always called "a bednight snack." Cindy had asked me to come over after the kids were in bed to coordinate family Christmas presents, but I'd seen very soon that what they really wanted was to know more about what had happened to Olive.

This was the night of the full moon. It was so bright through the bay window that I could recognize the shapes of leaves halfway across the yard. Normally the full moon keys me up, but right then I was having a hard time staying awake, in spite of the coffee.

Cindy had served a dreadful new blend she had bought from a catalogue. To me, it tasted like a combination of tea olive and Carolina jessamine, and I've never been fond of flowers in my coffee mug. I finished it, to be nice, but set down the mug with relief.

"I'm not sure you could call Olive and Edie friends," I answered Walker. "They were just bound by family and similar interests—the library, bridge, and eating out at night. Alex James thought Olive was jealous of Edie—she probably thought Edie had pots of money and didn't have to live on her librarian's salary."

"Olive doesn't live on hers, either. She expects Adney to pay for anything she wants that she can't afford—and he usually does." Cindy cupped her hands around her mug, like she was cold. "But Genna says Olive was jealous of Edie, too—not for the money, but because Olive was the best bridge player in her club back home, and she resented that Edie was better. I think she's jealous of Genna, too. Olive lived in an apartment next door to Adney until he and Genna got married and moved into a house, and the two of them have always been real close. Their parents died when they were little. Genna said one reason she wanted to move here was to get away from Olive, then Olive showed up one day saying she'd gotten a job at the Hope County Library."

I reached for one of Cindy's warm pecan chocolate chip cookies. "I still think she's the best candidate for murdering Edie."

Walker disagreed. "The sheriff knows who did it. Henry Joyner." He spoke in that dogmatic tone adult children use when correcting their mothers: part knowledge and part bravado, mixed with a hefty dose of "my turn has finally come."

"What makes you think so?" I was sure the sheriff hadn't been spreading that around.

"Shep Faxon was telling everybody at the country club this afternoon. Henry is actually Josiah's son—can you believe that? Who'd have imagined dumpy old Josiah would—"

That got my dander up. "You'd better not believe it, because it's not true. I don't believe Henry killed Edie, and I am pretty darned sure Henry's not Josiah's son—he's not even his grandson." I told them what Joe Riddley had figured out.

Walker rubbed his chin thoughtfully. "Shep *said* Edie claimed it was Edward, but then he laughed and said that a dead uncle is a real convenient thing to have sometimes."

If Shep had been within striking range, I'd have hit him right then, judge or no judge.

Walker continued, "Shep also swears Josiah is leaving Henry everything he has—the house, the grove, the whole kit and caboodle. That set the club on its ear—I can tell you that. In the locker room fellows were saying if Henry hadn't gotten caught for the murder, next thing we knew, he'd have been applying to join the club."

"And why not?" When he didn't immediately give the right answer, I lashed out. "What's the matter with you? We already have the technical college president, two black doctors, and one black dentist in the country club. What's so different about the owner of a pecan grove?"

"Nothing, if he'd been born to the grove. But his daddy was a foreman, Mama."

"Your granddaddy was a farmer," I said furiously. "My daddy had no more education than Pete Joyner, and nobody asked about that when your daddy and I applied. What do you know about Adney's daddy—or Shep's, for that matter? Furthermore, you were never raised to take part in that kind of talk. I don't care if it costs you the presidency of the club, you need to stand up for what is right."

He turned and looked out at the moonlit yard. I knew how he was feeling, caught in the predicament of any businessperson whose personal ethics are not always those of clients and customers. Like almost any mama, however, I didn't know when to stop. "I appreciate your struggle, honey—we've lived with it all our lives—"

He flapped an angry hand at me. "Enough, Mama. You've said what you had to say." He still didn't turn toward me.

Cindy got up nervously—she hates it when Walker and I fight. To my dismay, I realized she was about to refill our cups. I was delighted to be saved by the bell of the phone. She reached for it, and we heard her say, "Hi. No, we haven't seen her. Oh, dear. Maybe Olive—? Oh. Well, if she calls, I'll tell her you're worried."

She whisked the pot over and filled my mug before I had time to cover it with my hand.

"That was Adney," she told us, "wanting to know if Genna was here. They must have had a fight or something, because he said she left a couple of hours ago and hasn't come home, and he's real upset. He doesn't like for her to be out alone after dark."

"Adney needs to remember he's living in Hopemore, not Birmingham," I snapped, still angry but glad to have a new target. "I drive around this town at all hours of the night, and nobody ever bothers me."

"They're smarter than that," Walker said sourly. "Who'd dare tangle with you?" Then he reached over to muss my hair with a smart-aleck grin. Walker and I have the same tempers. They flare up and dissolve. Joe Riddley and Ridd can simmer for days.

"Dang right," I agreed, giving him a playful smack with a grin of my own. "But she's not at Olive's?" I picked up my mug, wondering how I could possibly get that coffee down.

Cindy put the pot down and regarded us both with her fine brows drawn in a worried pucker. "He said Olive had come over to their place and said she hasn't seen her. That's when he started getting worried. Maybe I ought to drive around and look for her. But where could she go?" Good question. Hopemore doesn't exactly roll up the sidewalks after dark, but stores close before suppertime, the Bi-Lo closes by nine, and even Myrtle's isn't open after eight except on weekends.

"The superstore," Walker suggested. "Isn't it open until eleven? Maybe she's walking up and down the aisles."

Cindy reached for her purse. "I need to get a few things there anyway. I think I'll run over and see if I can find her."

"Don't get involved in somebody else's fight," he protested. "She'll go home when she's ready."

Cindy pressed her lips together and traced little designs on the countertop. She seemed to be wrestling with herself about whether to speak or not, but finally she admitted, "I think she's worried about something. She's acted real strange these past few days."

"Everybody's acted strange these past few days," he pointed out. "We've just had a gruesome murder in town, and it was Genna's stepmother who got murdered. I know they weren't real close, but they were family. Adney said he had to go on the road the past couple of days just to take his mind off thinking about it all the time."

Cindy started drumming one fist silently against her thigh. "I'm scared Genna's heading for a breakdown, honey. She's all pent up, erupts over the least little thing—I'd like to go look for her. Okay?"

He went over and stroked her hair out of her face, then fetched his keys from the kitchen counter. "You aren't going without me. If Mama's right—and occasionally she is—there's still a murderer loose in town. I don't want you running around in the dark alone."

"I'm just going to the superstore. They have security guards in the parking lot at night. And we can't both leave the children."

I went through a mighty struggle between my druthers and my responsibilities, then reached for my cell phone. "I'll go with you. Just let me call Joe Riddley and tell him where we'll be. I promised I won't go anywhere right now without checking in. And don't you look at me like that, Walker Yarbrough. I do sometimes do what your daddy asks. Stop laughing!"

Joe Riddley had forwarded our calls, because he was down at Ridd's, helping Hollis, Smitty, and Tyrone with economics. I could picture them sitting around the big oak table in the kitchen, like he used to do with our boys and their friends. I sure wished I was down there making them all cups of hot chocolate.

Instead, ten minutes later, I was violating two of my principles. I was riding high above the world in a gas-guzzling, environment-polluting monster SUV, and I was headed for the new superstore. It took us almost half an hour to walk those brightly lit, overstocked aisles, and I'm embarrassed to admit how often I had to rein myself in to keep from buying a few things I needed. Only Cindy's anxiety about Genna kept me from trying on a soft, fuzzy sweat suit in a flattering shade of green.

We didn't find Genna, but we did see a friend of theirs with a piled-high cart. "Isn't it nice to be able to shop after the kids are in bed?" she greeted us. "Tim's watching television, but I think if the house burned down, he'd notice and save them."

She said she'd seen what she thought was Genna's car ahead of her coming down Oglethorpe, but it had turned down Whelan Grove Road at the intersection.

"Maybe she went to Edie's," Cindy concluded, heading for the door.

"Why would she do that?" I could hardly get the words out between pants. Cindy was slender as a greyhound and had long, strong legs. In a hurry, she was almost as hard to keep up with as Joe Riddley. "You said she's nervous about being alone at night, and that place would give even me the willies right now."

Cindy was already swinging up into the SUV. "I didn't say she was nervous about being alone at night. I said Adney is nervous about her being alone. Genna herself thinks he's silly. Besides, where else could she be going?"

"I-20? The world?"

Cindy didn't take me seriously. "We'll just drive by and see if her car is there."

I pulled out my cell phone and notified Joe Riddley of our change in plans. He said, "Well, we've finished down here, so I'm heading home. Keep me posted."

"This thing of phoning in seems restrictive and silly," I told Cindy, putting my phone back in my pocketbook, "but it keeps him happy."

She didn't answer. It takes a lot of concentration to drive a tank.

She pulled in, slowed, and peered at the house far down the drive. "Is that moonlight I see, lights in the house, or a reflection from that security light outside?"

I leaned forward to see better. "The light outside is at the back. I don't think it could reflect in the front windows. It could be the moon, but it looks to me like the place is lit up."

"Let's just look." She headed down the drive. As we got closer, we saw Genna's silver Mercedes pulled crookedly behind Edie's Saab.

I also saw a familiar friend, looking almost pretty bathed in moonlight. "There's the green tractor I chased Olive with."

Cindy's jaw dropped. "You drove that huge thing? That's incredible!"

I preened to have impressed my elegant daughter-in-law, until she ruined it by adding, "I guess it's just what you're used to."

"I'm not used to driving tractors," I said crossly. "I used to do it, but no more."

"Should we go in?" Cindy had stopped and was staring at the back door. "I don't know if she'd want us to . . ."

The kitchen lights went out, and a face appeared in the newly repaired window of the door. A trick of light distorted its shape, so I wasn't sure if it was Genna or not. But who else could it be? All doubt vanished when the door flew open and a figure stumbled across the porch. "Cindy? Oh, Cindy! I'm so glad it's you!"

In spite of the cold night, she wore only a pair of slacks and a silky blouse. I thought the blouse had an awkward neckline until I saw the top two buttons were missing. As she reached the light, we saw that it was no trick of the light that had disfigured her face. One eye was puffy, her lips were swollen, and a dark streak that looked like blood ran across her cheek from the left corner of her nose.

"Oh, honey! What happened to you?" Cindy jumped down from the car before I could stop her, ran to put her arms around Genna, and held her tight. Through the open car door, I saw that Genna wore only thin house slippers.

She sobbed and gasped as if she was experiencing a short-age of air. Her words came out in short bursts of fright. "He got so mad! I've never seen him like that. He kept asking, 'Where is it? Where is it, bitch?' Then he hit me and hit me—" She turned away from Cindy and covered her face. "I'm so ashamed for you to see me like this. He's not like that, really. He never talked like that before, and he never hit me." She lifted her tearstained, disfigured face to the halogen light and cried, "I've got to find it. Where could it be?"

"Where is what?" I called, climbing down from my high seat.

"Daddy's money," she said, as if I should have known. "I told Adney I'd gone to the lawyer and that Shep says there really isn't any money. But Adney doesn't believe me. He thinks I'm hiding it from him. Why would I do that? I only wanted it so he could start a business."

She started to blubber, and pulled the tail of her shirt up to wipe her nose. Then she took a deep breath and announced in a shaky voice, "Maybe Edie hid it. If I find it, he won't leave me." She turned and limped back to the house, whimpering in a voice that contained both determination and de-feat, "I'm going to find it. I know she has to have hidden it somewhere in there. Maybe it's in a safe-deposit box. I just have to find the key."

Cindy turned and looked at me. "Should we go in?"

I pulled out my cell phone. "Not until I've told Joe Rid-dley."

Cindy paced beyond the car while I filled Joe Riddley in on our last ten minutes.

"Adney's not there?" he asked.

"Not yet." He knew as well as I did that if we'd figured out where Genna was, Adney could, too.

"I'll send Walker over to talk to him."

"Cindy's here, so there's nobody to stay with their kids."

"We'll figure something out. Don't you let Adney in if he shows up. You promise me?"

That was one promise I had no trouble making.

As we turned toward the back steps, we saw headlights coming down the drive. Genna ran screaming from the house and nearly knocked us down. "He's coming! He's coming! I have to get away!" She streaked off through the grove.

Don't ask why I took off after her. I was following Cindy, who was leaving me in her dust. She and Genna ran every morning, remember. My favorite exercise is opening the refrigerator for another glass of tea.

The headlights got closer, and I looked over my shoulder to see how close they were. It wasn't Adney—it was Olive. She was headed straight for me.

❧ 27 ❧

Do you know how fast I can run in the moonlight? It depends on the size of the SUV behind me. That night, I'd probably have passed Frank Sparks's motorcycle.

I had no idea where Cindy or Genna had gone. My one thought was to put as many tree trunks as possible between me and Olive, and to find the darkest shadows.

I dashed. I dodged. I circled, and I backtracked. She followed me all the way.

My side ached, and my lungs felt like somebody had replaced the air with fire. Just as I was beginning to see black spots in front of my eyes—and yes, you can see black spots even in the dark—I heard somebody yell, "Hey!" and then I heard a thump.

I kept running.

Next thing I knew, Olive's lights swerved away from me and headed in another direction. I clung to the nearest tree and peered around the thick trunk, gasping. I watched in astonishment as somebody hung on to the luggage carrier on top of her car with one hand and leaned down to pound the windshield with the other. "Hey! Hey! Hey!"

Olive swerved again and ran right into a tree. The person shot forward, missed the trunk, and rolled on the soft grass between the trees. A bald head gleamed in the moonlight. For one startled moment, I thought Daddy had come back to save me.

Olive certainly looked like she'd seen a ghost. I heard her swearing as she tried to get past her air bags and out the bent driver's door. She finally climbed out the other side, stopped to retrieve something from the car, then stomped around to examine the damage. One fender was smashed against the tree, its headlight blazing high into the branches above.

She whirled and screamed into the night, "Okay, damn you, where are you? I know you're out here!" She glared around. I ducked behind the wide trunk. When I peeped back to where my hero had landed, he was gone.

"Where are you, Judge?" Olive yelled. "I was just playing with you. Come on out. I won't hurt you. Genna? Adney sent me to get you. He's worried about you. Where are you?"

"Down here. You scared me, driving like that." Genna's voice was a small, frightened sound in the night. I heard a rustling of nuts and saw her move onto the bright median from the shadow of a tree far down the row.

Olive laughed. "I was just having a little fun with the judge, getting back at her for this morning." She laughed again. "Come on. We'll need to use your car to get home."

I jumped as someone put a hand on my shoulder. I smelled cigarettes and heard a husky mutter. "She's got a gun. Count to fifteen, then start throwing these one at a time across the grass." He pressed several warm nuts into my hand. "One . . . two . . ." I turned, but he was gone.

On fifteen, I pitched a nut. To my astonishment, I hit a tree across the median.

Olive turned in that direction. "Judge? I was kidding, okay? You can come out now."

I pitched another nut, a little in front of the first. She turned, tense and alert.

I pitched a third, and a fourth. Each time she turned and listened.

It was a surreal scene, silver and black, dark shadows beneath the trees and bright moonlight between them. Not a bird or cricket spoke. Genna came limping from far away, her hair bright under the moon, clutching herself tightly against the cold. I wanted to cry out, to stop her from coming any nearer, but I didn't dare.

I pitched another nut, then another, making a rough pattern as if somebody were moving cautiously among the trees. Olive moved hesitantly toward the plops they made, then stood peering into the darkness.

One nut fell short. When she turned that way, I caught my breath sharply. The moonlight glinted on a short barrel.

She peered all around. "I know you are here," she muttered between her teeth. Then she raised her voice. "Hurry, Genna. I haven't got all night. It's cold out here."

"I turned my ankle. I'm coming as fast as I can," Genna called back.

My nuts were gone. I inched down, calves and thighs screaming, and gathered more in a terrifying game of pickup sticks in which the penalty for moving anything that rustled could be death. When I had a handful, I stood and flung several as far as I could, all at once. They landed in a noisy hail against a distant trunk. She whirled. "I know you are there!"

"Hi-ya!" He came from behind her, a black streak from blackness. He hurled himself at her and tackled her low. As she fell, she pulled the trigger. I heard a *nick* as the bullet hit a limb above me, and Genna's scream.

Sheltered behind the tree, wondering how I could help, I watched the two of them roll on the ground. Genna hobbled a little faster our way. Olive writhed, trying to get the gun in position. Suddenly he grabbed her wrist and twisted it without compunction. I heard a crack, a scream, then she lay still.

The gun lay across her open palm in the moonlight.

"You've killed her!" Genna screamed, clinging to a tree. "Miss Mac? Where are you? Are you killed, too? Please don't kill me!" She fell to the ground, sobbing.

He climbed shakily to his feet and stood panting, staring down at the form on the grass. "You can come on out, now, Judge. I didn't kill her. I think she fainted." He turned to face me.

"Smitty?" I approached him on trembling legs.

"Yeah." He brushed leaves and grass off his clothes and gave his trademark snicker. "Looked like you could use some help."

He bent down and picked up the gun, weighed it in his hand, then thrust it at me with obvious regret. I had to admit it was a pretty little piece.

"How did you get here?"

"On my bike. I saw her on my way home, after I left Ridd's. I heard Joe Riddley talkin' to you on the phone, and it sounded like something was comin' down involvin' the Harrisons, so when I saw her headin' out this way, I followed. It was easy. She drives like a little old lady."

He looked down at Olive again. "I would of used karate, but we haven't had but two classes. We didn't get to the part yet about how to defend against firearms."

"You did fine."

We sounded like a couple of frogs. He croaked because he was sixteen and winded. I croaked because my voice wasn't working right. My legs weren't working right, either. I backed up and leaned against a tree for support. "As soon as I can walk, I'll get my pocketbook from the car and call the sheriff. You're gonna be a hero."

He snickered again. "Think they'll put my statue up on the town square?" He looked around. "I wish I had something to tie her up. I didn't hurt her much, just broke her wrist."

"I wish you hadn't done that," I admitted.

He shook his head. "Can't play soft when it's you or them, Judge. You gotta do what you gotta do and get it over with." Remembering that ferocious, practiced twist, the crack of bone, and Olive's scream, I shuddered.

I called down to where Genna still huddled on the grass. "Genna, it's okay. You can come on, now."

She lifted her head, saw Smitty, and shuddered.

"He won't hurt you," I assured her. "We need to get back to Cindy's car and call for help. Where is Cindy?"

Genna looked around like she'd forgotten Cindy was

there. "When Olive started chasing you, she said she was going back to the house to call 911." She hobbled to where we were and bent down to speak to the silent form. "Don't worry, Olive, the ambulance is coming."

"Do you know if Edie had anything we could use to tie her up until help arrives?"

Genna stepped back, shocked. "Tie her up? Why? She wasn't going to hurt you. She was just teasing. And I wasn't running from *her.* I thought it was Adney."

I held out the gun. "She had this."

"Olive wouldn't shoot anybody!" When I didn't reply, she heaved a huge sigh. "I don't understand any of this."

I sighed. "You don't have to understand, but I do need something to tie Olive with until somebody comes."

She shrugged. "There's a clothesline in the utility room."

"You take Smitty to fetch it. He won't hurt you," I repeated firmly. "I'll stay here."

Me and the gun. I loathe and despise the things, but it felt solid in my hand as Olive began to moan and stir.

"Ow! My arm!" She clutched her right hand. Then she struggled to sit up, but that's hard with only one good arm. She peered up at me. "Mac? Where are we? What happened? What are you doing here?" She looked around at her damaged car, the sheltering trees, and pressed one hand to her cheek. "I think I went a little crazy back there." She attempted a laugh. "I must have acted a little weird, huh? I was just trying to get some of my own back, for you chasing me up that tree." She shook her head to clear it and looked down at her useless wrist. "That bastard broke my wrist! Who was he?"

"The secret avenger," I told her. "He appears out of nowhere to save the innocent. Just relax. The sheriff ought to be here any minute."

Her eyes widened in an attempt at innocence. "The sheriff? We don't need the sheriff. It was a joke. You aren't going to press charges for something that silly. You did the same thing to me this morning."

"We'll sort it out when he gets here." I leaned back against the tree. Shock from the chase and its aftermath was beginning to set in, and my knees were trembling.

"At least help me up. I can't make it with one arm."

"Just rest down there until help comes."

She gave me a furious glare, then wriggled around and propped herself on the elbow of her damaged arm, pushed with the other, and lurched to her feet.

"I've got your gun." I held it so she could see it. "And you need to know I was brought up shooting rats in my daddy's chicken house. I can still hit a moving target." I didn't bother to tell her we used a twenty-two rifle for rats, or how hard it is to hit a moving target at any distance with a little handgun. What she didn't know made life easier for me.

She backed up so she could lean against her car, breathing heavily. "So help me, if you tell the sheriff I was chasing you through the grove, I'm going to tell him I was looking for Genna and you just got in the way. Adney sent me to find her. She ran off this evening—"

"After he beat the living daylights out of her."

She shrugged. "That's between the two of them. Besides, it was a misunderstanding. He got mad because he thought she was holding out on him, pretending Edie didn't have any money when she did. But when I got there, I told him what you said about Wick losing all his money and Josiah still owning the grove, so he's not mad at Genna now that he knows she wasn't lying. Adney cannot stand people who lie."

How could a man who spent his life convincing people one brand of plastic pitchers was superior to another criticize anybody else for lying?

I'd think about that later. Right now, I had other things to think about, and I desperately wanted my cell phone.

I gestured with the gun. "Let's go up to the house. Walk slowly, and don't try to get away. I won't kill you, but you might wish I had."

I felt almost sorry for her as I trudged behind her to the house. Plain, not rich, not attractive to men, not endowed with the gift of making friends. Her shoulders slumped, and her hair hung stringy and lifeless at the collar of her gray jacket. What could Olive have been with a little encouragement and better wardrobe advice?

Smitty was coming down the steps with a clothesline. "After you tie her up, I've got an errand for you," I told him.

Smitty's knots weren't as expert as his fighting, but they would hold until a deputy arrived. When I explained to him privately what I needed, he gave me a quick nod. "I can do that." He went to get his bike and pedaled away. I retrieved my pocketbook and my phone.

Before I could push even the one button I needed, headlights came down the gravel drive. When I recognized Joe Riddley's car, I thrust the gun at my startled daughter-in-law. "Here. Guard her until the emergency folks arrive. And call Walker and tell him to meet you at the emergency room."

I ran to the car and pounded on the driver's window before he could open the door. "Slide over and let me drive. We've got to go somewhere, quick!"

On the way, I handed him my phone and explained what had happened. He made a couple of calls, then laid his head back and shut his eyes. "How can you sleep?" I demanded.

"I'm not," he replied. "I'm praying and trying not to see the speedometer."

Everything was closed when we squealed into the parking lot, but a familiar car sat near the front door. We jumped out and rang the bell. We were met by a slight man in a gray uniform, who held the door wide. "They're here. Just down to the left."

We hurried as silently as possible down the hall. As we reached the door, we heard a voice within shout, "Freeze!"

We ran in to find a police officer standing in the closet door holding a revolver. Across the room, Adney Harrison stood beside Josiah Whelan, holding a pillow over his face.

❧ 28 ❧

"I was just fluffing his pillows," Adney protested as the officer handcuffed him. "I was on my way home and stopped by to see him. I knew it was late, but thought I'd run in to say hello. He wasn't comfortable, so I was rearranging his pillows. Isn't that right, Granddaddy Jo?"

Josiah lifted his head from the pillow and shouted hoarse sounds nobody understood.

"If he could talk, he'd tell you," Adney insisted.

Josiah's eyes told us all we needed to know.

Sheriff Gibbons stepped into the room. "I hope we weren't too late?"

"Augusta's finest were on time," Joe Riddley told him and introduced the young officer who had been on watch. After the tedious procedures all arrests take these days, custody was transferred to our sheriff so he could take Adney home.

"You ride back with the sheriff and leave me the car," Joe Riddley told me. "I don't want to leave Josiah alone tonight."

I gave him a kiss. "I'm proud to know you," I whispered. "I can't imagine how terrified he must have been."

The sheriff told Adney he could call Shep to meet him at the sheriff's detention center. We could hear Shep clear up front. "Tarnation, son, three arrests in two days are downright tacky. I don't do tacky." After that, Adney leaned back in the corner of his seat and didn't ask to call either his wife or his sister.

After we'd ridden a few miles in silence, the sheriff looked my way and asked, "Tell me what happened tonight, and how you figured he'd be up there at Josiah's."

"I was with Olive and Genna out at Edie's, and Olive said Adney had sent her to find Genna. But if Adney sent Olive after Genna, that meant nobody was watching him. Genna had fled her home after a domestic dispute. She told Cindy and me that Adney hit her because he thought she was lying about Edie not having left her any money—he apparently thought she was hiding it from him."

Adney gave a snort of derision from the back. I ignored him and went on.

"We found Genna frantically searching Edie's house for stocks, money, or a key to a safe-deposit box. But when Olive arrived, she said Adney wasn't mad at Genna any longer, because she—Olive—had gone over and told him the truth: that Edie really didn't inherit any money from Wick—"

"You sure about that?" The sheriff doesn't like to be interrupted, but he's never minded interrupting me. "I always thought Wick was pretty well fixed."

"He was, until he became a drug addict who spent everything he had, and more, feeding his habit. If you don't believe that, you can check with Alexandra James at the library. She heard it from Edie herself, and says she'd already recognized the symptoms, because one of her brothers—well, never mind. What worried me more was when Olive said she'd told Adney that Josiah still owns the house and grove. I suddenly got very scared for Josiah." I hesitated, then admitted, "Tonight's mess is partly my fault. I was the one who told Olive this morning that Edie didn't have any money or own the grove."

The sheriff gave a grunt. "That thing about the grove is all over town. I'm surprised Adney hadn't already heard it."

"Would it surprise you to hear I think Adney killed Edie?"

Adney laughed in the backseat. "You seem to have forgotten, Judge. I was in Birmingham. Left a meeting at eight

Wednesday night, and I can produce witnesses. I also got a wake-up call at eight the next morning and was in the lobby twenty minutes later. I might conceivably have driven six hours here and six back, but when did I have time to kill Edie? Especially the way she was killed. Whoever did that had to have been a bloody mess afterwards." His voice grew faint. "I get sick just thinking about it. Poor Edie. I loved her, Mac. I did."

The sheriff looked over at me. "Well?"

"It's not a six-hour drive, it's a five-hour drive. It seems like six coming this way because of the time change, but that makes it only four going back. At night, when there's no traffic in Atlanta, it's more like four and a half hours each way. If he left at eight, he could get here by twelve thirty their time, one thirty ours. We know he called Edie at twelve thirty, but do we know where he was then? I don't think he was calling to see if she was all right. I think he was calling to make sure she was there and alone. He'd have an hour to kill her, clean himself up, and get out, and he could still get back to Birmingham by seven and have an hour's sleep before his wake-up call. I figured all that out while we were driving to Augusta tonight."

Sheriff Gibbons gave me a swift look. "While driving like a maniac? Next time concentrate on the road."

I ignored him. "Adney looked absolutely exhausted when he got here the day Edie died."

The sheriff thought that over. "His odometer checked out. He didn't drive that far."

"He could have rented a car."

"We could ask the Birmingham police to show his picture around some car rental agencies," he murmured to himself. "Somebody might remember him."

"They will if they're female. He's a handsome cuss. Aren't you, Adney?"

"Handsome or not, they already ran a check on my credit card. I did not rent a car in Birmingham. Why are you doing this, Mac? I always thought you and I were friends."

I bit my tongue and refused to be baited. Instead, I watched the silver landscape flash by in the moonlight. Finally I spoke to the sheriff. "He could have a credit card in the name of a business he was pestering Walker to give him insurance quotes on over Thanksgiving. Some kind of sports complex. He said he was asking for a friend, but I didn't believe that—especially after Edie told me Genna had been asking for her 'inheritance' to help Adney start a business."

That got a little rise from the backseat. "What Genna asked Edie was between them. I didn't ask Genna or Edie either one for money."

"But you beat Genna when she told you Edie didn't leave any. If Edie had told Genna she didn't have money left after she paid Wick's debts, would she be alive today?"

"Don't soil a beautiful lady's memory," he replied. "I did not love Edie for her money."

The sheriff told me, "We checked out those keys you found on the nail with the plastic bags. They must be Josiah's keys to all the outbuildings. One of them fits Henry's shed. I guess that's how he got Henry's machete and coveralls. But how do you reckon he knew about those keys?"

"Beats me. I guess you'll have to leave something for the prosecutor to figure out. The coveralls were decoys, anyway. Adney wouldn't need to wear them. He sells supplies to surgeons who mess around in blood all day long, then go home clean as a whistle. In a pair of scrubs, booties, a cap and mask—how many traces would he leave? I'll bet he dumped those things at the hospital he visited the next morning, but you might find traces of blood in the rental car, when you find it. Can you imagine anything more low-down than smearing Henry's coveralls in the blood afterwards to implicate him? Unless it's calling Edie to make sure she was home so he could come in and kill her. That was downright—" I stopped. I didn't want to say the kind of words I was thinking right then.

"You listening, Adney?" the sheriff called to the backseat.

"She's building up a pretty good case against you, don't you think?"

"I think she's got a vivid imagination." Adney leaned back and started to whistle.

"I *imagine* you'll look at Adney's cell phone records again," I replied. "I imagine that they, plus a conversation with the motel desk clerk in Birmingham, might elicit the information that Adney's request for a wake-up call came not from his room phone but from his cell phone. While he was driving to Hopemore, in fact. His cell phone records might also show that he talked to Olive after she was at Edie's Wednesday night. Olive could have told him Genna had left Whelan Grove."

"She could have," Adney agreed blandly, "but she didn't."

The sheriff looked over at me as we reached the city limits. "You want me to drop you off at your house?"

Not yet. I'd begun to realize there were holes in the story. I thought I knew how to patch them. "Can Adney call Genna, to see if she got home safely?"

The sheriff gave permission, and Adney punched the number. "No answer. Let me try her cell." He punched another number and we heard his side of the conversation. He started out nice as pie. "Hello, honey. You doin' all right? . . . I'm so sorry about that. I'll make it up to you. Listen, I went out after Olive left, and I ran into a little trouble, so I may not get home tonight. You're where? What are you doing there? What happened to her? She *what?*"

I wished I could hear Genna's side of the conversation. Was she telling him Olive was sitting beside a deputy, waiting to get a broken wrist set so she could meet him down at the jail? Or was she soft-pedaling the news, as he had soft-pedaled his own?

"Well, you all take care. Maybe she ought to go home with you tonight."

He wished. If I had anything to do with it, he and Olive would be sleeping under the same roof. Nobody attempted to kill me in my own county and went home to sleep.

He hung up. "You've been so busy making up stories, Judge, you somehow forgot to tell me my sister ran her car into a tree and broke her wrist. Genna said they have sat in the emergency room for nearly three hours, and Olive just went in to get it set. Oh, God, why am I here when I need to be there?"

I doubted very much that was a prayer.

"Cindy's probably with them," I said brightly. "Take me by there, too, Sheriff. Cindy can run me home."

As I got out of the car at the emergency room door, I turned and said to Adney, "By the way, did you play golf today?"

"No," he said curtly. "I was down in Savannah until nearly suppertime."

"Then you missed the excitement. Shep Faxon told the fellows that Josiah signed a new will last Tuesday, leaving everything he has to Henry Joyner. Henry's daddy, Pete, was Josiah's nephew. Walker said it made a real sensation at the club."

Nothing that day had been as sweet as seeing Adney's face.

⤳ 29 ⤳

The waiting room was almost empty. Walker, Cindy, and Genna were sitting in the far corner when I arrived, but Walker was halfway across the waiting room the second he saw me come through the door, and towering over me two seconds after that.

"What did you mean, shoving a gun into Cindy's hand and haring off like that? She's sitting over there"—he lowered his voice and got so close I could smell coffee on his breath as he hissed—"she's sitting over there with an illegal handgun in her purse!"

"Don't tell me about it, son. I'm an officer of the law."

"You're the one who gave it to her!"

"She was supposed to turn it over to the deputy as soon as he arrived and tell him we'd taken it from Olive. I guess I forgot to give her that part of the instructions."

"Mama! My wife doesn't know a thing about handguns. It's a miracle she didn't kill somebody."

I could see she hadn't shot herself or Genna. At the moment, feeling like a weary dog dragging its tail in the dust, I didn't much care if she'd shot Olive. Still, I figured I ought to ask.

Walker huffed out a stream of exasperated air. "Of course she didn't shoot Olive. But this is the limit, Mama. I've put up with you all my life, but you can't go on doing things like this."

"I never did anything like that before, and I wouldn't have then if it hadn't been absolutely necessary. Can we sit down before we continue this conversation? If I don't sit, I'm likely to fall. I am dead on my feet."

I tottered over and plopped down beside Cindy. She and Genna had obviously spent time in the ladies' room with those pounds of cosmetics they both carried around. Cindy looked as fresh and pretty as if she'd just come from a salon. Genna had managed to cover her purple eye and fluff up her hair. She'd even gotten a fresh shirt and shoes from somewhere.

I felt like something the cat had played with half an hour before dragging it in. "How's Olive?" I asked.

Genna leaned across Cindy to answer. "After making us wait three hours, they just took her back a few minutes ago." Her jaw moved funny.

"Did you ask them to look at that jaw?" She dropped her eyes, and I decided not to pursue it just then. "Did the deputy go in with Olive?"

That wouldn't have been strictly necessary, but I was impressed with his or her dedication to duty—until Cindy said carelessly, "Oh, we didn't wait for anybody to come. After you all left, I went ahead and drove Olive here while Genna stopped by her house, then came on over."

"But the deputy was supposed to arrest Olive."

She and Genna both stared.

"She threatened me with a gun," I pointed out grimly.

"You had the gun," Genna corrected me. "Olive was chasing you, then she wrecked her car, and when she got out, that guy started beating up on her and broke her arm, and you had a gun on her." She looked at me, obviously bewildered.

"Why did you think I wanted her tied up?" I demanded.

Genna shook her head. "I had no idea. We untied her as soon as you left."

I counted to ten. Maybe at that distance Genna hadn't seen exactly what was going on. Or maybe she didn't want to remember. I was so tired, it was all getting blurry for me, too.

Walker took the seat on the other side of me in the manner of a psychiatric worker sticking close to a patient. I remembered something I had forgotten to ask Joe Riddley. "Who's keeping your children?"

"Bethany and Hollis came over to stay when Daddy sent me off to talk to Adney. Adney wasn't there, and about then Cindy called to say she and Genna were heading to the emergency room with Olive, so I called and told the girls to bed down in our guest room for the night and came over here. Are you planning to tell us what this is all about? Or is it just the standard Yarbrough parental circus?"

I leaned back in my chair and tried to figure out what to say. For the time being, I settled for, "Your daddy and I had to go somewhere real fast." I lowered my voice so Genna couldn't hear. "And the reason Olive broke her wrist is that she was chasing me in the grove with her car tonight, until Smitty dropped onto the car to distract her and she ran into a tree."

Walker shook his head in disgust. "That Smitty. Somebody ought to lock him up."

"Somebody ought to give him a medal. He saved my life. Listen to what I'm saying, boy. Olive was trying her dead-level best to run over me. She—" I had to stop. Memories of that chase and my fear in those desperate minutes washed over me and left me trembling. "If it hadn't been for Smitty," I finally managed, "you'd have been visiting me in the ICU—or the morgue."

I could tell he didn't believe me. Heck, a judge wouldn't be likely to believe me, either, with Smitty as my only witness. But I hadn't come there to argue that case.

"I need to go find a Coke," I said. "Anybody want one?"

"I'll get it," Walker offered reluctantly, starting to get up. He is, at bottom, a good son. That time, though, I turned him down.

I waved him back. "No, I need to make another stop on the way."

If they figured I had to go to the ladies' room, that's all

right. What I needed was a private corner in which to call the sheriff.

He told me the chief magistrate had been at the jail when they arrived, so Judge Stebley had sent Adney to a comfortable bunk in the detention center on a charge of attempted murder, awaiting the leisure of a superior court judge. I told him what I'd found at the emergency room, and we discussed a few other items. As we closed, he asked, "You holdin' up okay?"

"'Bout as well as you can expect for somebody who hasn't eaten for eight hours or slept since six yesterday morning. I keep telling myself it's just like prom night, but there seems to be a certain lack of hilarity in the proceedings."

"We'll all party later," he promised.

I went back to my seat, stopping to greet a couple who were the only people left there besides us. He had a horrible cough, and I didn't know them well, but I felt so punchy that any familiar face looked like a friend.

I'd scarcely sat down good before I remembered something Walker had said. I leaned over and murmured to Cindy, "Meet me over by the front door. We need to talk."

Walker came with us. "You're not giving my wife any more fool instructions tonight."

I glared at him. "Why didn't I pinch your head off when you were two and I first realized you were going to be obstreperous all your life? Look, son, we're in the middle of something awful right now, and we don't need extra trouble. What I wanted to suggest was that Cindy quietly walk out to your car and put that gun in the glove compartment. It still won't be legal, but at least it will be safe."

"I'll take it."

He was already reaching for her purse when I asked softly, "You think you'll be less conspicuous carrying a purse across the parking lot? Walk her out, though. I want to talk to Genna."

The last couple went into the examining room as I sat down beside her. "You must be worn out, honey. If you want to go on home, we'll wait for Olive." I wasn't sure what part Olive might have played in Edie's death, but she'd certainly played one in tonight's events. Friends don't let friends go home with possible murderers.

Genna reached for her purse so eagerly I suspected she'd have left sooner if Cindy and Walker hadn't stuck around. "Would you really? I'd appreciate it." She yawned, then winced as it hurt her jaw. "This has been the longest day. First I had to get up early to let you folks in down at Edie's, then I had aerobics class, then I was dressing for the Junior League Christmas luncheon when I got a call from Adney saying Olive had taken some stuff out of Edie's room and I needed to call the sheriff and tell him it was all right, because she was bringing it to me. I don't know what that was all about, but it nearly made me late for the luncheon. After that I had a tennis match, then a bunch of us had a Christmas cookie swap. After supper, I had that stupid fight with Adney, and"—she waved one hand as if too weary to finish—"you know. All this stuff."

Except she didn't say "stuff," and hers was a more accurate way to describe her beating, my near murder, and Olive's broken wrist.

She covered her mouth to hide another yawn. "I am utterly exhausted, so if you don't really mind—?" She was already on her feet.

I watched her go, wondering why I was putting myself out to save her petty little life. But that was weariness speaking. Any life is worth saving. Tomorrow might be the day Genna decided to turn around and live up to her potential. Look at Smitty.

I smiled. The sheriff had told me that when his deputy got to the grove that evening, he found Smitty in a porch rocker, fast asleep. Unlike Olive, who had been desperate, Smitty hadn't been able to climb the pecan tree, so he had decided to wait until somebody came in the morning and see if they had a ladder. He'd taken the deputy to the tree, but insisted he had to go up first. "The judge told *me* to," he objected when the deputy started to climb. The deputy reported, "That was one dude I didn't want to disagree with unless I had to, so I just gave him a leg up." Halfway up, Smitty had found the envelope Olive had hidden in a broad crotch between two branches.

The workers hadn't shaken that tree, we would later learn. They feared it was unlucky because it drew the police. "Nuts no good," they would continue to insist. "Rotten. Cut it down."

Just as Genna reached the front door, Olive came out from the treatment rooms. "Genna? Wait!" Her right arm was bent and encased in plaster from her fingers to her upper arm. She looked mad enough to fight a pit bull and win.

Genna changed direction and headed her way. "Are you done? Then I can take you home. Adney called and said for you to sleep over at our place tonight."

"I'm done, all right. They nearly killed me, and didn't give me anywhere near enough painkiller, but I'm finally done." She flung a general glare around the waiting room as if it were full of people who all voted on emergency room procedures. In the process, she saw me over in the corner. Her glare turned to a deadly stare. "And where did you go?" she demanded, stomping across the room and standing over me, a harpy with mahogany hair and a sharp beak. "Why did you and Joe Riddley take off like that?"

"We had something to see about," I said in a level voice, wishing I'd been smart enough to move to a seat nearer the door. "We had to hurry, but fortunately we got there in time."

Her eyes narrowed. "I don't know what you're talking about." She turned away.

"Good. Adney won't be coming home tonight, by the way. He's been detained."

She whirled. "What do you mean, 'detained'?"

"Kept. Locked up. He's down at the jail."

Genna had followed Olive and overheard. "Jail?" she squealed. "You didn't say that before. Did you tell them he hit me? How could you? He didn't hurt me, really he didn't."

Olive grabbed Genna's elbow with her good hand. "We've got to get down there and bail him out."

"No bail," I told her. "The charge is attempted murder."

"Murder?" Genna squeaked.

I nodded. "When we got to the nursing home, Adney was trying to smother Josiah."

"Granddaddy Jo?" Genna's squeaks were getting tiresome, but I reminded myself that she was tired and hearing some really bad news for the first time.

Olive shook Genna's elbow, which she still held. "This is nonsense. He was probably fluffing his pillows. We need to get down there and talk to that sheriff. By the time I get through, he'll let us bail Adney out."

"Sorry," I informed her. "Only a superior court judge can make that decision. The chief magistrate will write the superior court tomorrow and ask them to send somebody down for a hearing."

"We can call tonight."

I shook my head. "We may live in the instant age for most things, but in this case, it has to be a written request from a county magistrate."

"You did this!" she spat down at me.

I shook my head. "No, Adney did it. The police caught him red-handed. I didn't even hold his hearing, since I could be called as a witness at his trial. I doubt he'll be out anytime soon. It is interesting, though, that you and Adney gave the same reason for what he was doing: fluffing a pillow. Makes me wonder if you discussed an excuse ahead of time, in case somebody came in."

Genna pulled her arm away from Olive to cup both hands over her mouth. Above them, her eyes were wide and dark. "Why would Adney want to kill Granddaddy Jo?"

"Ask Olive," I suggested. "She's the one who came down to the grove to be sure you didn't go home while Adney went to Augusta. She's the one who went by your house after you left and told Adney it was true Edie didn't inherit any money from your daddy, and that she didn't live long enough to in-

herit the grove. Adney seems to have been under the mis-
conception that Josiah had already given over everything he
owned to Edie."

Genna looked from Olive to me, puzzled. "She had his
power of attorney."

"That's not the same as ownership. She would have inherited the grove only after Josiah's death. Now Henry will
get it."

"Henry?" Genna and Olive spoke in shocked unison.

I nodded. "Josiah made a new will last week."

"Why Henry?" Olive demanded.

At the very same time, Genna protested, "It was Edie who
made a new will. She talked to Shep Monday night and
arranged to meet him Tuesday morning at his office."

I replied to Genna. "They went from there to Josiah's, so
he could sign a new will, leaving everything to her for her
lifetime and to Henry after that. Did you tell Adney Edie was
making a new will?"

"Don't tell her a thing!" Olive snapped.

But Genna had already nodded. "I was so upset, I had to
call him. I was worried Edie would leave all she had to Valerie, after everything Valerie and that Frank did to make her
think she was going crazy."

"Why did you think it was Valerie doing all that?"

Olive put out a hand, but Genna didn't notice. She said in
a bewildered voice, "Olive said so. She said whenever she
went down to Edie's to play bridge, Valerie and Frank were
always there, that Frank stayed overnight when Edie didn't
know it, and they changed things in her house to make her
think she was going crazy like Gramma Sally did. She even
saw them using Edie's computer one day, and the next week
it had pornography on it."

That raised an interesting question. "How could Olive see
them using Edie's computer? Wasn't it in her bedroom, at the
top of the house?"

If looks could kill, I'd have been ready for the hearse. "I

had to use the little girls' room," Olive snapped, "and some-body else was in the upstairs one."

"Or maybe you ran up to open a porn site or two on Edie's computer. Just like you went down and put blouses in the wash, dishes in the dishwasher, and magazines on the porch."

"Don't be silly." Notice that Olive didn't deny it. "Why would I do such a thing?"

"To help convince Edie to sell the grove, which you all thought she owned, and move into town. Valerie and Frank had no reason to want Edie to think she was losing her mem-ory, but Adney did. He wanted Edie's land, didn't he? He wanted her to sell the grove for housing developments and invest the money—which he thought Genna would eventu-ally inherit. And he wanted Edie to give Genna the strip along the road for his sports complex."

"That's ridiculous," Olive snapped—just as Genna said, "And a small mall."

"Did you know, Genna, that Adney wrote Edie a detailed letter, outlining how the investment income from the sale of the grove, added to investment income from his estimates of her profits from the sale of her house and the pharmacy, would take care of Josiah for the rest of his life and keep her comfortably for the rest of hers without ever touching the principal? And that he also warned her that the two of you were concerned about her deteriorating mental health and wanted her to be sensible and move into town pretty soon, because recent developments made you both question whether you should consult a lawyer to have her declared mentally incompetent to handle her own affairs?"

Genna collapsed into the chair next to mine, as if the idea was too heavy to contain standing up. "I didn't say any of that. I was worried about her, sure. She seemed to be forget-ting a lot of things. But I wouldn't have had her declared in-competent or anything."

"Adney told her you would. Edie kept the letter, of course—she kept everything. Olive found it this morning in a secret tray in Edie's chest—one that Adney probably didn't know about, right? I saw Olive take the letter, along with pearls and a gold chain. She left it up in a pecan tree, but the sheriff has it now. Maybe you told her about that secret tray—something like, 'I hope the robber didn't find that tray under the lid of Edie's chest, where she kept her pearls.'"

Genna's gasp was all the confirmation I needed.

"But Edie didn't respond like Adney thought she would," I went on. "She knew she wasn't incompetent, and she knew the grove belonged to Josiah. She found out something else the Sunday afternoon before she died: Pete Joyner was the son of her Uncle Edward. She decided that rather than leave the grove to you and Adney—who have no blood claim to it—she would arrange for Josiah to leave it to Henry, who does. That's why she called her lawyer—to change Josiah's will, not her own."

"But Adney said—Olive said—" Genna protested.

I sighed. "Honey, you'll do a lot better in life if you don't believe everything people tell you, no matter how much you trust them."

"Including all this crap," Olive spat out. "We don't have to listen to this. Genna can do what she likes, but you will hear from my lawyer. I don't have to put up with slander, even from a judge. Come on, Genna, take me home."

"Don't go with her, Genna," I advised. "Tonight she may have helped Adney attempt to kill Josiah. She certainly tried to kill me. It's entirely possible she even helped Adney kill Edie. I'd rather you went on home and left Olive to me."

And the deputy I expected any minute.

"You nosy old woman!" Olive lunged at me and caught my neck in the long fingers of her left hand. Even with one hand, she was amazingly strong. She shook me back and forth like a dog worrying a sock as she hissed, "I ought to break your neck! Somebody should have years ago. Adney deserves that business! He's worked and scrabbled all his life. What did Henry ever do to deserve it? And that old man—he can't even speak! If Edie had been sensible—"

My air was cut off, her fingers strong. I heard running feet and the desk clerk protesting, "Stop it! Oh, please, stop!" But although the two of us tried to break Olive's grip, her fingers were stronger than ours combined.

I'd heard of the strength of the insane. Now it clutched my windpipe, and the emergency room was going dark.

May Walker forgive me for anything nasty I ever said to him. If he hadn't grabbed Olive just in time, I wouldn't be here to tell this story.

❧ 30 ❧

For the rest of my life, I will remember and regret that I was the one who told Olive about Edie's finances and Adney about Henry's machetes. I know Adney would probably have found another weapon in the end, but sometimes knowledge is not enough. As penance for my big mouth, and for love of Edie, I sat through his entire trial—except for two hours. I just had to run over to the Hopemore Medical Center to see Meriwether's new baby. They named him Zachary Garlon DuBose, for his deceased grandfathers. Meriwether is trying to break Jed of the habit of calling him Ziggy.

Adney made a wonderful impression on the jury— friendly, honest, bewildered that anybody could think such evil of him. It might have gone differently if one of the jurors hadn't had an ex-husband just like that.

And if Olive hadn't gotten angry during cross-examination. Thanks largely to her temper and pride, Adney won't be building sports complexes in Georgia in my lifetime.

We were all surprised to find out how deeply Olive was involved in Edie's murder. She not only admitted it, she bragged about it. What got her goat was the prosecutor asking her, "Do you have any knowledge that your brother and Mrs. Genna Harrison conspired to kill her aunt?"

The defense attorney objected, of course. Genna wasn't on trial, and the witness had already taken the fifth with regard to what she knew about her brother. But Olive was incensed.

"Genna Harrison doesn't have the brains for that," she blazed out. She clutched the witness stand with both hands and glared at the prosecutor with those flat pewter eyes. She then informed the court that she, not Genna, had played the pranks that made Edie think she was losing her mind, and that she was the one who had persuaded Genna it was Valerie and Frank. She had sneaked into Edie's computer and contaminated it with pornography. "Genna doesn't know the first thing about computers!" She also boasted about what none of us suspected—that during Edie's final Sunday afternoon bridge party, while playing winning bridge, she left the game, took the keys from the pantry, and stole Henry's machete from the shed. She called finding the coveralls "a real bonus" and claimed that she'd kept the machete and coveralls in her trunk until she could get them to Adney.

"How did you know the key was there?" the prosecutor asked.

Olive tossed her head and put her nose in the air. "I, sir, am a trained research librarian."

When asked about the evening of the murder, she said she had come back from North Augusta because Adney needed for her to go down to Edie's. "He was worried Genna might be spending the night at Edie's."

"Why?" asked the prosecutor.

"That would have spoiled everything," she snapped. She also bragged on Adney for giving her explicit instructions about how to construct her own airtight alibi. I don't like Adney Harrison, but he did take care of his little sister.

Any research she does in the foreseeable future, however, will be done in a prison library.

For me, the case ended as it had begun, sharing tea and cookies in Alex James's office. It was a cold, dreary winter day with a hint of rain in the air, the perfect weather to sit with a friend sipping tea from china cups. She'd poured a third cup, in memory of Edie. Steam rose from it like gentle prayers for her soul.

As I reached for a cookie, Alex demanded, "So what would make Olive and Adney do those things? I mean, they both had good jobs, and he, at least, was handsome and charming. He had a great house, he had Genna—"

I noticed where she'd put Adney's wife on the list. That was probably higher than Adney had. I had asked Genna after it was all over, "Tell me something. How long did you know Adney before he found out your daddy owned the Hopemore pharmacy?"

"Oh, he knew from the beginning," she said in a dreary tone. Genna had not yet begun to find out who she could be without Adney. "He came by the hospital one day saying he'd called on Daddy the week before, and Daddy told him I worked at the hospital in Birmingham."

I didn't bother to color in the lines. One day, maybe she'd do that for herself.

Alex was still waiting for an answer, and it tied in with what I'd just been thinking about. "Adney was good at seizing the moment. Walker used to talk all the time about how good he was at really listening to what a customer said, then using some small point he'd picked up to put through a deal. When he learned that Whelan Grove Road was going to be four-laned, and knew the land on both sides might be developed—"

"—he thought Edie was sitting on a gold mine." Alex looked as sad as I felt.

"And when he heard she might be changing her will, he decided she had to die."

We both looked at Edie's cup for a moment of heartbroken silence.

"You got any happy news?" Alex finally asked.

"I do, actually. For one, guess who's going to be the policeman in the upcoming production of *Arsenic and Old Lace?*" I waited to be sure she didn't know. "Smitty. Ridd says Smitty is amazing onstage."

"Smitty as a policeman anywhere would be amazing. I'd have guessed him for the evil brother. Did I hear Ridd is playing the love interest?"

"Heck, no. He's the mad doctor. Want to go with us when we see it?"

"It's a date." Alex leaned back in her chair. "You know, Mac, I can't stop thinking about all this mess, and you know what I think was at the root of it? Entitlement. Remember when I told you I am dedicated to seeing that people get what they're entitled to? This has made me rethink that. It was because Adney felt entitled to own his own business that he killed Edie. And Olive felt entitled to have Adney take care of her, and thought he was entitled to whatever he could get because he'd worked so hard. From something she said, I think they came up as poor as I did."

I sipped my tea as I thought that over. "But Adney was never greedy. One of the things that made it hard for Walker to believe he'd kill Edie for money is that he says Adney was one of the most generous men he ever met. When they read that letter out in court, Walker literally turned pale. Until that minute, he had remained convinced that Adney was innocent, that he wanted Edie to move into town because he was genuinely concerned about her."

"Entitlement is different from greed." Alex wrinkled her forehead, as if working out what she was saying as she went along. "It's subtler, and easier for people to fall into. We all know it's wrong to be greedy, but our whole society teaches us we're entitled. Remember that old commercial, 'I'm worth it'? That's the real American dream. We think we are entitled to live in the strongest country, that we *deserve* to be affluent, live in better neighborhoods, and eat richer food than other folks. And why? Because of our color, or our religion, or where we were born. It's in the fiber of our being. The U.S. Constitution itself says everybody is *entitled* to life, liberty, and the pursuit of happiness."

"But the authors of the Constitution were smart enough to spell out the Bill of Rights, to ensure that people don't feel so entitled that they snatch what they want at somebody else's expense," I pointed out. "If you'll climb down off your soapbox a minute, I have another bit of good news."

"What?"

"I had a visit this week from Frank Sparks. He roared up on his Harley, stomped into my office, and sat down so hard he nearly broke my wing chair. He deposited his silver helmet on my floor, turned beet red, and asked me to preside at his and Valerie's wedding this spring, down in some pasture. He said he'll come pick me up in his sidecar."

For once in my life, I'd impressed her. "You do weddings?"

"I never have, but I'm entitled to. Dang, that word's contagious. What I meant to say is, magistrates *can* marry people. Joe Riddley never would, because it would have broken his heart if a couple he'd married wound up in divorce court. But I said I'll do it. I think this one might stick. Besides, I never rode in a sidecar, and I'm dying to meet Frank's mama. You needing a wedding anytime soon?" I added, trying to sound casual.

"Dream on, girlfriend. I told you, when it comes to men, I move like molasses on ice."

"But I'm the one who got Henry to fix your car. Don't you forget that."

She grew very still, and started doodling on her desk with one long magenta fingernail. "I'm gonna remember if this turns out bad. But right now, we're what my auntie calls 'keeping company.' " She ducked her head with a grin. "He's pretty good company, too. But speaking of Henry, I e-mailed several middle-school librarian friends up in South Carolina to see if they could learn anything about the whereabouts of Latoya, and they found her! Never underestimate the research skills of a bunch of librarians. Henry's driving up to see her next weekend. He said she's in foster care, and he thinks he and Daisy might have a good chance at getting custody."

"Tell him if he needs character witnesses, Joe Riddley and I are available."

I looked over at Edie's cup, which was slowly growing cold. "I sure wish Edie could have known how things would work out. Valerie and Frank getting married, you and Henry 'keeping company,' Daisy feeling brave enough to take on a teenager, this year's harvest safely in and sold, and Josiah able to smile a little when we saw him last week."

Alex snatched a tissue to wipe her eyes. I was getting too soppy for even me to stand, so I ended, "Even Genna's sort of happy. She found a safe-deposit box key after all—Adney rented one to store the antique snuffboxes and Edie's jewelry."

As I left, I paused by the door. "Don't forget I have a license to marry."

She grinned. "You don't give up, do you? But I'll keep it in mind. Natasha's already told me if I don't marry Henry, she's going to."

"What did Henry say to that?"

Alex threw back her head and laughed. "He said they're gonna live in the grove, and I can come see them every Sunday."

After supper that night, Joe Riddley came into the living room where I was sitting on the couch with Lulu. "Here." He dropped something in my lap. "You've been hinting about taking a vacation for months now—"

"I haven't been hinting," I objected. "I've been downright asking."

"Well, here's something right up your alley. I've already put down a deposit, so there's no use arguing about it."

I picked up a brochure. "Explore Your Roots!" it said in big letters. Inside were pictures of purple mountains and lovely lakes. "A tour of Scotland?" I looked at the little map and felt quivers of excitement in my middle. "Look! They're going to the village our branch of the MacLarens came from."

"Thought you'd like it." He settled into his recliner and

picked up the remote. "Laura MacDonald got this in the mail, and she's going, too, so you won't be all by yourself." Laura MacDonald, owner of MacDonald Motors, is my namesake, although I persuaded her parents that MacLaren MacDonald would be too much of a good thing. She is also one of my favorite people. But—

"You aren't going?" I never imagined going overseas without him.

He didn't meet my eye. "The boys have been talking about taking a deep-sea fishing trip down in Florida. Invited me to come along—" He added quickly, as if that made all the difference, "We're taking the little fellows. Crick and Tad."

"You are taking my only two grandsons on a deep-sea fishing trip? What if they fall off the boat? What if they get sunburned?"

"We'll call you in Scotland to let you know. I thought you'd enjoy detecting over there. I figure you can't get in too much trouble looking up dead people."

He was dead wrong, but that's another story.

Thanks

It is amazing what you need to know to write a book. I couldn't have written this one without several people who have specialized knowledge they were willing to share.

Fellow mystery author Walter Sorrells gave a fascinating presentation to the Atlanta Sisters in Crime on kenjutsu and how to forge blades of various types, never realizing he was inspiring part of this story. Thanks, Walter, for patiently answering all my questions and checking the manuscript, so Smitty and Tyrone could study at the Hopemore Budokan and Henry could make his machete. If I'm ever in bodily danger, you're the man I'd like to have at my side.

Thanks to Shigenobu Machida for translating various Japanese terms related to kenjutsu, so I didn't inadvertently put the wrong word in the right place.

I have always loved pecans and once had a tree, but I never appreciated how much is involved in raising pecans commercially until instructed by Bill McGehee of the Big 6 Grove in Fort Valley, Georgia. Thanks, Bill, for explaining complicated processes so I could understand.

Helen Rhea Stumbo of Fort Valley again let me visit the headquarters of *Camellia and Main*, one of the classiest home-furnishings catalogues I know. This time we toured the warehouse, and I saw what happens to merchandise from the time we place an order until it gets shipped. Thanks for a great day, Helen Rhea—both the tour and tale of the marauding kittens, which was so good I used it.

Thanks, too, to Sergeant Holly Lonergan in the Cobb

County sheriff's department, who helped me with Genna's arrest. "Who's this woman again?" she demanded.

"It's a book," I assured her.

I have tried to incorporate what each of them told me as accurately as possible. As always, any errors are my own.

Donna Linse is a real, live MacLaren fan who read my Web site, entered a contest, and earned the right to have her name in this book. Her name, however, is the only part of her I used.

My local librarians were so eager to have a librarian "do it," I wish I could have obliged. After all, when I called to ask, "What do you all call that little doo-hickey you use to de-magnetize the books?" they didn't tell me I was dumb. They just replied, "A magnet."

Thanks as always to Judge Mildred Palmer in Burke County, Georgia, who remains my inspiration. To my husband, Bob, for enduring weeks of angst, late meals, and, sometimes, no meals so this book could get written. To my agent, Nancy Yost, who always picks me up and keeps me going when I call to ask, "Why did I ever think I was a writer?" Finally, many thanks to Ellen Edwards, who is not only my patient and persevering editor, but has become a friend as well.

Read on for an excerpt from
Patricia Sprinkle's next
Thoroughly Southern Mystery

Who Brought the Coffins?

Coming from Signet in February 2006

Roddy Lamont charged into the dining room of the Heather Glen guesthouse, interrupting our midday dinner. "Father? Father! Fit's to be done wi' the coffins in the narthex, then?"

I remembered enough of my morning lesson in broad Scots to know that "fit" meant "what."

Father Ewan, who ate Wednesday dinner at Heather Glen on his housekeeper's day off, rose from the table. "Coffins? Whose are they?"

"I dinna ken." Roddy's petulant face was flushed and beads of perspiration dotted his forehead beneath a mop of ruddy curls. He must have run all the way up Schoolhouse Brae. "I just went in to mop the narthex, and the bl—" A quick look at his mother and he finished smoothly— "oomin' place is full of coffins. I was workin' in the back, y' ken, so I never saw them comin' in, but you shoulda told me if we're havin' a funeral—much less two." He pulled a blue handkerchief from his back pocket and wiped his face.

His mother twisted her hands under her apron and practically glowed with pride at how seriously Roddy was finally taking a job, until he added in indignation, "I'm off to the bike rally at three, and this has put me behind."

Father Ewan looked with regret at his gooseberries with vanilla custard. He'd already said how fond he was of gooseberries with custard. But he laid down his napkin and gave those of us around the table a slight bow. "Excuse me, Mrs.

Yarbrough, but I'd better go see what this is about. I've had no notice of anyone dying hereabouts." He motioned me with one hand. "Come along when you're done with your meal. This shouldna take long—there's obviously been some kind of mistake. And I can take you on that wee look 'round the chapel as soon as I sort this out."

I put down my napkin. "Why don't I come with you now? I can be looking at the grounds while you're occupied." It was a perfect excuse for me to skip the gooseberries, which lay in my bowl like pale green eyeballs. I'd been wondering how to get out of eating them.

I trotted after the two men as they strode out the back door and down the hill. Fortunately, the priest was as short as I am, and a little older, so I had no trouble keeping up. Roddy was still full of grievance. "1 saved cleanin' the narthex til the last, y' ken, so I could mop the flair and front steps last, then leave them to dry while I came up for my dinner. I must have been hooverin' at the back when Ian brought them in, but you'd think he'd have the sense to give me a shout. He shouldna just dump people like that and go away."

The priest and I were both panting from trying to keep up with Roddy's long legs. Father Ewan waved for him to stop opposite the schoolhouse, half-way down the hill—or "brae"—and reached into the pocket of his black suit for a cell phone. "Stop a wee whiley and let me give Ian a ring. Ian Gettys is our local joiner," he added to me as he punched in a number.

As he sidled away to talk, I asked Roddy, "What's a joiner?"

Roddy—who never stood if he could lean—propped himself against a house that abutted the sidewalk across from the school and gave me the look Middle Georgians would give somebody who asked, "What's a bird dog?"

"Y' dinna have joiners in America?" Clearly, he wondered how we managed to survive.

I shook my head.

He reached down the neck of his gray pullover and

brought up a crumpled pack of cigarettes from his shirt pocket. The way the sweater sagged, that must be a frequent habit. He held the pack out to me, and when I refused, he took time to light up and exhale slowly. The way his brow was furrowed, he was trying to figure out how best to explain something obvious to an ignoramus. "He's a sort of builder, y' ken? He makes coffins and kitchen cabinets, lays carpet, puts up wallpaper—he joins things." He flapped one hand to conclude the explanation.

Father Ewan snapped his phone shut, stowed it in a pocket, and came back to us with a broad smile. "False alarm, lad. The bloomin' things are empty. Ian is out, but Barbara said the coffins are for that play the Americans are putting on tomorrow night." He nodded my way.

Guilt by association made me say quickly, "I don't know anything about coffins, and we aren't putting on the play. It's just being put on while we're here. Our tour guide wrote it."

"Och, that must be the way of it, then." Roddy nodded with enlightenment. "The lass said to take them to the chapel, and that dunce Ian didn't ask what she meant by that." He squinted down at me through another cloud of smoke, "Folks not from here look at the sign that says St. Margaret's Chapel and think it's called 'the chapel'—never knowin' our lot's got the chapel and St. Margaret's is just St. Margaret's—not the chapel a-tall. Used to be Church of England, but nowadays it's just a meeting hall."

"I'm Presbyterian." I felt a continuing need to distance myself as far as possible from those "folks not from here" he was ridiculing.

"Och, then ye'll be goin' to the kirk, down by the manse woods." He pointed to the right, obviously glad to get all that cleared up for my benefit. Then he added to the priest, "Shall I shift them to one side, just, until Ian can fetch them? I've still got that flair to mop."

Roddy might not be good at working, but he was a master at complaint.

The priest hesitated, looking back up the brae toward

Heather Glen. 1 suspected he was debating the possibility of returning for his gooseberries. Instead, he turned on his heel and said in the tone of one successfully resisting temptation, "That's the way, lad. I'll just give you a hand."

At the bottom of the hill, we turned left onto the walk that led to the small Roman Catholic Church. I don't know when I've seen a prettier approach to a place of worship. The chapel itself was built of granite, like everything else in the village, but someone had rounded the outer edges of the stones just enough to replace severity with gentleness. A simple tower rose in the center and ended in a stone cross. A small rose window was set above arched front doors. Tall dark yews stood in an arc on the soft emerald lawn, arms reaching out to draw us down the walk, while welcoming masses of daffodils nodded on each side of the steps. "Quite nice those, aren't they?" Roddy nodded toward the daffodils as he reached for the giant ring that opened the dark wooden door. "Mum planted them a few years back, in memory of m' dad."

Father Ewan motioned for me to precede him up the stone steps. "Come along in. It won't take us but a minute to stack the boxes for Ian so Roddy can get on with his work."

I followed them into the narthex and shivered in the accumulated chill of three hundred winters. Even the floor was stone—what I could see of it. A third of it was covered by a long table holding pamphlets and various offering boxes. The remaining floor space was almost filled by two wooden boxes, one long and one short. In Georgia, people tend to be buried in great bronze or gray metal caskets, lined with velvet. I had never seen a plain wooden coffin before, but the shape was unmistakable.

The narthex was chilly and dim, lit only by sunlight filtering into the sanctuary through dark stained glass windows. I inhaled that smell of holiness which empty places of worship seem to have in common and tiptoed around the boxes toward the sanctuary while Roddy and the priest shoved one box over close to the right-hand table. Behind me, I heard them cross the narthex for the other, then heard Roddy exclaim, "Hold on! There's something in this one!"

"There can't be," Father Ewan protested. "Barbara said . . ."

"The lid's not nailed down," Roddy muttered. Hinges creaked. Then Roddy exclaimed, "Who the devil is that?"

"I dinna ken," the priest replied soberly, "but whoever it is is very dead."

Father Ewan raised his voice and called to me—as if he hoped I hadn't heard what they'd been saying, "You'd best go on back up to Heather Glen. I'll show you around another time."

He was obviously wanting to spare me the sight of whoever was in that coffin, but I had to pass it to get to the front door and Roddy was too slow in lowering the lid.

I saw enough.

What was it Joe Riddley had said just before I left Hopemore?

Wanting him to come along, I'd reminded him, 'You promised to go everywhere with me."

He'd replied, "I didn't *promise* I'd go everywhere with you, Little Bit. That was a threat, and it only applies around here. I figure you can't get into too much trouble in a country where you don't know a soul. Presumably you won't feel obligated to endanger your life trying to solve the problems of everybody in Scotland, and you aren't likely to be stumbling over dead bodies on a bus tour."

And now, here I stood in a chilly church in the heart of the eastern Highlands, with a member of our tour group lying dead at my feet.